THE SCANDAL SHEET COLLECTION: VOLUME 1

JESS MICHAELS

The Scandal Sheet Collection: Volume 1

The Return of Lady Jane

Copyright © 2019 by Jess Michaels

Stealing the Duke

Copyright © 2019 by Jess Michaels

Lady No Says Yes

Copyright © 2019 by Jess Michaels

THE RETURN OF LADY JANE

THE SCANDAL SHEET BOOK 1

For rekindled lovers and those waiting for their happily ever after. And for Michael, who is mine.

PROLOGUE

"She's a beautiful girl, Colin. No one could ever deny that."

Viscount Colin Wharton smiled as his cousin motioned across the crowded ballroom to Colin's new bride. Jane stood at the edge of the fray, surrounded by friends offering well wishes on their union, which was only a few hours old now.

When she noticed his stare, it was obvious. Her cheeks filled with a pink blush and she slowly let her gaze move to him. His smile broadened because the crowd did not know the secret they shared. No one else knew that he hadn't been able to wait and had already made her his bride in body as well as spirit earlier in the afternoon, before their wedding ball had even begun.

Her soft cries and passionate moans were a reward well-earned after months of erotic tension during their courtship. Although the match had been arranged, Colin had high hopes it would be a happy one. Jane was not just beautiful, but also witty and wise. Kind to all who met her and observant when it came to those she was close to. She was capable of softening him, taking the edges from his personality, and he couldn't wait to escort his beautiful bride back to their marital bed and make her his over and over again.

She smiled softly as her head dipped and the little tendrils of blonde hair that framed her slender face shivered. Her blue eyes swept away from him and back to her companions.

"I'm happy you've found such a good match," Arthur continued as he clapped Colin on the back. "After that mess with Cassandra, I thought you'd never recover."

Colin stiffened at the mention of that name. Cassandra had been his first love, a woman he'd once believed he'd marry. But when it came out she was bedding not only his former best friend but also any cavalry member who gave her a side glance, his world had been shattered.

"I do not wish to speak of that today of all days, Arthur," Colin said softly, clenching his fists at his sides.

Arthur inclined his head. "Sorry, mate, that wasn't well done of me. Of course you wouldn't want to think of Cassandra's betrayal. Certainly you can *fully* trust Jane, can't you?"

Colin shifted. Fully trust? Hell, he wasn't certain he could *fully* trust anyone. Cassandra had taken that ability from him. He'd seriously considered never marrying at all, letting the title and all that went with it slip to Arthur or his future heirs. He might have done just that, except that his mother had gotten involved after watching him grieve for nearly a year. She'd told him to stop moping, convinced him to let her arrange a union. A few months courting Jane, and here he was.

He let his gaze move to his wife again. She certainly *seemed* trustworthy, and there was no doubt she'd been an innocent when he claimed her earlier in the day. A passionate innocent, yes. He'd never seen someone so passionate.

He frowned.

"Didn't she have another suitor before your mother intervened?" Arthur pushed.

Colin folded his arms with a deeper frown. "Yes. Some rich, untitled fop. Martin, his name was. Her parents were happy to see them part, I think, in trade for a higher ranked match."

But now that Arthur had placed the thought in his head, Colin began to wonder…was *Jane* equally as pleased to end the flirtation? She'd never spoken of the man, nor seemed overly upset at their parting. She'd always seemed happy to spend time with Colin, as well, and her behavior today made him believe she cared for him… *wanted* him.

Yet there was a niggle of doubt in his mind, an egg waiting to hatch. He scowled.

"I'm certain it will all work out, old man," Arthur said, apparently oblivious to the uncertainty he'd placed in his cousin's head. He slapped a hand against Colin's arm and squeezed. "Now I'm off to dance with the lovely Lady Amanda. She's been making eyes at me all night."

Colin forced a smile as his cousin strode off through the crowd toward the lady in question. He remained in his place, watching Jane, but whereas before he had stared at her through eyes of excitement and anticipation, now it was with apprehension.

Had he made a mistake? *Could* he truly trust this woman?

As if in answer to his question, he watched as a man approached Jane. Colin's eyes went wide. The man was one he recognized, the very one he'd just been describing to his cousin: Jane's former suitor, Mr. Martin.

Tall and handsome, the gentleman sidled up to her as her companions drifted away. Jane's face read surprise for a moment, but she didn't look unhappy to see the man she had once allowed to court her. She didn't push him away, certainly. They spoke for a moment, then Jane nodded and allowed the other man to take her arm and lead her to the terrace doors. They exited, leaving Colin staring after them, his hands shaking at his sides.

What was Martin doing here? Had Jane invited him? Was this a planned encounter? The very idea of it turned Colin's stomach and pulled a veil of red anger over his eyes.

He had to know. In that moment, he *had* to know what her intentions were, where her heart was. So he slipped from the ballroom and around to a parlor that also exited to the large terrace that wrapped around the entire back side of the house. He shut the door quietly behind him and stepped forward across the stone. There was a little bend in the terrace that offered him some protection from the eyes of those already outside, and he flattened against the wall as he peered around the corner and found his new wife and her former suitor standing at the wall, looking up at the full moon overhead.

They were alone. No one else was on the terrace. Jane faced the other man, and in the moonlight, Colin examined him. Martin was handsome enough, he supposed. The kind of man some women wouldn't refuse.

They were talking, though Colin couldn't make out the words on the breeze. Just Jane's low voice murmuring softly and then Martin answering, his deeper voice obscuring hers. What he did know for certain was that they were standing too close together, and Colin's blood began to boil.

And then, slowly, Martin reached out and gripped Jane's bare upper arm. He pulled her forward, dipped his head and kissed her.

Colin caught his breath, staggering back into the darkness in shock. The last thing he saw before he spun away was Jane lifting her hands to embrace the other man.

The egg his cousin had placed in his mind hatched in a terrible instant. Jane was betraying him. On their wedding night. A mere few hours after she had surrendered herself to him as his bride. She might *look* the part of a virtuous miss, she may have even kept her virginity intact, but clearly she was *not* innocent. Not if she would tryst so brazenly with a former suitor.

He stumbled into the house, but didn't return to the ballroom with the others. He careened down the long hallway to his offices, where he threw himself inside and slammed his hands down on the sideboard.

"Cousin?"

He froze at the sound of Arthur's concerned voice behind him. "Not now," he croaked past a suddenly thick throat.

Arthur stepped inside and closed the door. "I was looking for you on your mother's behest. What is wrong?"

Colin looked up at him, hardly seeing his cousin's face through the fog of betrayal and disappointment and humiliation. "A short while ago, you asked if I could trust Jane...well, it turns out I cannot."

Arthur arched a brow. "What are you talking about?"

Slowly, Colin choked out what he'd seen on the terrace, watching as Arthur's eyes grew wide and his expression grave. "Great God, Colin," he said, shaking his head when Colin had sunk into a chair, covering his face with his hands. "I feel terrible that I brought up anything tonight about Jane's trueness when *this* was to follow."

"Don't be," Colin whispered. "After all, without that doubt being named, I might not have followed her and it would have been Cassandra all over again."

Arthur nodded slowly. "It is better to know the truth, I suppose. But what will you do now?"

"I have no idea," Colin said. "I cannot end the marriage. It was... consummated."

Arthur drew back in obvious surprise. "Was it?"

Colin felt heat rush to his cheeks. "Yes," he said softly. "But what do I do? Confront her and her lover?"

Arthur paced away. "It might be tempting to do so, I suppose, but what good would come of it? Perhaps there is a better solution."

"And that is?" Colin asked.

"Send her to the country," Arthur said.

"Banish her," Colin said, his tone flat and dull, even to his own ears. "That seems abominably cruel."

Arthur shook his head. "More cruel than what she did tonight, with no thought to how it would make you feel? How it would look were she discovered with her lover?"

How it looked. Colin's stomach turned. Others had known about Cassandra. Those whispers of her lack of fidelity had hurt him as much as the actual act had. And here Jane had been, still dressed in her wedding frock.

His stomach turned and he lifted a hand to his lips as he tried not to cast up his accounts. "Send her away," he repeated, the idea gaining merit with each moment he pondered it.

"Your country estate is secluded enough," Arthur encouraged gently. "If you were worried about her taking a lover there, you could have your servants report on her movements. It would allow you to move on with your life."

Colin winced. His life. The life outside of his marriage. He did have duties to perform, and he'd always taken them seriously. He served the House of Lords to his highest ability and he'd always planned on providing an heir if he married. But Cassandra had made him question that plan.

Tonight, Jane had destroyed it entirely, and his old desire to lock himself away, body, heart and soul, returned with even greater urgency.

He cleared his throat. "Sending Jane away is certainly far more palatable than listening to her lie to my face about what she was doing on the terrace tonight. Perhaps some time apart will help clear my head so I don't respond in rage and do something foolish."

"Yes," Arthur encouraged him. "It doesn't have to be forever, does it? Just until you decide what to do. How to handle her terrible betrayal."

Colin drew in a long breath and nodded. This was the right decision. "Will you fetch her?" he asked softly.

Arthur straightened his jacket. "Of course. I'll get her right away."

His cousin left the room and Colin paced the length of the chamber, his hands shaking and his blood pumping hard. He had to gather himself, as to not show Jane his emotions. He had to be cold and calculating, he had to shove feelings aside and simply do this duty.

This duty to send Jane away and with her, the pain that her

betrayal had caused. Pain that exposed a weakness he had sworn he would never allow again.

Now he wouldn't. Now he had finally learned his lesson. And that lesson was that no woman was to be trusted. Not with his name, not with his future, certainly not with even a fraction of his heart.

CHAPTER 1

Six Months Later

Jane shifted in her seat as the carriage came to a smooth stop at the doorstep of her beloved older sister, Alicia. Although she was thrilled she would get to see her family, she couldn't help but be nervous. After all, she had not been in London for half a year. Not since her husband had cruelly sent her to his country estate without so much as an explanation about why he didn't want her anymore. There had been none since her departure either, and any letter she wrote to the man went unanswered.

She shook her head as if that motion could clear the sting in her very soul. The carriage door opened and one of Alicia's servants helped her down.

"Welcome, Lady Wharton," the butler said as he opened the door and motioned her inside. "Your arrival has been most anticipated."

"Thank you," she said as she stripped off her gloves and handed over her hat.

"Would you like a moment to gather yourself, or—"

She laughed. "Cookson, I have not seen my sister in six months. I cannot wait another moment!"

The butler smiled. "Mrs. Beckford said you might feel that way. Come, they're waiting for you in her chamber."

Jane followed him up the winding stairs and down a twisting hall until they came to a tall door. Cookson knocked and said a few soft words into the chamber. When he moved aside, Jane took a long breath and stepped in.

Alicia sat in her bed with her husband, Charles, at her side. And in her arms, she held a little bundle, swaddled up in blankets that covered the precious face of their child.

"Darling!" Jane said as she moved forward. Alicia passed the baby to Charles, and Jane leaned down to embrace her as he stepped away. "You look wonderful!"

"I look like I had a baby two days ago," Alicia laughed.

Jane frowned. "I'm sorry I missed the birth. That trip from Applegate Castle is awful in a carriage and there was mud on the road. These autumn storms have made everything more difficult."

The estate where she had been banished was an isolated one. And yes, it was beautiful, overlooking cliffs and a violent ocean below it, but it was also very lonely. It had taken her months to adjust, though now it was better. She had developed relationships with her husband's tenants and ran the estate as best she could.

She had no choice, for Colin did not make any effort to do so himself. It was like she and the estate were being punished together.

"You are here now," Alicia said, motioning to Charles. "And *this* is Matthew."

Charles smiled at Jane. "Hello, Jane."

She laughed as she realized she hadn't even acknowledged her brother-in-law. "Oh, Charles, I'm sorry."

He moved forward and set the baby in her arms. "You had more important things to think about."

He brushed the blanket aside and Jane caught her breath in wonder at the beautiful, perfect, pinched and pink little face before her. "Alicia, he's…"

"Wonderful," her sister said with an emotional sniffle. "Isn't he?"

Jane nodded, unable to form any other words as she stared at the baby. She was so very happy for her sister, but deep in her heart, she felt something else, too. Pain. She had always wanted to be a mother. She'd prayed her one night of passion with her husband might result in a baby, but it hadn't. And Colin's cruel rejection of her made her believe that would never happen.

"You are crying," Alicia said, reaching to touch her arm.

Charles sent the sisters a quick look, then said, "I have a bit of correspondence to catch up on after the excitement of the past few days. Why don't I leave you to catch up?"

Jane smiled at his kindness and at the way he leaned in to gently kiss her sister before he left the room. Once they were alone, she shook her head.

"I'm being silly, of course. Babies make me emotional—who knew?"

Alicia speared her with a sharp look. "Why wouldn't they? After all, you are being denied your right to be a mother by that bastard you married."

Jane caught her breath. "Such language in front of your child."

"Don't tease," Alicia said, her frown deepening. "You have been sequestered in that estate for half a year, and it's ridiculous. What did you *ever* do to deserve such cruelty?"

Jane handed over her nephew and then got up, pacing away from mother and son as she tried to regain her breath. "I have no idea. I have reached out to Colin over and over, but he refuses to respond to me. I don't even know if he realizes I'm in Town."

Alicia made a little sound of distress and Jane turned to face her, finding her sister pale. "I-I don't know how to tell you this...have you heard of the *Scandal Sheet?*"

Jane nodded slowly. "I've had wind of it in letters from friends. It's some little weekly gossip rag that only circulates in London, isn't it?"

Alicia pursed her lips. "No one knows who publishes it. It just shows up on the doorstep every Tuesday morning. Well, today is Tuesday and...*you* are featured in it."

"What?" Jane gasped.

Alicia nodded at the table by the window and Jane rushed over to grab at the paper that had been left there. She read through it, finding the item about herself splashed across the front page.

"The gossip is *supposed* to be blind," Alicia said. "But it isn't as if that's a difficult code to decipher. You are obviously the Lady W. to whom it refers."

"How would someone know I was coming to London, down to the date of my arrival?" Jane asked, blinking as she read the item over and over again, like she could somehow erase it by staring at it hard enough.

Alicia shrugged. "It wasn't a secret. I told people about it. I'm sure you told friends, too, so that you may make calls upon your arrival. Someone might have mentioned it off hand or a servant could have told someone else's servant. Who knows how the publisher of this rag gets his information?"

Jane set the paper down with a scowl. "I'm sure it's not the first time I've been gossiped about since my exile. And I assume *Colin* gets this paper, too?"

"*Everyone* in Society gets a copy," Alicia said. "So I assume his lordship does, as well. We would be fools to think someone wouldn't give him the news even if he didn't bother to read it himself."

"Bollocks," Jane said under her breath, then turned with an apologetic blush for her sister. "I suppose I shouldn't scold you for language when I come in here like a sailor."

"Matthew is a baby—he has no idea what you're saying," Alicia said with a reassuring smile. "But what will you do?"

"I don't know that there's anything *to* do," Jane said with a sigh. "About this unexpected and very public humiliation or about my circumstances in general."

Alicia reached for her, and Jane allowed her sister to take her hand. She sat on the edge of the bed, feeling Alicia's gaze search hers.

"You've not seemed entirely unhappy in Applegate," Alicia said slowly, like she was being careful to feel out the situation. "But you don't...talk about...*him*. Has he truly made no effort to contact you?"

Jane covered her face for a moment. It seemed it was easier to remain distant and strong when she didn't have to look a most beloved sister in the face. Now she felt the truth bubbling up in her. Straining to be released.

"At first I was in such shock at what happened," she began with a long sigh. "It was like a dream...a nightmare. And I kept waiting to wake up or have him come to his senses. And then I got into a proper rage at him."

"He deserves no less," Alicia said with a deep frown.

"And yet I cannot forget the good times we shared," Jane whispered. "During our courtship he was...*good*. Oh, he was often formal, but I saw glimpses, here and there, of a man with deep principles. With kindness. I came to care for him, very deeply. I have no idea what happened to turn that man away, but I am married to him. I still want a future and he is my only path to one, isn't he?"

"I wish it weren't true, but yes."

"So I gathered myself and began to write to him. I have written the man thirteen times in the past three months. A letter a week."

Alicia's eyebrows lifted in surprise. "And what does he say?"

Jane bent her head and tried to ignore the pain that rushed through her. "*Nothing*. He has not responded even once. It seems he doesn't care what I do. So why would he care about my being here… except that I went against his decree that I would go to the country and stay there?"

Alicia's eyes narrowed. "Someone ought to have a word with the viscount! He *cannot* treat you this way. I feel well enough to get up for a bit. I should march over there and—"

"Oh no, please don't!" Jane cried. "You are hardly recovered enough for that, and it wouldn't make a difference. Whatever affection Colin once showed for me was obviously false. He pretended to care for me before we wed and he certainly pretended it on that day. For some unknown reason, his heart is hardened toward me. There is no fighting that."

She sighed as her mind traitorously took her to a sunny afternoon just after her wedding when Colin had been anything but cut off from her. He had made love to her and shattered her with pleasure unlike anything she'd ever imagined. She shivered at the memory.

"And what will you do while you're here?" Alicia asked softly.

Jane shrugged. "I know where I stand, don't I? He's made it very clear. I plan to stay out of his way. And hope he stays out of mine."

Colin tossed aside the little rag of a paper and clenched his hand on the table next to his plate. "She's here," he growled out loud.

His butler, Simmons, was standing by, checking on the food left on the sideboard, and he looked up at those words. "I beg your pardon, sir?"

"Nothing," Colin ground out as he pushed back from the table and the food he would certainly not eat now.

He stared out the window at the sunny autumn day that seemed to have been created to taunt him. Jane was in London. It was like a shot echoing in his mind.

"Is there anything I can do for you, my lord?" Simmons pressed.

Colin glared into the window. "What is on my schedule for today?" he asked through clenched teeth.

Simmons straightened. "A meeting with Lord Grimley about the legislation you want to propose to the House of Lords, and then a lunch at your club with your cousin. You are also to meet with your solicitor this afternoon about the autumn maintenance at your estates."

Colin frowned. All those things were important, indeed, and normally he would not let anything sway him from performing his duties and obligations. But right now he could think of nothing but that Jane was *here*.

And he needed to see her. No, not see her. Confront her.

"Cancel it all," he said, spinning away from the window. "And have my horse prepared. I have a call to make and I doubt I'll be in any mood for company once it has been completed."

If Simmons was surprised by this sudden change of plans, he didn't show it on his stern face. He merely nodded and exited the room with swift efficiency.

Leaving Colin to ponder what in the hell he was doing. Jane had sent him no word she was coming to London. She obviously had no interest in seeing him. He should have had equally little interest in seeing her, and yet he felt a pulsing drive to go to her. To hear her voice and smell her scent and look her in the eye as he hadn't for six long, tortuous months.

A foolish notion, but as a husband, it was his right. And that is what he would tell her when she faced him. That and nothing more.

"Sir?"

Colin jumped as Simmons reappeared at the door. "Yes?"

"Your horse is ready."

Colin nodded to the butler, collected his gloves and exited the house, his chin lifted and his shoulders back. He swung up on the mount and urged him forward, turning him toward the house of Jane's sister and her husband. He had not seen either of them since the day of the wedding either. He could not imagine he would receive a warm reception.

Currently he didn't give a damn. Jane was his only thought now. Jane and her bright eyes. Jane and her gentle smile. Jane and her easy lies.

He couldn't forget that last bit. Not if he wanted to come out of this encounter unscathed.

It took him a quarter of an hour to ride to the home of Mr. and Mrs. Charles Beckford, but his heart rate never slowed the entire ride. It still throbbed as he mounted the steps to their modest home and straightened his jacket before he knocked.

A butler appeared in a moment and looked him up and down slowly. "May I help you?"

Colin sniffed. "I'm aware that Lady Wharton arrived today from Applegate. I am here to see her."

The butler shifted slightly, guard entering his expression. "And who may I say is calling when I ascertain if Lady Wharton is in residence?"

Colin held out a card. "Her husband."

The butler caught his breath almost imperceptibly and took the card being held out to him. He cleared his throat and then stepped back, allowing Colin entrance. "Let me inquire as to the lady's whereabouts, sir. Follow me to the parlor to wait, if you will."

Colin shook his head as he followed the man. "You may let the lady know that if she sends you back with a claim that she is not in house, I will know she is lying and come to find her myself."

The butler was now bug-eyed, but he nodded just the same. "Certainly, sir. I will pass along the message."

He hustled from the room, leaving Colin to pace the chamber

slowly. He had been here once, over a year ago, when he and Jane had celebrated an engagement luncheon at her sister's home. He recalled sitting beside her at a long table, smiling as they were toasted by all in attendance. She had slid her hand into his under the table, and in that moment he had felt two powerful reactions. The first was a sense of peace unlike any he'd ever known. The second was desire that tore all propriety to shreds and made his body throb.

He blinked away the images that danced through his mind and turned to pace in the opposite direction. When he did, he came to a full stop, for there at the parlor door was Jane. She was dressed in a pretty pink gown that brought out the porcelain perfection of her skin and the honey-blonde brightness of her hair. Her blue eyes were locked on him, and she took a shuddering breath before she stepped inside the chamber and firmly shut the door behind herself.

Leaving them alone together for the first time in six long and lonely months.

CHAPTER 2

Jane stared at Colin, her body trembling and her breath hard to find. He was here. He was *here* in her sister's parlor, standing no more than ten feet away. And God, but he was handsome. He was impeccably dressed in a black jacket that accentuated his broad shoulders and a smart waistcoat interlaced with golden thread. His dark hair was cut close and not a lock of it dared to be out of place. His harsh jaw was smooth and clean, as if he had only just finished scraping his blade across any whisker that dared to make an appearance overnight.

He looked every inch the proper, upright gentleman, but then he always did even when there was no need for formality. Only once had she seen him undone and that was the afternoon he made love to her so sweetly.

She tensed her jaw and steeled herself against those thoughts. They would do her no good at present.

"Colin," she said softly.

His expression, which had been focused so intently on her, now went hard and bored. She remembered that look all too well. It was the same one that had been on his face when he'd told her she was to go to the country and not return.

"My lady," he said, his tone as icy as his demeanor.

She hardened herself in response, pushing aside her initial thrill at seeing him and reminding herself that not only had he sent her away so callously, but also ignored her for half a year.

"You didn't have to be so cruel to my sister's butler," she said, folding her arms as she glared at him. "You frightened the man half to death."

Colin arched a brow. "I wanted to make certain my intentions were clear."

"Well, you have done that in spades, my lord. As always, no one could possibly doubt your contempt for me. Now, what are you doing here?"

He took a step toward her and her heart stuttered. She hated herself for it. Hated herself for reacting to him at all.

"I could ask you the same thing, Jane," he said in a low tone that was not at all gentle. "I thought I made myself *very* clear that you were to remain in the country."

She shook her head. "Oh, you did, my lord. But Alicia and Charles had a baby. You know how close I am to my sister. I couldn't stay away—I *would* not, no matter what orders and edicts you gave."

His cheek twitched a little, but otherwise he remained impassive. "Perhaps you are right that I could not have expected you to stay away from your beloved sister at this happy time. Still, you could have let me know of your impending arrival."

She caught her breath at his arrogance. He had been ignoring her heartfelt letters for months and now he acted as if *she* had failed in her communication?

She narrowed her eyes further. "You have not acted like a husband, Colin. Why in God's name should I act as a wife?"

His jaw clenched and his entire body stiffened. His glare grew in intensity, sucking her into dark depths, dragging her to places she had convinced herself no longer existed. Perhaps they had never existed. And yet here she was, lost in his heat and his emotions and his obvious anger.

What she had done to deserve such censure, she still didn't know.

"Rumors have begun," he said after what seemed like an eternity had passed.

She let out a bark of displeasure. "Are you referring to the *Scandal Sheet?*" she asked.

He nodded once. "You have heard of it."

"Alicia showed me the paper when I arrived this morning. Surely you have enough discernment to see that it is drivel, Colin."

"Drivel or not, it does affect how I am seen. I cannot allow my reputation to be damaged. So you are correct, Jane. It is time for me to start behaving as a husband would."

She caught her breath. When he said that and his dark brown gaze flitted over her from head to foot, he almost looked like he… wanted her. Not that it was possible. Their one torrid joining had affected her, but clearly not done anything for him. He had walked away without so much as a backward glance while she woke sweating and aching, the covers tangled around her, her body pulsing with unfulfilled need.

"What do you mean?"

His gaze grew even darker and more intense. "Prepare your things, Jane. You shall move to my home today."

Her mouth dropped open in absolute shock and she stared at him, unblinking, as she tried to decide if she was losing her mind or her hearing.

"What are you talking about?" She choked on the words, barely able to formulate them.

"You heard me," he said softly.

She took a long step toward him and was hit by the spicy, warm smell of his skin. Her body began to tingle, but she shoved the reaction aside before it could overwhelm her and hissed, "You haven't wanted me near you in six months. *That* fact had to have caused gossip aplenty. Why do you give a damn about it now?"

"It is one thing to have a wife who remains in the country," he growled. "It is quite another to have her in the same city as I am and not living under my roof."

"Colin!" she ground out.

He shook his head. "This is ridiculous. Jane, you vowed to obey me—and you shall."

She flinched at the way he threw their broken vows in her face and snapped, "We both vowed a great deal. All of that means nothing to *you*."

She spun away from him, feeling his gaze hard and heavy on her back. But even though she was angry, so angry that she trembled, she recognized that arguing with him was futile. Colin got what he wanted.

If he didn't, he could make things difficult for Alicia and Charles. She wouldn't put it past him to do just that.

"I will go with you," she murmured when she could find her breath again, "If you will allow that I may return and see my sister, Charles and little Matthew."

She faced him in time to see a barely perceptible flinch cross Colin's expression. "Matthew. The child is a boy?"

Jane nodded. "Yes. And he's beautiful."

A slight softness entered Colin's face and he cleared his throat. "You may visit as often as you like," he conceded quietly. "I will send a carriage for you and a cart for your things after lunch."

He turned on his heel and made for the door, with her staring at him. She placed her hands on her hips. "That is all?"

Her words stopped him short at the door, one hand held out to the handle. He turned and faced her. "For now. Good day."

He didn't wait for her response, but marched out through the foyer, and then he was gone, leaving Jane to stare at where he'd last stood.

And wonder what the hell had just happened.

~

Colin urged his horse faster and clung tight to the reins so he wouldn't deposit himself arse over head into the gutter. He was shaking so hard he probably shouldn't have even been riding.

He'd had no intention whatsoever to demand Jane come live under his roof. He'd only come to chastise her, to see her and determine she was still the same as ever and then leave unscathed.

But the moment he laid eyes on her, everything in his world had changed. He'd spent half a year pretending Jane meant nothing to him. Six long months trying to make that lie into the truth. But seeing her here, even more beautiful than ever, smelling her lemony scent and feeling her warmth when she came near...well, he couldn't deny that he still wanted her.

That desire was dangerous, of course. Desire had made many a man commit terrible mistakes. But one could take desire and never allow it to control one.

Feelings were another thing entirely. And *that* was what made this situation with Jane worse. He saw her and he wished so desperately that he could go back in time. Back to before he saw her on the terrace with another man on their wedding night. Back to when he looked into her eyes and saw his future.

Those were feelings he *did not want*.

He turned his horse down a familiar lane and onto the drive of Arthur's home. He'd canceled their meeting through his butler earlier in the day, but now he needed to see his cousin. Arthur had always been a voice of reason when it came to women. When it came to Jane.

He needed that now.

He was let in by Arthur's butler and paced the room as he waited his cousin's entrance. When the door opened, he turned in time to see a scowl on Arthur's face. One that evaporated almost instantly as he stepped into the room, hand outstretched.

"Colin," he drawled, calling him by his first name, as always.

Arthur had never called him Wharton or *my lorded* him. "I thought you wouldn't be joining me this afternoon."

Colin shook his hand and nodded. "Yes, I know. Something happened and I thought I wouldn't be good company. But I have swiftly realized I need a friend's ear and you have always been one of the best to me."

Arthur's cheek twitched slightly and then he smiled. "I always shall be, Colin. Come, sit down. Tell me what has happened."

They took their places in front of the fire and Colin leaned forward, draping his forearms over his knees as he stared at the floor. "Jane is back in London."

He heard Arthur suck in a breath and looked up to see a troubled expression on his face.

"I had hoped you hadn't seen that particular item in the *Scandal Sheet*," Arthur said.

"I did." Colin scrubbed a hand through his hair. "I went to see her."

Arthur jumped up at that, nearly flipping his chair over in the process. "You did what?"

"I rode to her sister and brother-in-law's house," Colin admitted, his voice a moan. "God, it was stupid, I know, but I almost couldn't help myself. Knowing she was here, a few miles away, I *had* to see her."

"Why?" Arthur asked, his tone tense and shrill.

Colin shook his head. "She's my wife."

"Hardly," Arthur huffed out. "Need I remind you what she did on your wedding day of all days?"

Colin ground his teeth. "Of course not. I recall everything that happened that horrible day with perfect clarity, I assure you. But damn it, Arthur, it was six months ago. She has stayed in the countryside, just as I demanded, without so much as a peep to defend herself or demand anything. Word from my estate is that she has taken on her role as lady there with great gusto and purpose. The tenants and staff adore her."

Arthur arched a brow. "I'm sure they do, especially the male ones."

It was Colin who pushed out of his seat now and took a long step toward his cousin before he realized what he was doing. He stopped, the two men nose to nose, and his lips parted. "I'm...sorry. I should not vent my anger at you," he whispered. "You have every right to be so harsh considering what she did and how you've had to watch me suffer."

Arthur nodded slowly. "Yes. Your suffering has brought me no pleasure, cousin, I assure you. And I admit, I'm shocked that you would even consider seeing her again. Let her visit her sister and go back where she belongs."

Colin sighed and walked away from Arthur. He stared out the window, a hand clenched against the glass. "I told her she should come and stay at my home while she is in the city."

Arthur let out a great gasp and rushed up to Colin, grabbing his arm and spinning him around. "No!"

Colin wasn't surprised at his cousin's reaction, though the strength of it certainly set him back a pace. "The *Scandal Sheet* shall make the entire *ton* talk endlessly," he explained, even though the words seemed hollow to him. "My best course of action is to reduce their whispers by making it seem as though I *want* Jane here. That this is an invitation of *my* making, rather than a surprise sprung on me by my wayward wife."

"You and your reputation," Arthur spit out, his tone far harsher than Colin had thought it would be.

He held up his hands, almost as a defense. "My reputation is all I have, isn't it? It's how I manage to influence those in the House of Lords, it's how I generate respect and initiate change in Society."

Arthur rolled his eyes and Colin bit his tongue. While he took his duties to country and kingdom, as well as to those with less power than himself, very seriously, he knew Arthur thought him a fool. His cousin had often told him that if he held the title of viscount, he would do things very differently.

Arthur let out a long, put-upon sigh. "I *know* those things are important to you. But I worry about you in this situation, not whatever causes you have taken up this week. If Jane is coming to stay in your house, that doesn't mean you should soften your position toward her. Keep your distance, Colin. Don't get caught in her trap, for I'm certain she will try to seduce you with her wiles."

Colin tensed at the thought of Jane using her "wiles" against him. A very pleasing thought that was, actually. He often thought of the afternoon after they wed, when he'd stepped into her dressing room and dismissed her servant, and the two of them had passionately consummated their union.

He'd often dreamed of doing that very thing again, despite how angry he was at her.

And the fact was that she was his wife: he could certainly exercise his husbandly rights with her without forgetting what she truly was at her core. Perhaps it was his duty to do so, or so his mother kept reminding him by going on about heirs and Jane and the future.

"I won't fall into her trap," he murmured, as much to himself as to respond to Arthur's words.

His cousin seemed relieved at that statement and clapped him on the shoulder gently. "Excellent."

But as Arthur retook his seat and Colin did the same, he knew one thing for certain.

He didn't intend to keep his distance from Jane either.

CHAPTER 3

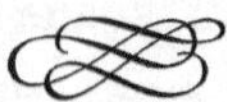

J ane stood in the lady's chamber in her husband's home less than six hours after he had called on her. She remembered this room well. It was where he'd first made love to her. It was where he'd left her to weep after he coldly dismissed her and told her she would be sent to the country only one day after their wedding.

She stared at the bed and shivered.

This was like returning to the scene of a crime.

She'd done just what he asked of her that morning. Against her sister's strenuous protests, she'd allowed her things to be placed in a cart, put herself in the carriage and ridden "home". But once there, Colin hadn't been in residence to greet her. For two hours, she had waited for him, feeling more and more foolish.

She turned away from the bed and found herself looking at the door that led to the adjoining sitting room and through it, to Colin's bedchamber. *That* room she'd never been in. She doubted he would want her to look, to snoop around in his things when he could clearly hardly stand her.

"It's his own fault," she muttered to herself as she strode through the door, into the sitting room and right up to his chamber entrance. There she hesitated, then steeled herself and pushed the door open.

The room smelled of him. That was the first thing she noticed. Something with a hint of pine and a whiff of masculinity. She shut her eyes and took a deep breath of that smell, then stepped farther into the room and turned in a circle.

The chamber looked like him, too, as if someone had designed it to fit the cool, sophisticated man she hardly knew. The furniture was simple, the colors muted and everything was in its place.

"Not a thing amiss," she said with a shake of her head. "God forbid there ever be a mess in the life of the Viscount Wharton."

"Messes are complicated."

She froze at the sound of Colin's voice behind her. She slowly turned to find him at the same door where she had entered not a moment before. He was leaning against the jamb, arms folded, eyes locked firmly on her.

"I don't like complications," he said, but his voice was rough. His gaze was heated and hooded as it swept over her. Once upon a time, she wouldn't have known what that expression meant. But now she remembered it well.

He wanted her.

She blinked at the realization and at the aching echo in her body that reminded her she wanted him, too, despite everything he'd done to her. Or hadn't? God, but it was a jumble now, all her disappointments and regrets.

"If you don't like complications, why bring me here?" she asked, her voice barely carrying.

He pushed off the doorframe and took a long step into the room. His expression still pulsed with wanting and her knees began to shake.

"You are..." He trailed off, and it was like he was trying to fight what he said next. "You are beautiful, Jane."

She drew back a fraction at that unexpected compliment, given reluctantly, but still given. And returned, for when she looked at him she saw more than the cold man who had banished her for untold crimes. She saw more than the man who refused to answer her letters and set her free from the prison of his contempt.

When she looked at him, she still saw the man she'd married with all the hopes in her heart. The man who had made love to her and woken her up to desires she'd never fully understood.

If he could look at her and see beauty, want her despite his negative feelings, perhaps she could change his heart by following the path of his desires.

She had to be bold enough to try if she wanted any kind of future at all beyond one locked away in a castle by the sea. Alone. Lost.

She took a step toward him, keeping her gaze locked on him. He stiffened as she made her way across the small expanse that separated them. But he didn't pull away, even when she stopped just in front of him.

Even when she lifted a hand to his chest and placed it there. His heart pounded beneath his jacket and hers leapt to join it.

"Is *this* why I'm here?" she whispered, lifting up on her tiptoes, going slowly as if daring him to pull away. He didn't. He held perfectly still as her lips brushed across his, and then let out a groan that seemed to come from deep within his chest, his soul.

His arms closed around her and he brought her up hard against his chest. His mouth opened and his tongue slid inside hers, sweeping across her, drawing her forward until her bones turned to water and her blood turned to fire.

She wrapped her arms around his neck, leaning fully against him and feeling the hard, heavy length of him pressing against her stomach. Her body responded with needy desire, wetness flooding between her legs and letting her know how much she needed him in this charged, unexpected moment.

As if he read her thoughts, he drew back, staring down into her eyes, seeking some kind of truth he'd never believed. She wasn't sure what he saw there, but when he let her go, he didn't leave.

Instead, he reached behind himself and slammed the door shut, giving them privacy.

She shuddered as he reached for her a second time, this time slower and gentler, as if before he had lost his senses and now wanted to savor the moment.

So did she.

He caught her hand and drew her across the room, toward the bed. *His* bed. He kept his gaze firmly on her face until they reached the edge, then he slowly turned her until her back was to him. She expected him to just open her gown, but instead he drew her back until she leaned against his chest. His arms came around her, hands cupping her breasts as he nuzzled her neck and pressed against her.

She sank into him, reaching a hand up to wind her fingers around the back of his neck and reveling in the warmth of his mouth on her flesh. God, how had she gone so long without this? At present, it felt as imperative as breathing.

He sucked at her skin and she gasped out his name on a broken breath. Only then did he slide his hands around to the buttons along her spine and open them one by one.

The warm air in the chamber slid along the skin revealed there, stirred the thin fabric of her undergarments, and she let out a low sigh of pleasure. He pressed his lips along the edge of her chemise, his tongue darting out to taste her there.

She shimmied to make the gown fall forward and clumsily pulled her arms free. He didn't stop her, nor did he stop her when she turned back to face him as she shoved the gown the rest of the way off her body.

His expression was still heated as he watched her do so, but she thought she sensed something troubled beneath it. She tensed at the sight of it, fear flaring in her that he would regain his ability to push her aside.

To combat that, she slipped her chemise from her shoulders and allowed it to fall at her feet with her gown.

Now she was naked before him. A state she had not been in for so many months. Heat filled her cheeks, but she forced herself not to cover up, forced herself to stay before him, under his slow, steady stare.

He reached out, and she caught her breath when she saw his hand tremble. For so long, she had resigned herself to the fact that she meant nothing to him, and here she was being proven wrong by that tremor. He trailed his fingers across her naked collarbone, then lower, across her left breast. When he touched her hard nipple, she couldn't hold back a hiss of pleasure.

His gaze jerked up as he repeated the action on the other breast. Those fleeting touches sent a ricochet of sensation through her heated flesh, and she caught his arm to keep herself steady.

That seemed to drag him into action again. He swept her up into his arms and laid her across his bed. He stepped back and stripped out of his clothing with swift efficiency. She stared as he revealed himself, shocked that his body was as magnificent as she had remembered on those heated nights alone in the countryside.

Colin was almost always formal in his dress, never a button or fold of his cravat out of place. But beneath that formal exterior there was a man who was wholly and wonderfully hard and perfectly formed. From his broad shoulders to his muscular chest to the erect line of his cock, he was carved from granite.

And she wanted to explore every inch of him.

He moved back toward the bed and she reached for him, sliding her hand over his chest, down his stomach and at last curling her fingers around his cock. He hissed in a breath as she stroked him, and she looked up to see that same expression of pleasure mixed with something troubled that she'd seen earlier.

She might have asked him about it, but he bent over and covered her mouth with his, silencing her before she even had a chance to speak. She sank back into the pillows, wrapping her arms around him as he maneuvered over her, covering her with that heavy, hard, hot body. She opened to him naturally, providing him a space between her legs that he settled into.

But he didn't just take her, which was what she'd half-expected and almost wanted, if truth be told. No, instead he focused on kissing her, deeply, thoroughly, until her mind emptied of all thought and protest and memory and all that existed was the pleasure he brought her in this charged moment.

And as if he guessed the moment she let go, that was when he moved, dragging his mouth down her throat as she lifted up into him, and lower to her chest, where he latched those same lips over her hard nipple.

She cried out his name at the electric jolt of pleasure that rushed through her entire body at the intimate touch. She drove her fingers into the thick waves of his hair, holding him there as he sucked and stroked the sensitive flesh.

She found her hips lifting as he licked her, her sex seeking relief as he built an inferno of pleasure and need with his mouth. A fire he seemed in no hurry to put out, for he slowly shifted his lips to the opposite breast, repeating his actions there until she was gasping and writhing beneath the weight of his body.

She stared down the length of her body, watching him at his work. When he lifted his gaze and their eyes met, he smiled. Her heart stuttered. He had not smiled at her in so long, and she ached for more of it.

But the smile was wicked this time, and he kept his eyes on hers as he slowly slid down the length of her naked body with his lips. His mouth crested over the flatness of her belly and she caught her breath, across the swell of her hip, and she stopped breathing entirely.

"Colin," she gasped out.

He smiled again. "Just lay still. Allow me this."

She didn't understand what he meant by those words. Allow him what? To kiss her all over, worship her like he gave a damn—

Her thoughts cut off when he gently spread her legs wider and settled his mouth between them. His lips brushed her wet and ready sex, and then he opened her with his fingers, exposing her to the first hot lick of his rough tongue.

She cried out in surprise and pleasure at the unexpected act, and found herself lifting her hips into him. He placed a big hand on her hip, steadying her before he licked her again, along the entire length of her sex.

She gripped at the coverlet as he repeated that action again and again.

Jane had felt pleasure before. Colin had made sure she experienced it that first time they made love, when she'd been afraid and nervous beneath his touch. In the months since, alone in her bed, she had found ways to create an echo of that pleasure, though it was never as satisfying.

But this...*this* was something different. It was as if all the focus in her entire body was suddenly settled at the bundle of nerves that Colin was now gently sucking. Pleasure flowed like water from her clitoris, making her body shake, her blood heat, the dam of pleasure strain, and finally it burst.

Wave after wave of quaking, intense sensation washed over her. She twitched against his mouth, keening cries escaping her lips as she surrendered to the intense pleasure he gave her.

It was only when her tremors subsided that he crawled back up the length of her body, kissing a path back to her mouth. When his lips settled on hers, she tasted the sweet and salty evidence of her release, and she made another muffled cry at the erotic knowledge of where his tongue had been.

She felt him shifting over her, positioning himself at her entrance. She continued to kiss him, allowing him to do as he would, bracing herself when she felt the head of his cock at the entrance to her body.

He stopped kissing her then and drew back, watching as he pressed forward.

It had been such a long time since he'd last taken her, and Jane gasped as her tight body slowly gave way to him. There was no pain like the first time, but she was certainly well aware of what he was doing. His eyes were wide as he pressed forward, forward, and finally seated himself fully inside of her.

His gaze was intense, but there was question there. As if he hadn't fully expected what he was experiencing. God knew she hadn't. She hadn't ever guessed this is how her afternoon would end when he pushed his way into her sister's house hours before.

She lifted into him, gripping him inside, and he made a strangled moan as his expression cleared of anything but pleasure. He began to rock against her, his hips swiveling so they hit that sweet spot his tongue had recently been teasing. She met his thrusts halfway, grinding herself against him to make the already exquisitely sensitive place even more stimulated.

The steady beat of pleasure that had begun to fade moments before came back now, building slower, but now even more intensely, because he was inside of her, they were together, and this was what she had missed all those months she was alone.

She cried out as release hit her a second time and he stared at her as he drew the pleasure from her. His thrusts increased until his neck strained and he pumped hot and heavy into her trembling body, and then collapsed down over her. He whispered wordless sounds of passion as she smoothed her hands over his broad back again and again.

And hoped against hope that this wonderful moment would bind them together and begin to repair all that had been damaged between them.

CHAPTER 4

Colin pulled his shirt over his head and stared down at his sleeping wife as he carefully rebuttoned it and shoved the tails into the waist of his trousers. Jane had slipped into sleep not long after they made love, and now she was sprawled naked across his bed, blonde hair tangled around her back and shoulders, a small smile on her beautiful face.

He wanted nothing more than to slide back into bed with her, curl his body around her and make love to her until she woke.

But passions had cooled. Reason had returned. And so had memory. Claiming Jane was one thing. Slipping into any kind of foolish belief that making love could fix all that was broken between them was quite another. He knew Jane's character, after all. He couldn't forget that fact.

He frowned as he pulled his jacket on. Jane was untrue, and yet her body had felt tight as a virgin's. Almost as if she had not had a man inside of her since he last took her on the afternoon of their wedding. Of course, none of his spies in Applegate had ever told him she had a lover, but he'd never believed that meant she *didn't*. Only that she was smart enough not to get caught at it.

He pinched his lips and grabbed for a blanket that rested on the back of a chair in his chamber. Gently he pulled it up over her, took one last look at her sleeping frame, and left the room.

It was foolish to muse too much on these things. Like he was looking for a way to absolve her of her past sins. Like he was searching for something that would make their marriage whole again.

That something didn't exist. Passions might, and there was a place for them, as well as for her presence in his home to stop any gossip that might arise from her being back in London. But beyond that...

"There is no going back," he murmured as he walked down the hallway to his office. "And I must never forget that ever again."

Jane opened her eyes, and for a moment she had no idea where she was. Early evening light was filtering through the windows of the chamber where she lay on a comfortable bed, but it wasn't her room in Applegate or at her sister's. It was...

It came back to her in a rush, and she sat up. She was in Colin's room. Colin's bed. Because Colin had taken her there.

But Colin was gone.

She frowned. Slowly, she rose and saw the evidence of the passion between them in the way her clothing was still strewn about his otherwise spotless room. His clothing was gone.

So he had abandoned her. Again.

She caught her chemise and pulled it over her head before she rang the bell at the door. The servant who answered told Jane she would fetch her maid, and Jane laid out her things on his bed as she waited for help.

Soon enough, Laura arrived. The girl seemed surprised to find Jane in the viscount's chamber, but she said nothing as she helped her dress and fixed her hair from its tangled reminder of Colin's fingers raking through the locks.

Once Laura had gone, Jane looked at herself in the mirror. She looked the same as she had that morning. And yet she felt so very different. Because Colin had claimed her, with a desperate, heated passion she'd long ago convinced herself didn't exist.

But if it still did, perhaps other things also existed. She sighed and smoothed her gown before she left the room and went downstairs to find her husband. A footman was standing at the bottom of the stairs, and she smiled at him.

"Do you know where Lord Wharton is?"

The man shifted. "His office, I believe, my lady. But he doesn't like to be disturbed before supper."

She waved off his admonishment and moved down the hall. She'd never had a chance to truly call this house a home, and that fact became stark when she could not find the study. In the end, it was the light coming from under the door that led her there. She stood for a moment to calm herself before she entered the chamber.

He was bent over his desk when she stepped inside, scribbling furiously. He didn't look up, but his face scrunched into a scowl. "Is my order not to be disturbed so very hard to follow?" he snapped.

She arched a brow as she shut the door. "I wasn't certain if it applied to me."

His gaze jerked up and his hand stilled in its writing. He stared at her, almost as if he had forgotten she resided in his house, then slowly rose.

"It applies to everyone. The time before supper is when I get my best work done," he said, but there was no cruelty to his tone.

"And what are you working on?" she asked. She knew from the past that he took his position in the House of Lords very seriously. More seriously than any gentleman she'd ever known. His passionate dedication to his place there had been one of the many things that drew her to him what seemed like a lifetime ago.

His mouth pinched and the walls came up between them. "Nothing you would be interested in, I'm sure," he said. "Is there something you need?"

She flinched at his suddenly icy demeanor. It seemed nothing had changed after all, and she felt herself filled with disappointment at the jab of that pointed truth.

But she also felt something else. Anger.

She folded her arms. "Yes, I suppose there is," she said. "I want you to tell me what it is you want from *me*, Colin."

He took a step toward her, his nostrils flaring slightly. He looked hard as stone in that moment. Not like the man who had passionately made love to her, but a different man. One who viewed her with nothing but contempt.

"I want nothing, Jane," he said through clenched teeth.

She shook her head. Letters hadn't changed him, time hadn't, even making love to her hadn't softened him in the slightest. Perhaps she was an idiot to believe she could ever break past all he threw between them.

Perhaps she should stop trying.

"If you want nothing," she said, wishing her voice didn't tremble, "then I suppose the best thing I could do is return to my sister's home so I will no longer be in your way."

She turned to step away, but his voice cut through the air between them. "No!"

She halted at his sharp tone and turned back. "No?"

"I command you to stay," he ground out.

She arched a brow. "You *command* me," she repeated, her ire raising, her frustration.

"It is my right," he said. "I'm your husband."

She caught her breath at the arrogance of that statement and the absolute falsehood of it. Without thinking, she took a long step toward him, fists clenched at her sides.

"My husband? Oh, no, you are not, Colin. You are a man who married me, then banished me without explanation. You do not *deserve* to be called husband. You are nothing but a cruel coward."

She saw that the barb hit its mark, for he recoiled ever so slightly. His eyes were wide as he looked her up and down.

"*I am the coward, am I?*" he asked at last, his voice dangerously low. "I could say worse about you, Jane."

She threw up her hands. "Then say it. For God's sake, Colin, say *anything.*"

~

Colin turned away. She was a fine actress, he would give her that. He almost believed she actually cared that they were estranged. That she actually wanted to bridge the gap between them and start again.

But when he thought of her on a terrace on their wedding day, letting some other man kiss her, his stomach turned and his heart hardened to her.

He would not give her his pain. He would not give her his emotions. She didn't deserve that.

"You said I wasn't your husband," he said, hardly managing to grind the words out as he slowly faced her. "That hasn't escaped the notice of others. So you ask me what I want."

She nodded, but her gaze swept over him. The desire hidden beneath her anger took him by surprise, just as it had in his bedroom not so very long ago. And it made him want her. It made him feel other things that he pushed aside with violence.

"You will stay here with me for the duration of your time in London," he explained. "And you will be my wife in public, until you go home."

She lifted her chin, defiance brightening her face. Making her look like a warrior. It was strangely erotic to see her like that. Certain of herself, challenging him.

"Only a wife in public?" she asked.

His eyes fluttered shut at the bold question. So she would try to use her body against him now. That was her best move yet, for it was the one thing he knew would be impossible to resist. Now that he'd touched her again, he couldn't have her under his roof and not do it again and again.

He would just have to be careful he didn't allow himself to be entangled in other ways. More dangerous ways. More impossible ways.

"You are trying to toy with me," he said softly, but found himself moving toward her.

She cocked her head, defiance in her stare, drawing him in even if it should have repelled him. "I think that's what you want, Colin," she murmured. "Or will you deny you desire me?"

He reached out and caught her hand, keeping his gaze locked with hers as he gently placed it on the placard of his trousers. His cock, which had been hard against his clothes since the moment she marched into his office, twitched at the pressure of her palm.

"Does it seem like I'm denying it?" he asked.

For a moment, he thought she might back away. Refuse them both this madness. But then she shook her head, almost as if she were as lost as he was, and leaned up into his chest. Her lips brushed his, and he ground out a curse as he cupped her backside and lifted her against him.

She made a garbled sound of pleasure as he turned around and backed her toward the desk. He set her up on the edge and slid his hands into her soft hair while he ground his mouth against her. She returned the passion of the kiss, the fever, arching into him again and again, teasing him with the drag of her body on his.

He was frantic as he shoved the skirt of her dress up her long legs, shifting so she could unfasten his trousers at the same time. His cock came free and she stroked him while their tongues tangled, warred, and he slid her forward on the desk so he could angle himself against her. The hot slide of her sex welcomed him, and their mouths parted as both of them let out a low groan.

This was madness, but it was a beautiful kind of madness. She was heat and slickness and *home*. He didn't want her to be home. He didn't want to need her. Yet he did, like he needed breath or food or water.

And he had her now so he took her, gripping her hips to thrust into her again and again. She lifted to meet him, mewling out pleasure as her fingers dug into his shoulders and her head tilted back in surrender.

He dropped his mouth to her exposed throat, sucking there. His thrusts increased and he loved how her pulse jumped beneath his lips and her grinding quickened until she stiffened, her body pulsing with release around him. He thrust through it, reveling in her soft cries, the grip of her fluttering body, the out-of-control way she jerked against him. His cock felt full and heavy, his balls tightened, and then he came with her, pumping hot into her as he moaned out her name.

For a long time they stayed that way, bodies intertwined on the edge of his desk, a desk he'd never look at again without remembering this heated and unexpected joining.

At last, she slid away, his body coming free from hers. He tucked himself back into place as she smoothed her skirts around her hips. Then she surprised him by reaching out her hand to him.

He stared at the offering and then looked up into her face in confusion.

She smiled. "Come upstairs, Colin. Come to bed with me."

He swallowed at the easy way she offered that temptation. At the way he wanted so much to take it.

"It isn't even supper time," he said softly.

She shrugged. "I don't care. And I don't think you do either. Come upstairs with me. If I'm going to play your wife, I want to be your wife. And I think you want that, too."

He hesitated, but then he found himself reaching out to the hand she offered, folding his fingers around hers, letting her guide him from the room. Up the stairs. Into his chamber. Into his bed.

And with every step, he tried desperately to remind himself that all he could give this woman was his body. Tried and failed.

CHAPTER 5

Jane rolled over and smiled to find Colin still lying beside her, facing her. His dark eyes were open and she was sucked into the depths of them. She was here, truly here, in his bed, after all the months they'd been separated. And while she couldn't read all of his intentions in his guarded expression, she could see the remnants of the desire that had been pulsing between them since her arrival in his home.

"Good morning," she murmured, reaching out to trace his shoulder with her fingertips.

He didn't pull away, but caught his breath at the touch. She could see his struggle, his war between wanting her and the contempt he still insisted on having. The contempt she didn't understand.

"Good morning," he answered, his tone slightly stiff and formal for a man who had made love to her long into the night, bringing her pleasure again and again, almost with the focus of a man possessed.

He pushed off the bed, giving her a grand view of his muscular backside before he found his trousers and covered himself.

"What are your plans for the day?" she asked, sitting up and not bothering to cover herself, for he had seen all of her and more. He sent a side glance her way and swallowed hard.

"I-I'm to meet with a few men about this...project," he said, turning away.

She tilted her head. "Yes, the project that you work best on before supper. Still don't want to tell me what it is that fills your mind so completely?"

He cleared his throat. "I can't imagine you truly care what I do in my duties in the House of Lords, Jane."

"Can't you?" she repeated. "You think I'm so cotton-headed that I cannot understand politics?"

He faced her, lips pursed. "We may have been apart a long time, Jane but I know you aren't foolish. I have always...always admired your intellect."

She lifted her brows. "A compliment, my lord, and you didn't even combust from giving it. Well, I will take it, for a sharp mind has always had more value to me than a pretty face."

"And here you are with both," he muttered.

She blushed at the second compliment, given just as reluctantly. But she was determined to build on them nonetheless. "Then tell me of your project. I am very interested."

He let out a long sigh. "There have been several accidents in the factories here in London recently. I've seen the destructive damage those incidents have done. So I am...working on improving the conditions of those who work in the factories. And I believe my work may be able to protect those in the fields, as well."

She caught her breath, shocked by that statement, but in only the best of ways. Colin was so straitlaced, so proper, she had never believed he gave the common man much thought, let alone put any time into his duty to protect anyone in a class below his own. But from the way he shifted, unwilling to meet her eyes, it was evident this legislation meant a great deal to him personally.

And it reminded her of the many things she had found attractive in him all those months ago. The kindness she had sensed in him that had long been turned away from herself. But it still existed, it seemed.

"Truly?" she said softly.

He cleared his throat in further discomfort. "You think me so cruel that I couldn't give a damn about anyone but myself?"

She shook her head. "I didn't realize that was your interest, that's all."

He ducked to grab his shirt from the floor and fiddled with the fabric as he said, "I have long fought for such things. It's an uphill battle, of course. Men of rank are often complacent in the torment of their lowers, or oblivious to it. Teaching them the facts and then convincing them to do better is a challenge."

She stared at him, handsome in his half-dressed state, but even more irresistible when she saw this softer, more caring side to him. A man who gave a damn about others, even if he refused to give one about her.

Regrets filled her. That they had been separated. That she didn't understand why. That he couldn't care for her the way he cared for strangers. She regretted it all and longed for the possibility of repairing it. Right now, lying in his bed, having a real conversation with him about his dreams, his goals, it felt like she could. If only she tread very carefully.

"I think it's a fine notion," she said at last, hearing the thickness of her voice. "In the running of your estate, I have seen how difficult it is for those in the positions you describe to survive. Certainly, you provide well for them, but there is little chance to improve their lot. How better to motivate a man than to give him the opportunity to provide a better life for his children?"

Colin cocked his head. "A good argument. Very good, actually. I'll use it today, if you don't mind."

She smiled at him. "I don't."

He shifted, and whatever headway she'd made with him slipped away as the walls came up between them. He motioned to his dressing room. "I'll go prepare for my day. And I'll see you later."

He moved away and she made no move to stop him. At the door, he turned. "Jane?"

"Yes?"

"There is a ball tonight, hosted by the Earl of Cornfellow. You will attend with me."

The words were said as a statement, but she heard the request in his tone. She nodded. "As you wish, my lord."

He stared at her a moment, then left the room and shut the door behind him. She smiled as she got out of his bed, wrapped her dress around her and moved into the lady's chamber to ring for her maid. But as she waited for Laura, she grinned at herself in her mirror. She'd made headway in re-establishing some kind of connection with Colin. And that gave her hope.

"I'm going to win him back," she said out loud, believing those words with all her heart as she said them. "I'm going to win my marriage."

~

Colin stood with his cousin Arthur and their host of this ball, the Earl of Cornfellow, but he wasn't attending to the conversation between them. Instead, he was staring across the room at Jane.

She was standing in a small circle of women, laughing and chatting. She was stunning, her blonde hair done in a complicated style that included ringlets which cascaded down in little tendrils across her back, giving him a path where he could later place his lips. Her gown was pale blue, matching her bright eyes perfectly and bringing out the perfection of her skin.

She was the focus of every stare. He supposed some of that had to do with the rumors of her return, as detailed in that *Scandal Sheet* rag a few days before. But he would wager much of it had to do with how beautiful she was, how charismatic, how fascinating.

"Look at him," Cornfellow said, his tone slightly teasing. "If I didn't know you better, Wharton, I'd say you were infatuated with your own wife, despite all the whispers about her long exile in the countryside."

Colin jerked his attention back to his companions. Cornfellow, who was at least ten years older than himself and Arthur, was grinning, but his cousin looked troubled. Just as Colin felt troubled.

"Oh, don't look so horrified that I know your secret," Cornfellow said, nudging Colin gently. "Warm feelings about one's spouse seem to be in vogue lately. And she's a beautiful woman."

Colin forced a smile on his face. "Indeed, she is."

"Yes, lovely," Arthur concurred, his face still lined with worry. Colin appreciated it, even though it didn't help his current situation.

"Still, the merits of my wife are not what you and I need to discuss, are they?" Colin said, forcing his mind to go back to matters at hand, not things he didn't want to ponder.

Cornfellow sighed and his smile slipped. "You are always working even when you are not working," he said. "Wharton, I just don't know if I can support your measure."

Colin gritted his teeth. This had been his entire day, poking and prodding spoiled aristocrats while trying not to be completely distracted by thoughts of his wayward wife.

The same wife who was slowly crossing the room toward him, her gaze locked on his and a slow smile on her face, which almost made his knees buckle. Damn her for being so irresistible.

"Gentlemen," she said as she stepped up beside him and slipped a hand into the crook of his arm. Her touch set him on fire and it took everything in him not to spin her into his arms for a wildly inappropriate kiss.

"Lady Wharton," Cornfellow said, smiling broadly for her. "You must have known your name was on the wind."

She arched a brow. "Talking about me, were you? Oh dear, for you all had such serious expressions."

Arthur made a noise in the back of his throat and Colin glared at him. His cousin was too protective—he hoped Arthur wouldn't do or say something foolish in front of Cornfellow. He didn't need any increased scandal during this delicate negotiation period.

"I'm afraid our serious expressions were born *after* the gentlemen were complimenting you, my dear," Colin said.

"Ah, so you were discussing business," she said with a light laugh. "Wharton's bill, I assume."

Cornfellow drew back in obvious surprise that she was aware of the topic. "Indeed. And what do *you* think of the measure, my lady?" He smirked, as if her answer would surely be a laugh for him.

Although Jane didn't know the specifics, Colin was surprised when she didn't even miss a beat. She leaned forward. "I admit I am not privy to all the nuances, but I do think that a man of position best shows himself by how he treats those below him, don't you, my lord?"

Cornfellow seemed to consider that. "I suppose I had not considered it that way. But do you think that by providing something more for those in the lower classes, we are encouraging rebellion? For those in lower position to grasp even higher?"

Jane's cheek twitched ever so slightly, the only betrayal that she found the question distasteful. "Think of the uprisings we've seen in recent years. Were they born of men who had been given too much, or too little? In my mind, you are preventing rebellion by supporting those without a voice, not courting it."

Cornwall drew in a long breath. "That is something to think about." He turned to Colin and looked him up and down with an appraising glance. "This is as shocking to me as it is to you, sir, but you may take my answer as a *tentative* yes, Wharton."

"Truly?" Colin gasped.

Cornwall nodded once. "Yes, your wife is very persuasive. Now if you will excuse me, I must attend to other guests. Let's meet at the club soon, shall we?"

"Certainly—good evening," Colin said, somewhat in shock by what had just happened. Here he had been working and massaging

Cornfellow for days, weeks even, and a few words from Jane's lips and the man was convinced.

He let his gaze slide to her. She was smiling broadly, and for a moment he couldn't breathe, she was so beautiful.

Arthur seemed less enthralled. He looked her up and down with a sniff. "Don't *you* have the ability to wrap men around your finger."

Colin jerked his face toward Arthur, and Jane also looked at him. For a moment her expression held hurt and confusion at the barely veiled accusation. Despite the fact that he knew it was a ploy, he felt a defensiveness of her.

"I don't know about that," Jane said slowly. Carefully. "Sometimes a person needs to hear the same words in a different voice for them to sink in, that is all. I'm sure Cornfellow was already nearly convinced by Colin's arguments."

Arthur shook his head. "I'm sure it had *nothing* to do with your smiles."

"Arthur," Colin snapped, his tone sharp. "Why don't you go find someone to talk to? I'm going to dance with my wife."

Arthur stared at him, almost in disbelief, before he executed a stiff bow. "Of course, cousin. Excuse me." He gave the barest of nods to Jane and then turned on his heel and marched away, his shoulders rigid and his whole demeanor frustrated.

Colin guided Jane to the floor and the orchestra began a waltz. As he pulled her in close and launched them into the steps, Jane let out a low sigh. "Your cousin seems to despise me," she said softly.

Colin frowned. "He just doesn't...*know* you," he said.

She stared up into his face. Her expression was calm even though there was a deep sadness in her blue eyes. "Like you? Do you know me, Colin?"

He flinched at the quiet question. In truth, he really *didn't* know her. She'd been an arrangement and then an attraction and then a betrayal and now she was...well, he didn't know what she was now.

But she'd never just been Jane. And he'd never just been Colin. And in that moment he realized just how much he wanted that.

Because in this moment he felt connected to her. Almost as if he was whole when he hadn't even known he was missing something.

"I want to go home with you," he whispered.

Her eyes went wide and she stumbled slightly in the steps of the dance. "But we only just got here, Colin, and we—"

He nodded. "I realize all that. And I don't care. I want to go home with you Jane. Now. Please."

~

Jane sat in the carriage, staring at the open door as she listened to her husband speak softly to his servants. There was a tension to his voice she'd never heard before. An intensity that matched what she'd seen on his face when they were dancing. Like he was fighting a battle he'd just realized he didn't need to win.

And she had no idea what that meant for her, for him, for *them*. Her hands shook in her lap as he finally climbed up into the vehicle and the door shut behind him.

He settled into his seat across from her and the carriage began to move. She searched the darkness, trying to see his expression, trying to read him so that she understood what was happening.

But it was impossible. The vehicle was dark. She only caught glimpses of his face in columns of light that sometimes passed through the glass.

She settled back and took a long breath. "Are you…angry with me?"

"No," he said, his voice surprisingly gentle through the dark. "Not at all. I just found I couldn't wait even one more moment to do this."

He moved to her side of the carriage in one smooth motion and cupped her cheeks. His lips lowered and she gasped as he kissed her. Not an ordinary kiss, but something heated and passionate and filled with dark desire and steaming, swirling pleasure.

She wrapped her arms around him, letting out a low moan as he pushed her against the carriage wall, his weight pressing into her, proving to her that he wanted her from the hard length of his cock against her belly.

He placed a hand against her thigh and began to tangle her skirt into his fist, sliding it up her leg to reveal her stockings, her skin.

"I need you," he admitted, his tone taut and filled with tension.

She stared at his face, clearer now that he was so close. She saw desperation there, emotional as well as physical. It mimicked her own.

"Then take what you need," she murmured as she leaned up to capture his lips once more.

He let out a low sound, something between a moan and a sob, and then he wrenched at his trouser placket, freeing himself. He shifted her on the seat, pulling her backside half off as he knelt between her legs and positioned himself at her entrance.

She gasped when he entered her, sliding into the slick evidence of her need as he whispered her name against her neck.

She lifted against him, rocking her clitoris against his pelvis and sending a shot of awareness through herself. He grunted and then began to move. They were short, hard thrusts, ones that ground against her as she lifted into them. Ones that claimed and captured and ripped pleasure through her body with unexpected ferocity and speed.

She came without warning, a release tore through her as she cried out, the sound muffled against his jacket, his shoulder. He wasn't far behind, spending deep within her with a broken grunt.

"You test me," he growled against her throat as he shuddered one last time.

"I like testing you," she whispered back, unable to keep a smile off her face.

He tensed at that statement and drew back as the carriage came to a stop. He moved to his side of the carriage, breaking the connection of their bodies and quickly pulled his clothing back together.

She did the same, frowning at his silence and the accusatory fashion of it.

It was like she was offered a chance to repair the breach between them and yet something always happened to ruin it. Something she said or did or didn't say or didn't do. A puzzle to solve, only she wasn't being given all of the pieces.

The carriage door opened and the footman appeared. Colin climbed from the vehicle first, then took her hand to help her down. She met his gaze as she exited, but he looked away as soon as he could and began the short walk into the foyer.

"Colin," she said as they handed over their coats and gloves and hats to waiting servants.

He frowned. "I find I'm tired," he said. "It has been a long and eventful few days."

The servants departed and she folded her arms as she stared at him. "So you will not speak to me?"

He stiffened at her direct method of approach. "I'm uncertain what there is to say, Jane."

She caught her breath. "Uncertain what there is to say? How can you mean that when there is half a year between us? When there is such anger in you at times and such gentleness at others? How can you look me in the face and pretend there isn't something to say?"

He almost looked chagrined at her accusation. He bent his head briefly, and there was a moment where she held her breath, waiting for the dam to break, for the truth to be revealed. But then his expression hardened.

"I recognize you want more," he said softly. "But this is all I have for you, Jane. It is likely all I will ever have. And there is nothing else to say."

He turned and walked away, leaving her standing in the foyer, staring after him, utterly lost and utterly broken.

CHAPTER 6

Jane sat in her parlor, staring at her empty cup of tea with unseeing eyes.

"Jane?"

She jerked her head up to find Alicia staring at her. "God, this is your first call since delivering the baby and I am quite possibly the worst hostess of all time. I'm so sorry, Alicia."

"I'm not worried about your hostessing skills," Alicia said, taking her hand. "I'm worried about *you*. Jane, what in the world is going on?"

Jane tilted her head back. "I don't know if I *can* talk to you about it."

"Why?"

"Because you hate Colin," she said, leveling her gaze on Alicia and daring her deny the charge.

Alicia sighed. "I admit, I despise what that man did to you. Dragging you out of London, banishing you to the countryside without explanation, tearing you away from me? But...he is your husband. There is no changing that now. And if talking about it would help, I will do my level best not to allow my feelings on the matter to come into play."

"Feelings," Jane mused, shutting her eyes.

Alicia sucked in a breath. "Are you saying yours have become involved?"

Jane looked at her. "Perhaps they always were. I felt them growing as we courted, they bloomed when we wed and then…I was crushed after he sent me away. But there were always dreams of him, Alicia. Always these secret hopes that one day he might see me, want me…care for me. And now I'm here and—"

She cut herself off, for the line of her thoughts was very dangerous, indeed. Unspeakable considering that she still didn't know anything about the man's mind.

"Are you in love with him? Despite all he's done?" Alicia asked, and Jane stiffened at those words she had not dared to think to herself, let alone say out loud. Now they hung in the air, a beautiful mirage that felt so very out of reach. "Jane?"

She shook her head and dropped her gaze from Alicia's seeking one. "Yes," she said, that one word snapping between them. "I…love him."

Her sister's eyes went wide. "Oh, Jane."

She nodded. "It's desperate, isn't it? To feel such a thing for a man who seems to hate me. Even when he touches me, even when he holds me, that hesitation is there."

"And that makes me wonder how it is possible that you could offer him something so precious as your heart."

"When Colin and I were first introduced, after the arrangements had been made, he was…he was so very kind. Gentle. We could talk for hours and never run out of topics of conversation. He laughed, he smiled. He was a different person."

Alicia frowned. "Very well, I *do* recall that somewhat. In fact, when you first became engaged, I was actually hopeful for you, that you would find the same love I had found."

"As was I," Jane said. "And then he changed."

"Why, though?" Alicia asked.

Jane threw up her hands. "I have no idea—that's the problem.

One moment he was declaring how happy he was to have me as his bride, how hopeful he was for our future. The next, he pulled away and banished me. I have never understood why. I even wrote to him, after I'd been away a while. Every week for the past three months, I wrote. He never replied, never explained it."

Alicia folded her arms. "You have not gotten to the point of the story where he is worthy of your love."

Jane let out a long breath. "Being here with him now, I see him struggling. It's like a push and pull between us. He wants me near and he can be so tender, so passionate. There are moments when his walls come down and I still see that man with whom I could have had a happy future. But then he pushes me away, almost as if he is compelled to do so."

"Have you asked him for an explanation?" Alicia asked.

She nodded. "I have tried, but it's as if he expects me to already know whatever sin I committed. So I feel as though I'm always on the edge of knowing him, knowing anything. But I never go over."

"It's unfair of him to do that to you," her sister insisted. "I know you, and I know you could never do anything so wrong as to deserve what he's done."

"Even if I did, there is no making up for something I don't even understand." Jane sighed. "It is infinitely frustrating, this loop we're in."

"I imagine so," Alicia said. "And I'm sorry."

There was a knock in the parlor door and Jane nodded as the butler, Simmons, stepped into the room. "My lady, there is a missive that just arrived for you. It was declared to be urgent by the servant who delivered it."

Jane wrinkled her brow. Could it be from Colin? He had gone out today, gone to do more work on his proposal and, she thought, to avoid her after their encounter the night before.

"Thank you," she said as she took the letter. She looked down at her name, scrawled across the folded papers.

"Who is it from?" her sister asked as Jane broke the seal and began to read.

"Arthur Wharton, Colin's cousin," she explained, distracted as she read the words he had scratched out. "He asks that I join him today at two for a meeting. Odd. The man clearly doesn't like me any more than Colin does. Perhaps even less."

"Curious," Alicia said, taking the paper as Jane held it out and reading it for herself. "There is no indication as to what he wishes to discuss. Will you go?"

Jane shuddered at the thought of spending time with yet another man who seemed to hold some unnamed crime over her head. "I don't know."

Alicia drew back in surprise. "Even after all you've said to me today?"

Jane stared at her. "What do you mean?"

Her sister got to her feet and paced across the room to her. "Lord, Jane, you have been talking about all you feel for Wharton and all you do not understand about what stands between you. Has it ever occurred to you that his cousin might be exactly the person to answer that question, since your husband will not?"

Jane shifted. "They *are* close. I'd call them friends as much as relations."

"Well, there you have it. I'm certain Mr. Wharton must know why Colin keeps you at arm's length. He might even be calling you to his home with the intention of speaking to you on that very matter. If you go, you could find your answers and then you'll know exactly what the right response is."

Jane bit her lip. Her sister was not wrong. But in that moment, she was terrified. What if the answer she sought was not one she could overcome? What if Arthur told her something that broke her heart and ended things between her and Colin forever?

"At least you will have tried," Alicia said softly, almost in answer to Jane's unspoken question.

Jane nodded slowly. "You are right, of course. I can look back with no regret if I do this. So I shall send him word that I will join him. I just hope with all my heart that whatever he wishes to speak to me about is something that can change the course of my future."

~

Jane sat in Arthur Wharton's parlor, waiting anxiously for his arrival. She worried a handkerchief in her fist, trying not to focus too much on what he might want from her when he called her here.

"You're going to rend that thing in two."

She jumped from her seat and turned to watch the man, himself, enter the parlor. To her surprise, he reached back and closed the door nearly all the way. She wrinkled her brow, for the increased privacy was anything but proper. And it made her think this conversation was going to be very serious if he didn't want anyone to hear it.

"Good afternoon, Mr. Wharton."

His lips thinned as he went to the sideboard. "Arthur, please. After all, we are *family.*" He emphasized that word as he motioned to the teapot. "Drink?"

She shook her head. "No, thank you. Perhaps in a while."

He smirked and she drew back a fraction at the odd expression. There was something so cold in his eyes. Oh, he'd always been standoffish toward her, at the party the night before he'd been flat out rude, but this went beyond that.

Still, she was here. She had no choice but to face him and hope he would help her out of love for his cousin in the end.

"I was surprised to receive your summons today," she said.

He laughed. "My *summons*. I like that. As if I am a king."

She forced a smile. "I-I suppose."

"But here you are," he said, taking a seat across from her. She retook her own chair and shifted uncomfortably as he looked her up and down. "In the flesh."

"Y-yes," she said, still very confused by his demeanor. It was not what she had been expecting. "I assume that since you and I have never enjoyed a social connection, you called me here to discuss Colin."

"In a matter of speaking," Arthur said, setting his glass aside. "I suppose the topic is my *dear* cousin. And his relationship with you."

"You don't approve."

He caught her eye. "I do not."

She bent her head. "I wish I understood why. I feel as though you and Colin believe I *should*, but I don't. In fact, I thought that by coming here, perhaps I could learn more about the barriers which separate me from my husband. Perhaps I could find a way to earn the trust you don't yet have for me. That *he* doesn't have for me."

Arthur's eyes narrowed, and then he surprised her by breaking out into a long, chilly laugh. When he had regained his composure, he leaned forward, fingers steepled on his knees. "Even after all he's done, you care for him still, don't you?"

She blinked, for there it was. Oh, Arthur mocked with his tone, of course. But he had said it nonetheless. And if she wanted to overcome what stood between her and Colin, she had to admit he was right.

"Yes," she said softly. "I do care deeply for your cousin. Despite all that has happened, I want our marriage to be real. To be happy. I know you care for him, Arthur—please, won't you help me?"

He arched a brow. "You *know* I care for him?" he repeated.

She nodded. "Of course."

He smiled, and Jane caught her breath. There was something so sinister in his expression. And in that moment, all her nervousness rushed back to her. Not because of what she was here to do, but because of his demeanor. She suddenly felt like she was in the room with a dangerous animal, one she had underestimated.

"Then you know only what I *wish* you to know," Arthur said, his voice rough and hard.

"I...don't understand," Jane said, rising slowly and backing away because it felt like the right thing to do. The thing that would protect her.

He got to his feet too and moved toward her without hurry. "You think I called you here because I might be able to help you repair your marriage? You stupid girl, I'm the one who broke it in the first place."

CHAPTER 7

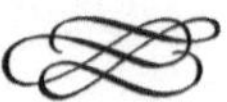

Colin shrugged out of his coat and handed over his gloves to Simmons with a sigh.

"I hope your appointment went well, my lord," the butler intoned.

Colin flinched. He wouldn't say it had gone *well*. Arthur had set the entire thing up for him, convincing him that meeting with Lord Massingale was the right thing to do and that the important earl could be moved. His cousin had been wrong, though, and the exercise had been in futility. Not only did Massingale have no interest in his legislation, but he had never even considered it. Worse, Colin had not been able to argue his case thoroughly because he was too distracted.

Too distracted by thoughts of Jane. Thoughts of the past, but also thoughts of what they'd shared since she returned to London. The night before, after the ball, she had seemed truly confused by his anger toward her. Completely unaware of any reason he might have to hold her at arm's length. She had begged him to explain it to her. To say those things that had hung between them in silence for half a year.

He had not done that since their wedding. At first because he was too sick to say those words out loud. Later, whenever he'd been tempted to confront her, Arthur had been the calm voice of reason, guiding him away from such foolish notions.

But Arthur was not in that carriage last night. Arthur was not in this marriage, in the end. A marriage that was beginning to feel real. If he did what she asked, if he sat down with her and told her everything he knew...he was beginning to wonder if there wasn't some way they could work out the past. Overcome what she had done, perhaps find a way to move forward...

Together.

With those thoughts burning in his addled mind, he'd left the meeting hours early in order to come home and finally talk to her. *Really* talk to her. His heart throbbed at just the thought of it and what it could do to change his life.

"Where is Lady Wharton?" he asked the butler.

Simmons wrinkled his brow. "I'm sorry, sir, I thought you'd be aware. She received a message from Mr. Wharton to meet with him. She should be there now."

Colin drew back. "My cousin, Mr. Wharton? *Arthur?*"

"Yes, sir."

The butler withdrew from the foyer, leaving Colin to stand there in confusion. Why would Arthur wish to speak to Jane? He'd never made his contempt for her anything but plain. He'd only ever encouraged Colin to stay away from her and not be taken in by her wiles.

But perhaps that was exactly why he'd called Jane to his side. Arthur wanted to protect him and now he foolishly thought he had to save Colin from her.

"Damn it," Colin muttered. "Simmons!"

The butler rushed back, Colin's things still in his hands. "Yes, sir?"

"I'm sorry, but I'm going back out again." He took back the items and ran to the drive. He motioned to the boy who was just trotting off with his horse and swung up on the beast.

As he exited his drive and raced back onto the street, he couldn't ignore the fissure of worry in his chest. And wonder at the cause, beyond a fear that Arthur would scold Jane or tell her to leave Colin alone.

His worry felt more driven than that. It felt more serious and he couldn't place why.

~

Jane stared at Arthur, uncertain that she understood what he had just said. Praying she didn't understand, for the alternative was just too awful.

"What do you mean you broke my marriage?" she asked, her voice shaking.

He rolled his eyes and turned to the sideboard a second time. He bent down and opened the cabinet below. "Do I need to use smaller words? I thought you were supposed to be clever. I interfered in your marriage, Jane. *I'm* the reason Colin banished you."

He turned back to her as he finished that sentence and Jane skittered farther away, because he now held a pistol in his hand. He leveled it on her.

"What are you doing?" she cried out as her backside hit the wall and she had nowhere else to go.

He smiled, a thin and empty expression. "Sit down, Jane."

She stared at the gun again and drew in a long breath. She'd have to run past this man to get to the door and escape. If he truly wanted to hurt her, he would shoot before she made it three steps to freedom.

So her best option was to do exactly what he said and try to understand *why* he was doing this. Perhaps once she did, she could reason with him and escape.

She moved forward in slow, wary steps, and retook her place in her chair. He did the same, never moving the pistol from its place pointing straight at her heart.

"What is this, Arthur?" she whispered, her voice shaking. "What are you doing?"

"*This* is called finally getting what I deserve."

His voice was cold and calm and terrifying, but she forced herself to stay in place, keep her hands folded tightly in her lap.

"Please," she whispered. "I don't understand what you want."

He nodded. "I realize that. I realize that no one understands what I want. Which only makes me an accomplished liar and actor, I suppose. After all, you believe that I care for Colin. That alone should earn me an award."

"*Don't* you care for him?" she asked in utter confusion.

"With his heart that bleeds for justice?" Arthur snorted, his tone thick with contempt. "With his superior attitude? I don't give a *damn* about him. I never have. *I* should be viscount. I should have the money and the title and the lifestyle he wastes on his so-called good works."

The hatred practically dripped from his voice, and Jane shook her head. "Arthur, you cannot mean that."

"But I do." Arthur shook his head. "Do you know how hard I worked to twist him? To break him? First with Cassandra."

Her lips parted. "Cassandra?"

Arthur grinned. "Oh, that's right, ladies are *protected* from such things. I knew what she was from the beginning and I encouraged Colin to court her. Then I helped her along in entering into an affair with every man who gave her a pretty bauble."

Jane caught her breath. She'd known that Colin had courted a woman before her and there had been whispers it had ended badly. But she'd never imagined what she was hearing now. That Arthur would purposefully cause the kind of pain he was describing.

"Why would you do such a thing?"

"To have what I wanted, of course." Arthur shrugged, as if his actions were harmless, meaningless, understandable. "I thought I had him then. I thought certain he'd *never* marry. I encouraged that path. Hell, there were times I even thought he might end it all."

Jane jerked her hand to her lips at that idea and the pain it caused her. "You cannot mean that."

He nodded. "He was very upset. And if he had put a bullet in his own brain, it certainly would have been less messy than all this."

"You are a monster," Jane whispered.

He smiled. "And you are a fool. But a frustrating one. You see, your family came along, his mother became involved and this arranged thing between you was set. So I had to break that, too."

She blinked. "I still don't understand. What do you mean, *break* it?"

"Do you remember the terrace, the night of your wedding?"

She thought back and her eyes went wide. There had been one thing that happened at her wedding ball that she'd never told a soul.

"*There* it is," Arthur chuckled. "You know what I'm talking about. Todd Martin."

Jane gasped. Her old childhood friend, Todd Martin, who had not been invited to the soiree, had approached her in the ballroom, demanding to speak to her.

"I went out with him," she murmured. "Wondering why in the world he was there. He was acting like there was something urgent that could not wait. But when I got outside, he changed his mind."

"And then you were waylaid by another guest," Arthur encouraged. "A lady who drew you into an adjoining parlor to talk to you."

She nodded. It had been an odd series of events, but one that had hardly stuck in her mind when she was so anxious to get back to Colin's arms.

"Your husband saw you exit the ballroom with Martin," Arthur said. "And then he saw you two kiss."

"I *never* kissed him."

"Of course you didn't. You were being kept busy elsewhere. But another lady, one with honey-blonde hair and a gown exactly like yours, kissed him."

Her mouth dropped open as she understood the full horror of what he was saying. She was now beginning to understand not just

Arthur's motives, but everything that had transpired between her and Colin since their wedding. "You invited a man to whom I had once been linked, and then you created a situation where Colin would believe I betrayed him."

"I did invite Martin. Well, smuggled him in is a better description." Arthur chuckled, like the whole thing was a wonderful joke. "He and the lady of the night who was so easily mistaken for you were paid well to do exactly what they did at the exact moment they did it."

Tears welled up in her eyes and she blinked to clear them. She would not give this monster her tears. "You wanted Colin to believe I was no better than this Cassandra woman who broke his heart."

His smile grew. "You are not as stupid as I thought. Brava, Jane. Exactly. Now I *thought* this would make him annul the marriage, but it had not occurred to me that he would have already bedded you."

Jane flinched, turning her face as heat flamed into her cheeks.

"That threw me off. Disrupted my plans. But I adjusted, as any true man of intelligence must do from time to time. I switched tactics, and it was easy as child's play to convince him to send you away. To convince him to hate you."

Jane's stomach rolled and she covered her mouth in horror. "You...you..."

"Arthur."

He jumped to his feet and swung around, turning his gun toward the door. Jane looked in the direction of the voice, that voice she knew so well, and gasped as she looked at Colin, standing in the entrance to the parlor, his face pale and his hands shaking.

"Arthur," he repeated, his voice hollow. "How could you?"

Colin stared in disbelief at his cousin. He'd come to the house, thinking he might encounter a scene, but this was not the one he'd pictured. No one had been at the door when he entered, no servant even seemed to be in the house. So he'd come down the hall, looking for Arthur and Jane. He'd overheard Arthur's confession in the hallway, about Cassandra, about Jane and the bitter lie he'd believed since their wedding day.

But when he entered and saw the gun trained on his wife, his world had come crashing down around him.

Arthur sneered. "Don't get so self-righteous, Colin. You never gave a damn about her or else it wouldn't have been so easy to convince you to throw her away."

Colin winced at the statement, at the way Jane trembled as she looked at him in fear and horror. He had done so much wrong to her. He had lost faith in her, hurt her, and now when she needed him most, he hadn't kept her safe.

"Keep the gun on me," he said softly as he edged into the room. It took everything in him not to rush Arthur, to pour out the rage that now bubbled within him.

But that would result in getting shot. Or worse, Jane being shot. And he couldn't risk it no matter how much he wanted to pummel Arthur to the floor.

"Did you truly make me believe Jane was unfaithful?" he asked, though he recognized already that it was true. The fact that he'd let himself be so easily manipulated by such lies was another thing entirely.

"Yes," Arthur hissed. "But you ruin everything, Colin, just as you've *always* ruined everything. But this time I was careful. I planted the seeds, I took my time. And it worked for a while. You sent Jane away and it bought me time. But then she showed back up in London and you were tripping over yourself to reconcile with her even though you thought she was little better than a whore."

Jane sucked in her breath through her teeth. Colin met her eyes, praying she would be comforted by his expression. That she would believe he would fix this.

He *had* to fix this.

"Arthur, put the gun down," he said softly. "What is done is done. It's in the past. You don't have to do something you will regret."

"I won't regret it," Arthur insisted, placing his finger on the trigger. His hand didn't even shake as he did so. "Because this has been the plan all along. I'm going to have to kill you, Colin."

Colin swallowed hard. "No," he said, knowing how dangerous it was to call the bluff of a man who was currently leveling a pistol at him. "You won't."

Arthur laughed, but didn't depress the trigger. "And why won't I?"

"Because you have clearly wanted my title for years," Colin said. "And you haven't done it yet. Something stops you."

"Are you calling me a coward?" Arthur hissed, but his eyes filled with tears.

"No," Colin responded, gentling his tone as much as he could considering the circumstances. "Just not a killer."

Arthur bent his head. "I've tried, you know. I've tried. That riding accident when you were seventeen? The duel you refused? That illness two years ago?"

At that Jane slowly got to her feet. Colin stared at her, for her eyes snapped with anger. Anger on his behalf. Protectiveness he did not deserve.

"You?" she growled. Arthur pivoted, pointing the gun toward her again, and Colin's heart nearly stopped.

"Sit down, Jane," he ordered sharply. "Arthur, Arthur, please. Aim the gun at me. I'm the one who you have the quarrel with. Aim the gun at me."

"Colin," she whispered, but she took a shaky place at the edge of her seat.

As Arthur did as he'd been asked, swinging the gun back at him, Colin nodded toward her. "It's all right, Jane. I promise you."

"All right?" Arthur burst out. "All right? None of it is bloody all right! I was never able to finish."

Colin moved toward his cousin a step, praying Arthur's hand, which now did shake, wouldn't cause the gun to fire and kill him where he stood.

"Ending a life is not to be taken lightly," he said softly. "Perhaps you struggle because you don't really want to do this."

He took another step closer.

"Yes, I do. Stop walking toward me!" Arthur all but screamed. He began to depress the trigger as Colin lunged for him.

In that moment, Colin knew he was going to die.

Except that when the gun fired, it missed him. Because Jane let out a screeching cry and swept out a leg, kicking Arthur hard in the back of the knee and causing him to topple and misfire.

Colin jumped on him at once, wrestling the gun away and tossing it aside before he punched his cousin as hard as he could in the face and knocked Arthur unconscious.

Jane rushed toward him as he flipped his cousin over and placed a knee in his back to hold him steady. She wrapped her arms around him, pulling him into her chest, whispering his name as she smoothed her hands across his arms and back to make sure he wasn't injured.

"I'm fine," he reassured her. "Are you?"

She drew back at last. "Yes. Thanks to you."

"Thanks to *you*," he corrected as he looked up into her face and saw her, really saw her, for perhaps the first time. No longer was he looking through the glass of Arthur's manipulations and his own doubt.

He saw Jane and knew how badly he had failed her, even if he'd managed to save her life.

It was like she read his mind in that moment. She took a long step away and her gaze flicked away from his. "I-I should get a servant to call for the guard."

"Yes," he agreed, knowing this wasn't the time or the place to address what he now knew. "Though Arthur may have sent them away, so you might have to go to the next house. Hand me the gun, will you? Just in case."

She nodded, handing him the pistol before she gave him one last look and hurried from the room. He watched her go as he stood up and trained the gun on the still-unconscious form of his troubled cousin.

And he prayed that once this had been resolved, he could find some way to make everything up to her.

CHAPTER 8

Jane sat in the hallway, staring at the door to the parlor where Arthur had tried to kill her, tried to kill Colin. He had been taken out nearly an hour before by the guard, struggling and screaming as they did so. He would be taken to the prison…or perhaps to Bedlam, judging from how incoherent he was.

Either way, she had been reassured that he would not ever have the opportunity to hurt her again.

But those reassurances had not been delivered by Colin. Her husband had been in the parlor ever since they were attacked, explaining everything to the guard. Maybe even paying them off so this scandal wouldn't get out.

But then, Colin had always known how to handle a scandal. Even one that hadn't really happened.

Her stomach turned at what she now knew. That Colin had, for a half a year, believed her capable of betraying him. Without asking her, without confronting her, he had just…turned away.

It broke her heart. And it made her so angry she could hardly breathe.

Emotions she pushed aside when the door opened and Colin stepped out with the two members of the guard behind him. "Thank you, gentlemen, for your assistance," he said as he shook their hands.

"We've a few more things to manage here, my lord, but you and your wife are welcome to go," one of the men said, inclining his head toward her.

"Please feel free to call on me at any time of night or day if there is anything else you need," Colin said.

Then he at last turned and looked at her, his face drawn and pained. She felt for him in that moment. She had been hurt by what had happened, but she could recognize just how much he had been as well. And she loved him, despite this turn of events. She wanted to comfort him.

She rose, holding out a hand to him in silence. He took it, his expression filled with surprise, and allowed her to draw him toward the carriage she had ridden over in what felt like a lifetime ago. At the door, she turned back and acknowledged the guard before she and Colin walked out and climbed into the vehicle.

It was a silent ride back to his home. Colin stared out the window at the dark that had fallen during the hours they'd been at Arthur's. He said nothing. Neither did she, for she feared once they started, it would be a difficult conversation that could last a very long time. She didn't want to start it where the servants could spy.

They arrived at his home at last, and it was evident that news of what happened at Arthur's home had already spread. Simmons was sober as he welcomed them and took their things. "Would you like supper, my lord?"

Colin barked out a sound of humorless laughter. "No. I'll drink my supper in the parlor. Jane?"

She shook her head and smiled at Simmons. "Thank you, you may leave us." He bowed his head, and Jane looked at Colin. "To the parlor then."

He sighed and led the way, shutting the door behind them before he crossed to the liquor lined up along the sideboard and opened a bottle. "I'll begin with scotch. What is the lady's pleasure?"

"Nothing for me," she said, watching him as he splashed a hefty dose of alcohol into a glass and slugged half of it in one gulp.

He caught her eye and frowned. "I'm sorry. I know I'm being rude."

"No," she said. "I cannot imagine how you feel at present."

He moved to a chair by the fire and sank into it like he could no longer support his own weight.

"What can I do?" she asked, longing to move to him and rub his shoulders. To kiss him and help him forget. To make love to him and reassure each other they were unharmed after the near-tragedy that had taken place that afternoon.

But she found she couldn't. There were walls between them, just as there had always been. Only now she was the one who erected them for her protection.

"Nothing," he said in answer to her question at last. "I am in…shock."

She sank down in the chair near him and shook her head. "Of course you are. You and Arthur were so close."

"Were we?" he asked, staring off into space, his expression telling her he was reliving those moments in the parlor with his cousin. "It seems we were not. Not truly."

His agony was palpable, and even Jane's own pain couldn't keep her from reaching out. She touched his cheek with a trembling hand and he leaned into it, his eyes fluttering shut.

"He broke us," he murmured, his voice cracking.

She pursed her lips, but pushed aside all she wanted to say. "We don't have to speak of that tonight, Colin."

He looked at her. "But we do, Jane. I know now that you didn't betray me."

Anger began to burn in her chest and Jane lowered her hand from his face. She smoothed her skirts, trying to maintain calm. "You know it because you heard Arthur say it."

He nodded. "Yes."

"But why didn't you ask *me* six months ago, Colin?" The anger made her voice higher, and she stood up and paced away. "Why did you judge me guilty without so much as a trial?"

"I saw—" he began, standing and holding out a hand like he wanted to touch her. She didn't allow it, staying out of his reach.

"You saw *nothing*," she snapped. "You know that now. And if you'd had any faith in me whatsoever, you would have asked me right then and there. I would have explained myself and we could have resolved this and moved on."

He squeezed his eyes shut and grabbed the back of the closest chair, like he needed support to stand. "Perhaps I wasn't capable of faith. Arthur told you about Cassandra."

"A bit," she said. "Who was she, exactly?"

"A woman I…well, I once thought I loved her. But she betrayed me with other men."

She folded her arms and speared him with a glare. "Are you sure?"

He winced. "In her case, *yes*. I caught her with someone else. In my bed, of all places. I know now that Arthur orchestrated it, of course, but it doesn't change that it…broke me, Jane. Just as he wanted it to. So when I saw you on the terrace—"

"When you saw what you *thought* you saw, this Cassandra's punishment became mine," she whispered. "Without hesitation, you locked me away in a very pretty prison, Colin. You refused to respond to my pleas for amnesty, for a chance."

He shook his head, his brow wrinkling. "Pleas?"

She huffed out a breath. Had he not even bothered to read her letters? It only made this worse. "That other woman betrayed you," she said, fighting tears. "But you betrayed *me*."

His face twisted. "Because of Arthur!" he cried.

"In part, perhaps that is true. But in the end, you made your own decisions."

He moved toward her a step and her heart stuttered. He had never looked at her with such openness before. Such emotion. And the reason why he'd kept himself so guarded until now was exactly why she couldn't trust him.

"I'm sorry," he said, taking her hand.

She stared at their clasped fingers, his darker, larger ones intertwined with her pale, slender ones. Once she would have given anything to be bound to him in physical and emotional ways.

Now she was too hurt to let him in. To trust him.

"I'm certain you are," she whispered, and then tugged her hand away. "But sorry isn't enough."

His face grew panicked. "Jane—"

"Oh, Colin," she murmured. "We were an arranged marriage that quite possibly could have been so much more. But now, I just don't know. Perhaps there comes a point when two people can hurt each other too much to overcome it. Either way, I'm going home."

The color left his cheeks. "No, Jane. No. *This* is your home."

"But it's not," she argued. "It's not because you never allowed me to make a home here or in your heart."

He caught his breath and his voice shook as he said, "You can't leave."

"I will leave. Please let me go." She met his gaze and held steady there, even though it hurt so much. Even though it made her waver in her resolve to walk away. There was so much of her that wanted to accept his apology and just pretend the rest had never happened.

But she couldn't. She needed to step back. To truly evaluate all that had occurred. To decide her future without being swayed by his past.

He stared at her for what felt like a lifetime. Then he bent his head and nodded. "As you wish, Jane. I have done enough to you—I know I don't deserve your consideration or your affection. In some ways, I never did. If going is what you need to do, I shall not stand in your way."

She was shocked by his acquiescence. Even more shocking was how much she wished he would fight for her instead of bend to her will, just as he had bent to Arthur's a year before.

But she didn't tell him that. She didn't tell him anything. She just slipped past him into the hall to call for her maid and go back to her sister's.

And away from the man she loved. Away from the promise of a life that had never been and could never be again.

CHAPTER 9

Colin sat in his dressing gown and nothing else, staring at his empty bed and listening to the throbbing pulse that echoed in his aching head. A night of drinking had done nothing to make him forget Jane. In fact, it had only made the emotional pain become mirrored by the physical version.

"Nothing less than you deserve after what you did to her," he muttered to himself. There was a knock on the door and he sighed. "Yes?"

"My lord," Simmons said, cracking his door partly. "You have a visitor."

Colin jumped to his feet. "Jane?"

The butler refused to meet his gaze. "I'm afraid it is not Lady Wharton, my lord, but an inspector from the guard. He says that you told him to call if he had anything further to report on the… situation yesterday."

Colin tensed. He *had* said that to the inspector the day before. Only a day? It felt like a year. A decade. A lifetime. But Arthur's mess would have to be dealt with, no matter how bereft Colin was over Jane.

"Show him to the parlor and see if he would like some breakfast," he said with a sigh. "And send in Drake to help me ready. I'll be down as soon as I can."

"Yes, my lord."

His butler left, and in short order his valet came in. He picked Colin's clothing, asking his usual questions about waistcoats. Normally Colin participated in his morning routine, but today he waved the questions off, allowing Drake to choose everything. What did appearances matter? *Appearances* were what had gotten him in this mess in the first place.

Eventually he was dressed. He thanked his valet with an apologetic nod and then collected himself as he strode downstairs to the parlor where the inspector waited.

He drew a deep breath, trying to put on the visage of Viscount Wharton rather than a grieving husband at a loss. He wasn't certain how well he did when he opened the door and the inspector turned, pastry in hand, and frowned at him with concern.

"Good morning, Inspector…" Colin said, entering the room and holding out a hand.

The other man shook it without putting down his croissant. "Hyde, my lord."

"Of course," Colin said. "My apologies for not recalling that."

"I understand, my lord," Hyde said, finally putting aside his breakfast with a blush on his round cheeks. "Yesterday was a trying one, I'm sure."

"And I think your appearance here must signal that today will be little better. Is there an update on my cousin?"

He braced himself for the news, but Hyde shook his head. "Nothing much, my lord. He was taken to Bedlam in the end."

Colin frowned. "I thought as much. Perhaps better for him than prison. I'll ensure he is taken care of comfortably. God, his mother will be devastated." Hyde nodded somewhat uncomfortably, and Colin shook off his musings. "But if there was no update beyond that one, what is it you came for, Inspector?"

"Ah, yes," Hyde said, digging into his inside pocket. From it, he withdrew a packet of letters, bound with worn ribbon. "When we searched your cousin's offices yesterday evening, one of my men found these."

Colin held up a hand. "I assure you, sir, I have no need to read my cousin's private correspondence. I'm certain if you think—"

"I'm sorry to interrupt, my lord, but these aren't letters to your cousin. They are…they're addressed to *you.*"

Colin took the packet, untying the ribbon even as he stared at the inspector. "Me?"

"Yes, my lord. It appears your cousin was intercepting certain correspondence before it reached you, keeping you from receiving it."

Colin looked at the hand on the top folded sheet. It was in *Jane's* handwriting. He flipped to the next letter, the next. They were all from Jane.

"Mr. Hyde," he said, hearing the hollow sound to his voice. "How many letters were there from my wife?"

"We counted thirteen, my lord."

Colin's stomach turned. Thirteen. And judging from the dates written on the back of each envelope, this time in his cousin's hand, they had been sent every week for the three months before Jane made her unexpected return to London.

Now her comment the night before about her pleas for forgiveness, for starting over, made sense. She had written to him every week for half the time they had been apart.

And his silence had been a rejection to her. A verification that he didn't care for her. That her words meant nothing to him. When, in reality, they meant everything.

Hyde shifted under the weight of Colin's silence. "That's all I came for, my lord. I should leave you to your day."

"Thank you," Colin said, barely registering as the man stuffed what was left of his croissant into his mouth, bowed awkwardly and left.

Colin sank into a chair when he was alone. Carefully, he

arranged the letters along the tabletop, in order of the dates scrawled across them. The inspector was correct that there were thirteen.

He broke the seal on the first and began to read. And sat there for an hour, turning page after page, his eyes stinging as he read Jane's pleas for an explanation, her apologies for unknown crimes, and also her description of her life in Applegate. Although she always asked him to respond and sometimes there was a desperate tone to her letters, there was also a conversational way to them. Like she hoped that if she shared the minutia of her day, it would open his heart to her.

And it did. God, how it did.

He stood and refolded the letters, binding them again as he called out for Simmons. "Yes, my lord," he asked as he entered the room.

Colin held out the letters. "Take these to my chamber. And have my horse brought around. I have somewhere I need to go immediately."

Colin sat in Alicia Beckford's parlor, shifting uncomfortably in a chair as he awaited the arrival of his wife and her family. He had no doubt her protective older sister would not welcome him here.

He knew full well he didn't deserve their warmth or their welcome. But he would bear their censure if, in the end, he could somehow make up what he'd done to Jane.

The door opened and Alicia Beckford stepped in. Like Jane, she had blonde hair, but she wasn't as delicate as her sister. Her eyes were brown rather than blue. At present, she also looked like she was very capable of breaking a chair over his back.

He stood quickly. "Mrs. Beckford," he said. "Very nice to see you. Felicitations on the birth of your son."

Alicia's face remained drawn and angry, and she didn't offer a hand of welcome to him as she paced inside the room. "Get out of my house, Lord Wharton."

He froze at her cold order, gathering his composure in the face of her anger. "I understand your rage with me, madam. I know I deserve it. But I *must* see my wife. Please."

Her eyes narrowed at the please, but she shook her head. "Even if Jane were here, I would not allow you to see her."

"*If* Jane were here?" he repeated, his stomach sinking as a dozen horrible possibilities flashed through his mind. "Jane isn't here? She did make it here last night, didn't she?"

Alicia scoffed. "Are you pretending you care for my sister's well-being now, after what you did to her?"

"I *do* care," he insisted, his voice elevating slightly. "Please tell me she arrived here last night."

She pursed her lips. "She did," Alicia admitted at last. Colin almost sagged in relief. "And she left very early this morning. So you have stolen her from me not once, but twice."

Colin stared. "She—she left?"

"Yes, at dawn," Alicia said with a pained sigh. "As she was sobbing in my arms last night, she just kept saying she wanted to go home. As if *you* ever provided her with a home. But somehow she loves that Applegate place of yours. She feels safe there, out of the line of your disdain. So you should congratulate yourself, my lord. It seems you've gotten rid of her just as you always wished."

Colin couldn't help himself. He sank back into the chair, putting his head in his hands as he tried to process what had just happened.

"I don't want her gone," he muttered through his fingers. "I know you don't believe me. I don't even blame you for that. But the last thing I want is for her to leave."

Alicia laughed. "Which is why you banished her based on a lie." He lifted his gaze and found her nodding. "Oh yes, she cried out the whole sordid tale to me last night. I could hardly understand what she was saying through her hysteria." She took her own seat.

"Though you *did* save her life yesterday. That is the only thing I will ever thank you for."

Colin shook his head. "I don't deserve even that. Damn it, Mrs. Beckford...*Alicia*...I know I've bungled this terribly. In ways that were in my control as well as ways that were not. But I promise you, the last thing I want is her gone."

Alicia stared at him, reading him. "Why? Why would you want her to stay? For your reputation? Your pride?"

He swallowed. "None of those things. They're the last on my mind. I want her here because I...I care for her."

Alicia got up and paced away. "How utterly romantic. You *care* for her."

"The first time I admit I love her, it isn't going to be to you," he snapped.

She spun around at that statement and stared at him. Her defensive posture didn't change much, but her expression softened ever so slightly. "If you feel as you say you do, I won't tell you that you don't have a chance," she admitted, almost reluctantly. "But you will have to work at repairing this. I have never seen Jane so hurt to her core."

He nodded. "I hate myself for causing it, I assure you. I'm going to follow her."

"She's only half a day ahead of you. In a carriage. It's a long trip—on horseback, you could likely catch up with her at her first stop at an inn tonight. I can tell you which one she intends to take a break at."

He considered it for a moment, but then shook his head. "No. What I have to say, what I must do, it can't be done on the road. At an inn where there is no privacy. Jane wants to go home, so I will let her go home. I will give her a few days of peace, which is what she asked of me. On horseback, I can get to Applegate a day and a half ahead of her. Which gives me time to prepare. I must prepare."

He realized he was musing aloud when Alicia cleared her throat.

He looked at her sheepishly and found her looking at him, her demeanor and expression now far less hostile.

"I-I want my sister to be happy," she said. "If you intend to make this up to her, if you intend to make amends, I just hope you'll allow her to come back to London. I miss her, Lord Wharton."

He bent his head. "I have failed her and all who love her. And I give you my word that I will do everything in my power to make it up to all of you."

She nodded at last. "Then you best be on your way, my lord. After all, it's a long ride."

He followed her as she got up and motioned him to the door. "And I have a stop to make before I leave London. A very important stop, indeed."

CHAPTER 10

J ane climbed down from the carriage and drew in a long breath of brisk evening air as she stretched her back. It had been five long days of travel through wet and cold conditions back to Colin's country home. *Her* home for the past year.

But five days of travel hadn't done what she'd hoped they would for her. Despite the time alone, she hadn't forgotten what Colin had done. Or what he'd come to mean to her during their time together. She had been restless all along the way, unable to stop replaying her entire ill-fated visit to London over and over again.

"Damn you," she whispered to herself as her servants approached, welcoming her home. She greeted them with as happy a smile as she could pretend and walked up the stairs to the foyer where the butler, Chadwick, was waiting.

"Welcome home, my lady."

"I know you were not expecting me back so soon," she said. "I hope my note did not arrive too late and that you didn't have to rush much to prepare for my arrival."

The butler shifted, refusing to meet her stare, and her heart sank. He was going to reassure her, but she could tell that this change of plans had upended the household. She would have to do something kind for the staff to make it up to them.

"Of course not, my lady," he said, his expression still odd. "And we are *very* pleased to have you back."

"I assume there was not much correspondence during my absence," she said as she moved toward the stairs.

"No, since you were meant to be in London, hardly any," he said. "What little there was is awaiting you in your chamber."

"Excellent. I know Laura is seeing to the bags. Tell her I will tend to myself this evening and not to worry about putting things away. I'm exhausted and I think I'll just go straight to bed."

"Of course, my lady," Chadwick said, stopping at the base of the staircase. "Good night."

She nodded as she trudged up the stairs. She only had to keep this brave face on another few seconds. In her own bedchamber, without her maid watching, she could collapse at last and have a good cry. She felt like she'd earned that.

She reached her door and went inside, toward the blazing fire. But before she could reach it, something caught her eye and she stopped. There was a vase filled with roses on the table next to her bed. The servants did keep fresh flowers in the house, but not in her bedchamber and not during the autumn months. Which meant these were from the hothouse, brought in specially.

"Do you like them?"

She froze. It was Colin's voice behind her. But that was impossible. It had to be impossible. Wasn't it impossible?

Slowly, she turned and found it to be true. He stood in the doorway to the sitting room between their two chambers. He wore no jacket, waistcoat or cravat, his sleeves were rolled up and his feet were bare.

Her heart began to race, not just because he was here or because he was so damned perfect in the firelight, but because she was *happy* to see him. She was a fool to have that reaction, after all he'd done.

And yet there it was, a joy that clawed up her body and forced her acknowledgment.

"What are you doing here?" she whispered. "And *how* are you here when I left you at your home in London?"

"The ride is five days in a carriage, but only a little more than three on a horse," he said. "As soon as I knew you were heading to Applegate, I made chase to arrive here before you."

She shook her head. "Well, that explains Chadwick's odd expression and tone when I arrived."

"I asked him not to reveal my being here to you. I thought you might...you might leave if you knew I was waiting for you."

"So you manipulated the situation to your benefit," she said.

He stiffened. "I...I suppose that is true. And perhaps it was unfair. Would you...do you want to go?"

She bent her head. There was no use trying to lie. "No. I don't want to leave, nor would I have left if I'd known you were here."

Relief flowed over his features and for a moment he was younger, less stern, more the man she'd always hoped he could be. "Good. That means I have some small chance."

She clenched her hands before her and forced herself to remain in her place. "Why did you come, Colin? After everything that happened between us, after everything I said to you, why not leave it be, as I asked you to do back in London?"

He held her gaze steadily and drew in a ragged breath before he said, "Because I love you, Jane."

She heard a little cry escape her lips, but his expression didn't change as she processed that declaration, as it wound its way into her heart. There was so much of her that wanted to walk across the room to him and fall into his arms. To accept what he told her and surrender to him.

But when she thought of how he'd been so willing to believe the worst of her, how he'd sent her away and hadn't even bothered to respond to her when she pleaded with him to give her even a moment of his time...

She had to harden herself.

"Perhaps you believe you do, or think that you must after treating me so callously," she said, hands shaking before she shoved them behind her back. "But love is not abandonment."

His face crumpled. "Yes, I do have a great deal to make up for. I want you to understand that I come here with no expectation that you will forgive me quickly or easily. I know I'll have to earn your trust and your love after all I did to hurt you. But I must tell you one thing that may make it easier."

She tilted her head. "And what is that?"

"I never received your letters," he said, stepping into the room for the first time, closing just a fraction of the distance which separated them. "Arthur intercepted them, as part of his plan to keep us apart. So your pleas, the ones you mentioned in London...I now understand what you meant. And I didn't respond to them because I didn't ever know they were being made."

Her lips parted in surprise. There was some part of her that was softened by that truth. At least she knew he hadn't been ignoring her directly. And yet she still couldn't fully let him in.

"Colin, this is your home and I have no right to tell you what to do or if you should leave. But whether you knew about my letters or not, you still made *no* attempt to bridge the gap between us, judging me harshly without even allowing me to defend myself." She lifted her chin. "Right now, I have nothing else to say."

He nodded. "I understand that. You deserve your feelings. But you are right that I remained silent for a long time, based on a lie. A good portion of that fact is held on my shoulders, no matter how I was manipulated into it. If you have nothing to say, then allow *me* to speak at last."

He drew a long breath, then moved forward, pulling a letter from his pocket and holding it out to her. She stared at the folded sheet and then up to his face. "What is it?"

"Please take it," he whispered, his voice cracking just a fraction.

She blinked as she did so, and he stepped away as soon as she had, granting her the space she claimed she desired. The space that felt less needed now that she'd felt his warmth so close to her.

"You—you wrote me a letter?" she said, forcing herself to remain focused.

"A response," he clarified. "One long overdue. Read it at your leisure. Read all of them at your leisure. I will not push you, I will not interfere with you. But Jane, I'm not leaving. I'm simply waiting. Just as I made you wait." He walked to the door where he paused and turned back. "Good night, my love."

He departed the room, closing the barrier behind him and leaving her in a state of utter confusion. She shook her head and broke the seal on his note, unfolding the sheets. Within, she was surprised to find the first letter she'd written to him, over three months before. She read over it, flinching at the raw pain in her words, the pleas for an audience with him.

Then she turned to his response.

Dearest Jane,

This response is long overdue and for that I am endlessly sorry. I am sorry for a great many things. In truth, perhaps I wouldn't have responded to this first letter had I received it six months ago. I was hurt and angry, poised on the edge of a cliff where I had no faith in anyone. Pushed over that edge by a manipulator I called a friend. But that does not excuse what I did and all I failed to do for you. I hope that somehow I can find a way to make up for it.

Yours forever, Colin

She gasped as pain flooded her, and she read his words again and again until they were blurry from her tears.

She set the letter aside and paced her room, confused and torn. His first response had been honest and she appreciated it. But she was still hurt by him. His words didn't change that. She was so confused. So hurt down to the core of herself that she didn't have the strength to do anything at all. Not respond to his letter, not think about what she felt.

She let out her breath in a long sigh, then set the letter aside on the bed, eyeing it as she unbuttoned her gown and stepped out of it. She set her dress on the back of her dressing table chair, then shed her underthings and walked naked back to the bed. She stared at the letter, re-reading it until the words felt seared on her mind and her soul.

She glanced back toward the adjoining door. Colin had made no attempt to return to her. She didn't hear him in the sitting room that acted as an antechamber between their bedrooms. It seemed, against all odds, that he truly meant to give her the space she needed to process all that had happened between them.

She sighed and slid between cool sheets, blowing out the candle as she clutched his letter in her hand. Sleep was what she needed. A good night's sleep. Only as she stroked her fingers over the thick vellum of his letter, she wasn't sure sleep would come easily.

Not when there was so much more than a door to separate her from her husband who now claimed he loved her.

Jane tightened the tie of her robe around her waist and sat down at her dressing table with a sigh. It was a bright and happy morning outside her window. The leaves were turning red and coppery orange and a slight breeze blew in from the sea. On any normal day, she would have thrilled at the idea of taking one of her long walks through the estate, calling on tenants and enjoying this place she had come to love.

Today, she couldn't. Today she could only look down at Colin's letter, still reading his words as if they would somehow rearrange themselves and give her the answer of what to do next.

There was a knock at her door and she jumped as she faced it.

She hadn't heard Colin moving around this morning. Even if he were up, he would likely come to the door that connected their rooms, but her heart still raced as she slipped up and opened it.

Laura stood on the other side. The maid's eyes were wide and she blushed. "Good morning, my lady."

Jane forced a smile and stepped aside to allow her servant entry. "Good morning. I trust you slept well after our arrival?"

Laura gave her a side glance and cleared her throat. "I-I did."

"Well, we ought to start our day, yes?" Jane asked, turning away to move to her wardrobe and pick a gown like this was a normal day in her normal life.

"Er, of course, but I must tell you that Lord Wharton has asked that I deliver you a message before we do anything else."

Jane caught her breath and pivoted to face her maid. Laura had come with her from London after her marriage. The young woman had probably seen more of her heartbreak than anyone. Now she held out another letter, folded just as the first one Colin had given her was.

"I see," Jane whispered, and stepped forward to take it, feeling the weight of it in her palm. She wasn't certain she was ready to read what Colin had written next, so she clung to it instead. "He called you to him?" she asked.

Laura nodded. "He did, to his chamber next door early this morning. I thought perhaps he was going to sack me, but he was actually very kind. He asked after our travels."

Jane shut her eyes. "Did he?"

"Yes. And after I told him how uneventful it was, he asked me to deliver this letter to you when you were readying yourself."

Jane's lip trembled and she pressed them together to stop it. "Was there anything else you observed while you were with him?"

Laura shifted. "I saw a stack of other letters on his desk, and paper and a quill."

Jane caught her breath, and the maid looked uncomfortable.

"There is more, I suppose?" Jane asked, trying to set aside her curiosity at the idea of Colin being surrounded by letters that were apparently to her. "Did you hear something below stairs? I'm sure the servants must be going wild with this strange turn of events."

Laura worried her lip. "I wouldn't want to repeat gossip..."

Jane arched a brow. "We've known each other a long time, Laura. Repeat away. I need to know."

"Well, the servants *are* confused, I admit. After all, Lord Wharton does not come here often and never since your marriage. Carson, the third footman, said..." She trailed off. "Perhaps I ought not."

Jane let out the breath she had been holding. "I already told you, I want to know. What did Carson say?"

Laura leaned forward, her voice a whisper. "He told me that Lord Wharton arrived here completely unexpectedly. He gave Chadwick a list of a dozen preparations to make and then locked himself in his chamber next door."

Jane wrinkled her brow. "What has he been doing in his chamber?"

"Writing. All he does is write," Laura said, clearly taken in by the tale she was telling. Clearly oblivious to how much it affected her mistress. "Carson said he eats at his desk in his chamber and he only calls for servants when he needs more paper or supplies like a quill or ink."

Jane shut her eyes. Colin had been writing since his return and there were thirteen letters she had sent the man in their time apart. Surely he couldn't be writing her the same number of responses.

She sighed. "If he calls you to him again, please tell him I asked him to slip the letters beneath my door. There is no need for him to disturb your other duties."

Laura nodded. "As you wish, my lady. Though I don't mind going between."

"I mind," she muttered. "Now, why don't you pick out a gown for me. I plan to take a long walk through the estate later."

"Of course."

Laura stepped away to the wardrobe and Jane let out her breath in one, long shuddering exhale. She stared at the letter in her hands and then turned it over and broke the seal. Just as before, Colin had included her letter in the pages of his own. Hers had been another message asking him for kindness, pleading with him to come to her or allow her to return to London. As she read the plaintive words, she felt the raw agony once again, like she was transported back in time before she turned to his response.

Dearest Jane,

I would have responded to this letter. I may have looked like I had a cold heart in the time we were apart, but I can admit to you and to myself that I thought of you every day. I tried to remain angry with you, to hate you as Arthur wished me to do. But this letter could not have gone unanswered.

Still, I cannot lie and say that I would have opened myself entirely. My situation with Cassandra changed me, but I was already wary of strong emotion even before I was betrayed in love. My father, you see, punished the expression of my feelings. I learned to hold them inside, to deny them. I once thought that was a strength, but I can see now that it is a failing of the highest order, thanks to you.

Jane left off reading with a gasp. Colin had never shared any depths like this with her before. He was a proud and proper gentleman. And yet he was inspired to give her a glimpse of his true heart now. To pour it out in paper in an attempt to show her how earnest he was about winning her back.

She glanced over to find Laura brushing a pretty dark green gown free of lint. She would have a moment's privacy to finish his missive, and she ducked her head to do so.

I might have told you that I wasn't sure if you should come to London, the letter continued. *I might have told you that I knew you had betrayed me and that I couldn't trust you. Of course I would have been wrong, but my God, at least it would have been out then. You could have been given a chance to explain and defend yourself against such bitter lies. I regret that deeply, Jane. And I love you.*

Yours always,

Colin

She dropped her head back over her shoulders and let out her breath in a long, heavy sigh. His honesty was appreciated even if it stung her. As did his words of love. What would she have said if she received an answer months ago that claimed she had betrayed him? Would she have asked for clarification of his terrible accusation? Would she have had the strength to go to London over his protests and confront him?

They would never know. Thanks to Arthur. Thanks to Colin, himself.

"Are you ready, my lady?" Laura asked, her tone laced with hesitation. Jane took another deep breath and then smiled at her servant.

Laura came to her and helped her as she dressed. Normally, Jane would have talked more, but today she remained silent as she pondered what Colin had said to her in both his letters. Laura did not push and her toilette was finished in no time.

"I know you have a great deal to do after our travel," Jane said. "I will go and take a walk through the estate. I have no idea if Lord Wharton will demand my time, but if he inquires after me, tell him I intend to be back for luncheon."

Laura's worried gaze pierced briefly, but she did not press. "Yes, my lady. I will share that message if he inquires."

Jane gave her one more smile that she wished was more

comforting than it felt. Then she slipped from the room. She glanced down the hallway toward the door that led to his chamber, but ignored the tug to go there. She still needed time. Still needed to think. She had placed both of Colin's letters in her pelisse pocket after getting dressed and she pulled them out now, smoothing her thumb along the paper as she slipped through her halls and toward the crisp autumn morning.

She could only hope the fresh air might give her some clarity. Right now she needed it desperately.

CHAPTER 11

Colin stared out the window of his study, watching as the lithe form of his wife moved across the estate grounds, toward the pathways that twisted to the sea. He couldn't help but smile, even though his chest felt tight when she walked away. She was going to walk on the beach. How he'd loved to do the same as a boy. It was the place where he often thought on his more pressing problems, allowing the sharp air to clear his mind.

He swept up the spyglass on his desk and glanced through it. Now he had a clearer view of Jane. She wore a pretty green gown, and a lighter green shawl was wrapped around her shoulders. He caught his breath and leaned closer to the window.

She was holding his letters in her hands. Well, letters of some kind—he had to assume they were the ones he'd written. She was reading as she walked.

He set the spyglass aside and went to his desk. Papers were strewn across it. Not the normal day to day accountings of his fortune or his political aspirations. No, they were notes for his letters to her. He still had so many to write.

He picked up the next in the series that Jane had written and smiled. It was the sixth missive she'd sent. This one was about the lighthouse along the shore. How she sat in the window seat in the middle of the night and watched the flickering light that kept the sailors safe from the rocks.

He'd done the same so many times. He hoped they'd have a chance to do these things together. To celebrate this beautiful estate, to explore London together, to just spend time making up for all the days he'd wasted on irrational anger.

He sat at his desk, writing for the next hour, then got up. He'd leave this letter here, add it to his pile of responses up in his chamber in a while. For now, he wanted to take his own walk. He would avoid the seaside path, let Jane have her privacy, no matter how much he wished to intrude, press, push.

He smiled and acknowledged the servants as he passed through the halls, then walked out the front door and around the path that led to the woods. Away from the sea. He drew in long breaths of fresh air, trying to clear his mind, though it was an impossible endeavor. He'd been out close to half an hour when he made a turn and came to a halt.

There, sitting on the tree stump, was Jane. She looked up at the same moment he noticed her and jumped to her feet.

"My lord," she said, her hands shaking as she shoved his letters behind her back, like she didn't trust that he wouldn't comment on them, force her to do the same despite his promises. He had earned that, of course. Now he had to show her she was wrong through his actions.

"I'm sorry, Jane. I did not mean to intrude upon your privacy. I meant to allow you that as long as you needed it."

She worried her lip for a moment, and he couldn't help but look at her mouth. Remember how it tasted. How it felt on his.

"You knew I was out walking?" she asked.

"I did. Your maid told me this morning and I saw you from my study window not long ago. I thought you had headed to the beach, though, so I believed I would not disturb you if I took my exercise in the woods."

She nodded. "I intended a walk along the beach, yes. But when I started down the dune path, the wind was too high."

"Ah," he said. "Say no more. The breezes can be fierce on the water this time of year, even when it feels still above. I shall leave you to your place here."

He turned to go, though he ached at the idea of leaving her, but her soft voice kept him from walking away. "I am not ready to discuss our…situation," she said.

He forced himself to turn slowly. "I would not dream of asking you to advance whatever timetable you need, Jane. That is why I will not trouble you."

"We could walk back up together," she suggested. "If the topic of your letters, of our separation, will not be one that requires pressing."

He stared at her, with her wide blue eyes and her soft lips. The woman he loved. Truly, deeply. She was offering him a connection, despite her misgivings. He would be a fool not to take it. To take anything she was willing to give and hold on to it with both hands.

"I would be very happy to walk with you," he said softly, and stepped forward to offer her a hand.

She blushed as she placed his letters into her pocket and then took the hand he held out. He tucked it into the crook of his elbow, and together they turned back toward the house. For the first few moments, he let the silence hang between them. It was not entirely uncomfortable, to walk with her and not chatter on, though she glanced at him from the corner of her eye more than once.

At last she said, "You have a fine property, Colin."

He nodded as they crested the hill and the castle rose up before them, gray and craggy and mysterious. "I loved it here as a boy. I imagined a thousand ghosts running through the halls, found a dozen hidden places to explore."

She smiled. "It is hard to picture you as a child, my lord. You are such a…a *man*."

He laughed. "When you say it like that, it does not sound like a compliment."

Her smile broadened. "I only mean you are so very serious."

"I am that," he said with a sigh. "I took on a great deal of responsibility at a young age. I had to behave in a way that was seen as 'right' or feel the consequences. I put away the ghost stories and hidden passages a long time ago." He glanced at her. "I admit, I… miss that. Miss being carefree."

She turned toward him as they entered the garden maze with the house looming up above them. "You could always be carefree when you chose to be. No one has to be serious at all times."

He could not help himself. Slowly, he reached out a hand and traced her cheek with his fingertips. She tensed, but didn't pull away and he saw her pupils dilate with pleasure, with desire, with even more. It gave him hope.

"Perhaps one day you can help me better remember that."

She swallowed hard. "Perhaps," she said.

That one word, said so softly, almost so that it didn't carry on the breeze, had so much power. Enough to nearly knock him off his feet because it held in it all the promise that there could be a future. That there could be forgiveness.

That there could be a marriage to this remarkable woman.

"I will take that," he said, stepping back. "Thank you for the walk, Jane. If you…if you need me, I will be here. Waiting."

She nodded slowly and then turned toward the house, leaving him to watch her as she stepped up the stairs and onto the veranda. Just before she disappeared from view, she stopped and looked back at him. Her blue gaze held his, and then she slipped away.

Leaving him to hope, to pray, that the future was closer than ever.

Jane nodded at Laura as the maid gathered up the gown she had been wearing that day and folded it over her arm. "Will that be all, my lady?"

Jane nodded. "Yes, thank you. I'll see you in the morning."

Laura bobbed out a curtsey, then stepped from the room, leaving Jane alone. Alone as she had been most of the day. Her walk with Colin aside, she had not seen him otherwise. She had eaten alone, read in the parlor alone, walked the halls alone. Like her husband wasn't haunting these halls like the ghosts he had described imagining as a child.

She smiled at the thought of a young Colin, playing here. Wished she had known him then, before whatever harshness and responsibility that had been laid upon his shoulders had changed him.

Laura had drawn her covers back, and Jane threw herself onto the bed without pulling them up. She flopped an arm over her face, trying to calm her wild mind before she allowed sleep to come.

"Ha," she muttered. "As if sleep will come easily before this situation with Colin is fully resolved."

She had no idea how long she lay there, her spinning mind reminding her of every word he'd written, of every kindness he had ensured for her while they were under this roof together. Thinking of London and the way he had touched her there, physically and emotionally.

She knew she loved him. That had been true for a long time, and the depth of her feelings meant she couldn't just forget it. Or him. But was she a fool for love if she let him in after what had passed between them?

"Is love enough?" she whispered, the words hanging in the air like a crack of a whip.

There was a sound at the door that connected their chambers, and she sat up. A letter now rested on the floor close to her door, which meant Colin had slipped it under. Was he still standing there?

She stood and walked over, crouching down to take the letter and peeking at the space beneath the door. The light from the other room looked unimpeded. It seemed he had walked away after delivering the missive. Aside from their chance meeting in the woods today, he was serious about not forcing his presence on her physically.

Just his words.

She broke the seal and drew a deep breath before she read over her letter to him from so long ago. Her hand had shaken less as she wrote this one. And yes, it contained continued pleas for him to respond, but this was where she had shifted her approach. It had been so very lonely in Applegate. She was liked by the tenants and the staff, she knew that. But they all saw her as lady of the manor. None could be counted as friends.

In her quiet, in her loneliness, she had decided she would write to Colin and tell him about her life. Partly she had hoped it would soften him to her. Partly it was to share something with someone other than her sister, who wrote back regularly, but mostly to protest her being sent away.

So she had written this letter and told him about the state of his estate, the kindness of those who served him, and one funny story about their minister, who had not noticed that he was wearing two different shoes when he got up to the pulpit the Sunday before she wrote.

Dearest Jane,

You don't know how this glimpse into the life you led while we were apart made me smile. I would not have been able to keep myself from doing the same had I read it when it was meant to be delivered to me months ago. After all, Reverend Lancaster has been serving the Applegate community since I was in short pants, and I recall his forgetfulness. I hope to one day tell you stories of pranks we played on the poor man and what a good sport he was.

I would have written to you by this point, Jane. I would have begun to open my heart and questioned whether or not the lies I believed were true. I must hope I wouldn't have been so cruel in the face of your sweetness, your light. God, I hope I would not have been.

That you love Applegate means the world to me, you know. I adored coming here as a child. I have a hundred stories to tell you and a dozen hidden gems to show you if I ever earn the privilege. I cannot wait to read more about your time here, despite all my regrets.

All my love, Colin

Jane felt a tear slide down her cheek and wiped it away with the back of her hand. It was funny that this was the letter he had written to her, considering their encounter earlier that day. Those moments in his company had shown her how they could explore this place they both loved together. To merge their experiences, share them while they laughed. Perhaps create some new ones together. That future felt so real, so powerful that she could almost grasp it in her hands.

She crossed to her bed and climbed up, setting the third letter beside the first two. She stared at them, lined up in order, then picked up the first and read it, followed by the second, followed by the third. With every word, with every swirl of his hand, with every moment that passed, her resolve against him weakened.

"Could you not grasp your future in your hands?" she asked out loud, letting the words hang around her. "Could you not find a way to face this, not alone in this room, but with him at your side?"

She closed her eyes and rested back against the headboard of her bed. Colin had always been such a formal presence. He was proper except for those moments when he was overcome by desire. And yet in his letters, he allowed himself to be open. To reveal parts of a painful past to her. To reveal himself as he offered his apologies to her, his explanations, his heart.

Allowing her eyes to open, she looked at the door that separated her from Colin's chamber. All of her wanted to open it. To open to him. And yet a tiny, niggling doubt remained. A fear that kept her from going to him.

"Sleep on it," she advised herself, knowing it is what her sister would say if Alicia were here to talk to. "Sleep on it one more night and let tomorrow come. And with it all the risks that could come from letting him in."

With a sigh, she leaned over and blew her candle out, burrowing into her covers as her fingers clutched Colin's letters, her mind ran over Colin's words and her heart throbbed in time to all the hopes she had for what every tomorrow could bring.

CHAPTER 12

Jane arched into Colin's body, feeling his warmth swirl against her as his mouth sought hers, his hands ran over her. It was everything and she sank into it, opening to him as he positioned himself over her and—

She jerked awake and stared at the canopy above her bed, her breath coming short and her body throbbing as her dream faded and reality returned. She was alone in her bed, her sheets tangled around her legs. And what had woken her was the scrape of something coming under her door.

She bolted upright, dragging the covers up as she stared across the room. There, sitting on the wooden floor waiting for her, was the fourth of Colin's letters to her. And suddenly all her questions from last night were answers, all her hesitations erased. She wanted to see her husband. She wanted to start anew with him.

She wanted it all now.

Throwing back her covers, she leapt from the bed and raced to the door, but she heard Colin's chamber door shut before she could open it. With a sigh, she caught up the missive on the floor and tore it open. Her message to him, folded within the pages of his, was about her life in Applegate and more requests for an audience.

When she began to read his response, her breath caught.

Dearest Jane,

This is the point where I would have stopped responding to you. Not because I cut myself off, but because this letter would have inspired me to get on my horse and come to you. I would have come to you, Jane. I would have told you those lies about you that I believed. You would have deserved the same anger you feel now, but we would have had so much more time to overcome the falsehoods Arthur told. And the mistrust I allowed to separate us.

I would have come to you, Jane. Because I love you. I love you to the core of me. And I hope you will eventually forgive me.

Yours Always, Colin

Her hands shook as she stared at his words. They were written in a messier hand. Like he was writing fast, driven to get out what was in his heart and his head. It was so strange to see that, because normally he was so composed, so calm.

His love for her had changed that. Made him desperate. It had opened his heart, broken down his walls and the shell he put around himself. It made everything he said all the more real. All the more important.

She set the letter aside and stared at the barrier before her. The door was all that separated her from him now. Not any secrets or lies, not his icy disdain, not even her pain. Just a door. And doors were meant to be opened.

She did so, her hands shaking, and slowly stepped into the antechamber. It felt like it took days to cross through the dim adjoining sitting room and reach Colin's door. Another barrier to cross. Behind it, he waited for her. He was writing to her.

And when she opened the door, she would be opening her heart. If she opened her heart, he could hurt her. Or they could set each other free. And it was worth the risk to see which one would come to pass.

She turned the handle and stepped inside. Colin sat at his desk, hunched over a quill and paper. He was writing, just as she'd known he'd be writing. And he didn't seem to hear her as she entered the room, he was so focused on whatever it was he was sharing with her next.

She stared at him a long moment. He was so handsome. So very strong. And from his work in the House of Lords, she also knew he could be caring. He could be just. Fear had kept him from showing her those things, but they lived in him. He was offering them, a bit late, perhaps. But now. In this moment.

She couldn't walk away from that. Walk away from him.

"Colin," she said, her voice rough and low.

His hand froze in midsentence and he slowly turned. His eyes widened when he saw her there in his doorway, and he pushed his chair back like he would rise.

She held out a hand to stay him, keep him in his seat as she walked across the room to him. If he stood and towered over her, all that masculine heat and energy swirling around her, she might not be able to get out what she wanted to say.

"You're…you're here," he said, his voice shaking, filled with disbelief.

She nodded. "I am."

She stopped at his shoulder and leaned over, looking at what he had been writing when she entered the room. She caught her breath at what it was. Over and over, he had written, *I love you, Jane. Please forgive me.*

He shifted and his gaze darted away. "Not very creative, I suppose, but I knew I would have come here by then, you see. Though I love reading your stories of your time in Applegate, I know that I would not have ever written a response to any more of your beautiful letters, because I already would have been here, making up for the pain I caused."

She blinked at the tears that welled in her eyes. "And when you came to me, when you saw me here in person, what would you have said to me then?"

He gripped his hands against the arms of his chair and slowly eased to his feet. His breath came shallow, almost labored. His dark eyes were filled with fear and pain and honesty and hope…and love. She saw the love there, burning bright.

"That I'm so sorry," he whispered, leaning in so his face was close to hers. "That I know we lost so many months together and that is *my* fault, Jane. No one's fault but mine. I hate that I can never get that time back, nor erase the scars my actions have put upon your soul."

She caught her breath, her eyes burning with tears. He smiled just a little as he reached up to wipe one away with his thumb. He smoothed it across her cheek, cupped her chin, tilted her face closer.

"And I would tell you, I *will* tell you, that I'll work every day for the rest of my life in order to make the time we have left perfect for you. To leave you with so many good memories that these bad ones will fade and eventually have less power. If I could be given a chance which I know I don't deserve to earn your love."

She stared into his earnest face, and a calm washed over her. It washed away all the rest, replaced it with gentle certainty. She smiled up at him and saw him catch his breath. Felt him lean in as she lifted her hands to cover his.

"Neither of us can erase what happened before," she whispered. "And it will take some time for me to completely forgive you, to completely trust you again. But I must tell you one thing, Colin. You don't need to *earn* my love. You've had it all along, despite everything. You have it now. I love you."

C olin stared at Jane, his heart swelling with emotion and his mind clearing of anything and everything but her.

"You—you love me?" he repeated. "How can that be after what I did?"

"I know you're better than that," she said softly. "And I am going to put faith in the belief that you will prove it to me over time, over the years we spend together. Just as I have faith that I will slowly ease the pain of your past, until you know that I am not related at all to what your former love did, or your cousin, or anyone else who damaged your heart."

He wrapped his arms around her waist, holding her to him. "I wish—"

She lifted her fingers to his lips and the press of them was filled with gentle power. "No, no regrets. Let's start anew. From this moment, Colin. It's all we have in the end and I don't want to waste it."

She lifted her mouth and he lowered his to meet her, kissing her at first softly, but then with more purpose, more drive. She slid her fingers into his hair, tilting his head as their tongues tangled. She ground against him, whimpering when his fingers dug into her hips.

"I want you," he whispered as he dragged his mouth down her throat.

"I'm yours," she said in return, a great shiver of pleasure racking her as he sucked the delicate skin.

He continued to kiss her as he backed her toward his bed. *Their* bed. She didn't resist—in fact, she actively participated, unfastening the buttons on his shirt, sliding her fingers inside to brush along his bare skin.

He did the same, clenching his fingers along her spine and bunching her night-rail as he tasted her and tempted her and made her promises with his body that he intended to keep for the rest of his life. At last, he pushed the gown from her shoulders. It pooled at her feet, leaving her naked before him.

He stared. He couldn't help it. If they were starting from today, from this moment, he wanted to see her, to look with new eyes, fresh eyes unblocked by lies and deceptions and foolish fears.

She was exquisite. Perfect. And somehow, despite it all, *his*. He had every intention of celebrating that fact.

She reached for his open shirt, smiling up at him as she pushed it away, then moved on the buttons to his trousers. She had to work around his hardening cock to unfasten him, but she managed it at last and the last of the clothing separating them fell away.

She caught her breath. "I have always marveled at your body," she murmured. "When we were apart, I dreamed of it and you."

"You think I didn't do the same?" he asked, guiding her backward, laying her across his bed, leaning in to press hot kisses to her throat, her chest, sucking a hard nipple into the cavern of his mouth.

She arched beneath him with a mewling cry before she gasped, "Did you?"

"Oh, yes. My body knew what my mind refused to believe. That I belonged to you. And that nothing would be complete until I—" He parted her legs gently and nudged into the space there, feeling her wetness as he stroked his cock back and forth against her entrance. "—until I did this again."

He slid inside her wet heat, feeling her shudder around him as he came home to her.

"Colin," she whispered, her nails digging into his forearms.

"There," he said. "Now I'm whole."

She lifted into him, grinding against him. He let out a low moan of pleasure and then began to thrust into her, feeling her sex cling to him, her inner muscles massage every hard and sensitive inch of his cock. That felt like heaven, but the true pleasure was watching her face while he took her. She was utter surrender, she was complete trust and she was building pleasure.

Her lips parted as her body began to rock in a more urgent and broken rhythm, her hands clenched at the sheets, and then she shattered. Her beautiful face almost glowed as her body lost all control. It was too much for him to hold back, and he surrendered to his own pleasure, crying out her name as he filled her with his essence and his love and his everything.

And knew that he would never lose her again. He'd never let himself.

EPILOGUE

One Year Later

J ane rested a hand on her swollen belly and smiled as Colin brought her a second plate of her favorite breakfast treats.

"You spoil me," she said as he leaned down to kiss her gently.

"You deserve it," he said, smiling down the table at their guests. "I'm sure Alicia and Charles agree."

Jane cast a glance toward her sister and brother-in-law and blushed at their stares. But they were friendly stares. Loving. Since her reunion with Colin, since their return to London together, he had worked hard to prove himself not just to her, but to her family and friends.

It was paying off. Alicia had thawed to him considerably, and he and Charles were becoming friends.

But more than that, Jane, herself, knew she could trust him. She could surrender to him, she could fail or be imperfect around him because he loved her. In all her shades and looks and moments.

He loved her as she loved him.

"What will you name the baby?" Alicia asked as she took a bite of her own breakfast. "Matthew has suggested Ba-ba-boo, but I feel like it doesn't fit."

Jane laughed, thinking of her nephew and how thrilled she was that her child, boy or girl, would be surrounded by love from all sides.

"We'll put it on the list," Colin said with a smile.

"I'm certain you are wishing for an heir," Charles said.

Colin met Jane's stare, holding steady, holding true, as he had been for a year. And his smile grew. "I don't have a care in the world about that. As long as the child is healthy, I'll be perfectly happy."

She leaned forward and cupped his cheek as pure love and joy filled her. "Perfectly happy," she agreed.

STEALING THE DUKE

THE SCANDAL SHEET BOOK 2

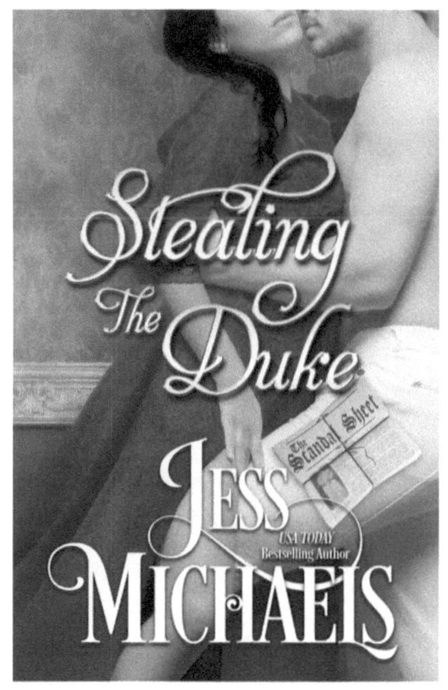

For Michael, who always steals my heart.

CHAPTER 1

The recent death of a certain Earl has unleashed a torrent of scandal that not even this publication has seen before. This is not the usual gossip which hints at mistresses or debts, but of something much darker. It seems this gentleman was guilty of robbing his own friends and neighbors of prized possessions. Many items have been returned since the dreadful news got out, but we must wonder how these terrible acts will affect his remaining heirs, from the nephew who now inherits his title to the daughters who will be forced to live with his humilia-tion. We shall see if the Robbing Earl has done more harm than can ever be fixed, even by time itself.

Marianne stared at the paper before her, the words swimming across the page as she read them over and over. Her stomach turned, and she nearly heaved up what little breakfast she had choked down already.

The Scandal Sheet was a paper that was delivered weekly to the most influential houses in London. Its blind items of gossip about those with titles and power were often cruel. Marianne had always flinched as her father read them out loud, his laughter booming.

And now here was one about him. A few lines so obvious that no one would doubt for a moment to whom it referred. What he had done was bad enough. Discovering the cache of stolen items in his personal effects after he died had been the worst moment of her life. She still went dizzy and her hands went clammy when she thought of it.

What she'd done about it made her nausea increase. She'd called the watch in the hopes they could handle the matter with discretion.

They had not. One grasping captain—one who looked at her like she was guilty just for sharing her father's name—one bastard of the highest order—had seen to that. Captain Black clearly viewed returning the items with much fanfare was a way to further his own relationships with those of power. In doing so, he had destroyed her.

Within hours, the truth had begun to spread throughout Society. There had been whispers, rescinded invitations. Her father's funeral had been poorly attended, and even the vicar had sniffed down his nose at the earl's gravesite.

And now *this*. This public final nail in her father's very recently buried coffin. Only it didn't only bury him. As the paragraph about him implied, it also crushed her in its wake. And her younger sister.

"Mari!"

She jolted as the very person she had been contemplating flew into the room. Marianne forced a smile and flipped over *The Scandal Sheet* so it was face down on the table, for she didn't want Juliet to see her pain. At ten, she didn't deserve the burden of adult problems.

"Poppin," Marianne said, opening her arms so Juliet could hug her and press a kiss on her cheek. "I didn't realize you would be back from Nora's until after lunch."

Juliet had spent the night at a friend's and Marianne expected her to leap into a spirited description of everything the two girls had done during their special night. Instead Juliet's face fell.

"I…" Juliet's eyes filled with tears. "They sent me home. And I heard Nora's mother whispering that I should not be invited again."

"Why?" Marianne said, her heart sinking, for she already guessed the reason.

Juliet's gaze flitted to the paper next to Marianne's hand and slowly moved to turn it right side up. She nodded toward it. "This."

Marianne ducked her head. She had tried to keep her sister from the truth, but now…well, there was nothing to do now. All illusions were shattered. As were both their lives.

"You read it?" Marianne asked softly.

Juliet nodded, and Marianne sighed and motioned to the chair beside hers. Her sister took it and stared up at her with wide eyes that were the exact color of their late father's. Odd to see his eyes again when he had been buried a week already.

"Did Papa *truly* steal?" Juliet whispered.

"Oh, poppin," Marianne said, trying hard to find words to explain the unexplainable. "How do you know this nasty thing in that rag of a paper is about him?"

Juliet lifted both eyebrows. "I'm not stupid, Mari. And I'm not a little girl. Please don't hide things from me. I know you have been, and I don't want there to be secrets between us. *Please* tell me."

Marianne worried her lip. If Juliet's friendships were already being affected by the truth, if they would soon suffer other consequences of their father's actions, she supposed she owed Juliet the facts.

"Papa had a compulsion," she began softly. "I think he always had it. He took things. Little things, but also big things. Mama tried to break him of it, but he didn't seem to be able to stop, even when he promised he would. Her death only made it worse, it seems."

Juliet's face crumpled, and Marianne hated herself for shattering her younger sister's illusions. She hated her father for giving her cause to shatter them.

"But…but can't we just give them back?" Juliet pressed. "After all, you and I didn't take anything. If we give everything back, perhaps Nora's mother will see I'm not like him and let me play with her again."

Marianne bent her head, pain swelling in her. "Well, darling, you see, I *did* give the things back. As soon as I found the piles and piles of stolen items, I arranged to have them all returned. But…but it didn't matter. In fact, it only made things worse." She clenched a fist in her lap. "I should have just kept them hidden or burned them. My better instincts have caused nothing but heartache."

Juliet's eyes went wide. "Mari, you don't mean that!" she gasped. "Stealing is *wrong*. And if you'd just kept whatever he took or destroyed it, wouldn't that have been stealing just as he did? You gave things back, that was the right thing to do."

Marianne sighed. Trust sweet Juliet to see the world as black and white. It was a child's prerogative to do so, she supposed. And in truth, she rather agreed with her sister. Perhaps holding her tongue about what she'd found would have saved her and her sister some grief, but living with that might very well have killed her. She'd never been good at lying.

That was something she *hadn't* inherited from her father.

"You are correct, my love," she said with a weak smile. "Giving back what he took was the right thing to do, whether it harms us or not. But some will only see the sin, not our attempt to remedy it, nor our innocence in the initial act."

"People like Nora's mother," Juliet whispered.

Marianne tried not to show her pain and anger. "Yes, I'm afraid so. There are consequences to what Papa did. They will be visited on us, it seems, since he is no longer around to pay them."

"Is that why Cousin Samuel is asking us to leave the house in a month?"

Marianne froze. It seemed her sister had been *very* busy finding out information she'd been trying to keep a secret. "How did you hear that?"

Juliet cast her eyes away in guilt. "I...I listened a little after you asked me to leave the room when he came to supper two nights ago. I didn't hear everything, but he was very angry, wasn't he?"

Marianne let out her breath in a long burst. "Samuel inherits Papa's title now, and with what our father did, he'll have a long road to walk to bring the name Martingale back to any kind of respectability. He believes having us away from London, out of this house, will help people forget."

"He thinks it's our fault?" Juliet wailed.

"He's a blustering blowhard who only cares about himself," Marianne burst out, shaking her head. "That he would cast a child out onto the—"

She stopped herself, for she saw the fear light in Juliet's eyes.

"Mari?" she whispered.

Marianne caught her hands. "I am making arrangements, my love. We have a little money from Papa's estate." A very little, but she didn't mention that. "And we will find a happy spot where we can live together. With time, people will forget about what our father did and it will all be...fine."

She said the words, but didn't believe them. But from the way Juliet's eyes lit up with faith and hope, it was clear her sister did. Juliet launched herself into Marianne's arms.

"You'll fix it, Mari! I know you will," Juliet whispered. "May I go up to see Miss Bennett?"

Marianne smiled at the mention of Juliet's beloved governess. "Of course. I'll see you later, dearest."

Her sister left the room, her troubles abated for the moment. Marianne's, of course, were not. The settlement she and her sister would be allowed thanks to their cousin was hardly enough to pay for their own expenses. She would not be able to retain Miss Bennett, who was the light of her sister's young life. In truth, she might not even be able to retain her own maid.

She rubbed a hand over her eyes and got to her feet, fighting the nausea and anxiety that rose up from deep within her. She stumbled from the breakfast room and down the hallway toward her father's office. There she had collected all her financial documents and some inquiries she'd made about a new residence. Perhaps if she looked them over again, she could stretch the funds just a little further, for her sister's sake.

She entered the office and tears leapt to her eyes. This place still held the spirit of her late father inside its walls. She smelled the scent of his tobacco still on the air. She could all too easily picture him in the leather seat behind the desk, smiling up at her.

She was angry with him. But she had loved him. She still loved him.

"How could you leave us like this, Papa?" she murmured as she walked to his chair and sank into its soft cushion. "How am I to carry on?"

She let herself sit like that for a moment, eyes closed, the smoky scent of the air filling her lungs. Then she pushed her shoulders back and focused on the papers strewn out in front of her. The numbers on them were terrifyingly stark. They wove a tale of the desperation she was trying hard to tamp down.

She searched the desk for a quill, but frowned when there was none to be found. An ink bottle, yes, but somehow the quill was no longer where she'd left it.

With an exasperated sigh, she began to open drawers on her father's desk, digging through his disorganization for the one thing she sought. In the third drawer she opened, she blindly pressed her fingers toward the back of the drawer and smiled. She felt them brush a long, thin handle of some kind, probably a quill crushed back in her father's distracted hurry. She tugged, and to her surprise, she did not bring forward a pen, but there was a tiny click and a hidden door inside the drawer itself slid partly open as it caught on the myriad of papers on top of it.

She snatched her hand back and stared at the tiny sliver of an opening beneath the obviously false bottom of the drawer. Her heart began to pound as she lowered a shaking hand to push the papers aside and examine the opening more closely.

She could only think of one reason why her father would have such a hidden space in his desk. Only one reason he'd want to hide something.

Because he'd stolen it.

"Please don't be something horrible," she whispered as she pressed the opening wider and looked inside. There was a box there, like something that might contain jewelry. She drew it out and set it on the desk, staring at the tiny thing like it might bite and feeling the accusation of its presence even before she dared to open it.

At last, though, she couldn't escape the drive to see what was inside. To open that box and hope she would find something innocent.

Her fingers shook as she unhinged the tiny clasp on the front of the box, then pressed it open. What she found made her catch her breath. It was a brooch. Beautifully made in ivory and gold. The lady whose profile it depicted had dainty features. Marianne drew the piece out, feeling its weight in her palm, the coolness of the metal back against her skin. Slowly she turned it and realized it was engraved:

Happy birthday, Anne
All my love from your brother Alex

She caught her breath. Anne was not her mother. Alex was not her father. In fact she knew of no one in her family with either of those names.

Which meant her fears were likely true. This was a stolen piece, one her father had hidden. She turned it over again and realized the brooch had a clasp, as well. She opened it and revealed two portraits inside, one of a beautiful young woman, one of a handsome man.

She stared at their faces and caught her breath. She knew the woman. She was almost certain of it. It was Lady Anne, the sister of the Duke of Avondale. She and Anne had been of an age, though they hadn't been friends. The young woman had died a few years back after an illness.

Her brother, the duke, had not been seen in Society since. Once a dashing rake with a reputation of taking whatever he desired, he had disappeared. Rumors abounded that the man had gone mad. Or had been horribly injured in some way. Or perhaps even died.

And *this* was the brooch of Avondale's late sister. How in the world had her father come to possess it? It had been so long since anyone saw the duke, her father likely would have had to break into his home and take it right beneath his nose.

"Damn it," she muttered as she put the brooch back into its place and slammed the box shut so she wouldn't have to look at it anymore.

She got up and paced across the room, staring into the fire for a moment before she turned back to the item. The box was still there, no matter how she wished it away. And now she had to decide what to do with it.

"You have four options," she said out loud to herself as she glared at the offending little cube. Talking things out had always helped her. "You could call the guard again. Only then that *loathsome* Captain Black will likely take great pleasure in leveraging our family drama for his own good. Just like he did last time."

She shook her head. No, that wouldn't do. The damage already caused was so great. Further information leaking into Society could be the death of any future Juliet might have.

"You could put the box back," she continued. "Just place it in Papa's desk where you found it, close the drawer and never speak of it again."

It was a temptation to do so, indeed. But then what would happen? She wouldn't truly forget she had found this thing and she knew she would likely forever wonder what had happened to it. Depending on who found it in the future, the damage she feared it might cause could still be out there, only waiting for some inopportune moment to strike and destroy her and her sister.

She huffed out a breath. "You could…sell it," she continued, with uncertainty in her tone.

Certainly there must be unscrupulous people who would buy such a fine piece. The money she collected would help her and Juliet in their dire straits.

Only the idea of doing that made her stomach turn. She would be no better than her father if she benefitted from his thievery. That kind of blood money could bring no luck, that was for certain. She would have to live with what she'd done. Not to mention that if selling the piece was ever traced back to her, the ruin she feared would be even more certain.

"I could not live with doing such a terrible thing," she muttered. "And that leaves me with my last option. I could…I could return the brooch to Avondale's house here in London."

Saying those words made her entire body quake with terror. By God, just the idea of it was enough to make the blood drain from her cheeks.

But the fear didn't mean it wasn't a good idea. As far as gossip said, Avondale was not in Town at present. His London estate was shut up, with likely only a servant or two in residence to manage it. If she could find an unlocked door or window, she could sneak in and leave the brooch somewhere it would be found. The duke would have his sentimental item returned, so she would have no guilt to hang over her head. And as long as she wasn't caught, she could rest easy, knowing the brooch could no longer be traced to her father.

It was a risky option, but no more than the others. And at least she could live with herself when it came to returning what her father had taken.

She nodded slowly, wishing that action could convince her she wasn't a fool, and walked back to the desk. She opened the box, took out the brooch and thrust it into her pelisse pocket. Then she tossed the box into the fire, watching the evidence burn away.

Now she just had to find a way to break into the Duke of Avondale's home. But perhaps that was something that would come naturally once she got there. After all, she *was* her father's daughter.

CHAPTER 2

Alexander Wittingham, Duke of Avondale, sat in the far corner of his office, watching as his fire burned down to nothing but faint embers, leaving the room in almost total darkness. He gripped a glass of scotch in his hand, but had not taken a sip of it in nearly an hour. The room was quiet but for the faint ticking of the clock. The house was quiet, too. He only kept a servant or two, just the bare minimum. Most of the time no one even knew when he was here in London. He came, did his business, and returned to his country estate like a ghost.

In some ways he *was* a ghost, living only half a life. He deserved no more than that. He probably deserved less.

He lifted his glass to his lips at last and swigged back most of the liquor in one gulp. As the drink burned down his throat, he froze. From the corner of his eye, he thought he'd caught a bit of movement from the door to his office.

He turned toward it and watched as his door opened, letting in a sliver of light from the hallway that outlined a shadowy figure who slipped into the room. Although he couldn't see the intruder's face, he knew it wasn't one of his servants. They were all trained to stay out of his private rooms. He didn't even allow them to be cleaned, and he trusted his staff implicitly.

So this was a blackguard who entered, not a friend. The figure hung at the door a moment, then stepped forward slowly, moving toward his desk. There the person stopped and there was a rustle of fabric in the silence. The shadow of his intruder's hand reached out and took something.

At that, Alexander moved. He jumped up and lunged forward, catching the person before they could abscond with anything of his. But as he wrapped his arms around the shadow, he caught his breath. He had expected to tackle a man, but the figure now trapped in his arms was a woman. He felt her curves pressed against his forearms as he held her from behind and her backside wriggled against his pelvis.

"No!" she cried out in a musical voice that broke the silence of the room and shocked his senses. "Please!"

A whiff of the scent of her hair wafted to his nostrils as he dragged her toward the fire. She smelled of vanilla and cinnamon, spicy and sweet and that, coupled with her continued movements in his arms, inspired the strangest reaction.

Deep inside of him, in a place he had long thought dead and buried, desire stirred. A strange and misplaced desire to turn the stranger in his arms and look into her eyes. Touch her skin and see if it was as soft as the curves of her body were. The fact that she was a stranger and a thief be damned in all of it.

But he didn't do either of those things. He wrapped a hand around her arm, holding her tight as he reached down with the other and grabbed a log. He threw it onto the dying fire, then caught a candle from the mantel and lowered it, lighting it from the growing flame.

Only then, when the light raised in the room, did he look at his intruder's face. And that face did nothing to reduce the strange longing that hardened his cock and made his long-dead heart throb back to life.

She was exquisitely beautiful, with silky dark hair which had partly fallen from the bun at the nape of her neck in their struggle. Her eyes were bright and wild with fear. Green eyes, darkest green, the color of summer leaves.

Eyes that went even wider when the same light hit *his* face. He knew what she saw. The scar that slashed from his temple, down his cheek, across his lips and down to his chin. The scar that reflected perfectly the monster that he was inside. He fought the urge to turn away from her gaze, to back into the darkness again so she wouldn't see him and the ugliness that went far beneath the surface.

She let out a gasp and twisted in his arms even further, then darted out one daintily slippered foot and crushed it down against his boot. Although it didn't hurt, he was surprised by the action, and for a moment his grip slipped. She didn't hesitate to shrug from his arms and dart back toward his door.

Marianne could hardly breathe as she ran. Just a few more steps and she'd be in the hallway. A few more after that and she'd be back in the parlor where there had been a window unlocked. Out that and she'd be free. Free of the dark and dangerous man who had—

She didn't get to finish the thought. She didn't even make it to the first door when he caught her again from behind and crushed her back against his broad, muscular chest once more. She felt his breath stir her hair, the steaminess of it against the shell of her ear as he whispered, "Stop running."

His voice was deep and rich, and its hardness stopped her struggle immediately. They stood there like that for a moment, his arms still around her, his panting breath in her ear, her body pressed intimately against him. Then he reached forward and pushed the door to the office shut.

He turned her in his arms, not releasing her when he did so, and she shivered as she stared up at his scarred face once again. It was a handsome face despite the harsh, raised mark that marred it. He had a well-defined jaw, full lips and bright eyes that were as blue as a cloudless sky. Her lips parted as those eyes bore down into her, holding her as hostage as much as his arms did.

"Who are you?" he asked.

That rough voice swirled into her ears and she stared at him harder, struck dumb by the command he held with so few words. He held her gaze for a moment, his frown deepening.

"I may look like a beast, girl, but I have no intention of hurting you. But you *will* answer me. Who are you?"

"M-My name is…" She trailed off, knowing that the moment she gave her name she would be lost.

"By God, you will tell me," he hissed, lowering his face closer to hers and filling every space until there was only him.

"Marianne," she whispered. "My father was…he was the Earl of Martingale."

He didn't react for a moment. Then he tilted his head like he was trying to read her. "If you run again, I will tie you to a chair, do you understand?"

"You know who I am," Marianne said as the reality of the situation settled heavy in her chest. "There is no point in running now. Everything is over."

His fingers loosened their grip on her and he stepped back, folding his arms across his chest. "You are the daughter of a nobleman."

She wrinkled her brow. At present she didn't know many who would call her father *noble*. "He was titled, yes," she admitted.

"Was?"

"He is dead, Your Grace. A week ago," she said, shocked that he was pretending not to know who the Earl of Martingale was. Such scandal like that which surrounded her father could not be avoided.

"My condolences for your loss," he said, inclining his head ever so slightly. "But why would a lady such as you break into my house and try to steal from me?"

Now she stared openly at him, her mouth slightly open. "You pretend not to know—is that by design? Are you sporting with me, sir? If you are, it is infinitely cruel."

He lifted both eyebrows. "*I* am not the one who broke into your home, my lady. I think you ought to be careful in your outrage. I am not sporting with you at any rate, I only think I have a right to know the situation of my thief."

She let out a sigh. "Do you *really* not know who my father was? I thought everyone in the world, or at least the world of the *ton*, knew about it all. About the scandal that surrounds him…me…*us*."

"Look at me, Lady Marianne," he said softly. "Do I look like I roam free in Society, giving a damn about some foolish little scandal?"

She caught her breath. He *truly* didn't know what was happening. He *truly* didn't know anything about her. He was the first person since her father's death who was so far removed from the whispers. The first person who did not automatically judge her for what the earl had done.

Of course, the duke judged her now for what he believed *she* was here to do, instead.

She stared up into his face, past the shocking scar, into those blue eyes, and for a wild moment she knew what she would do. She knew she would tell him everything. Because she needed so desperately to spill herself out to someone who had no preconceived notions. Someone who wouldn't whisper anything she said down the lane until her own words came back to haunt her.

"May I sit down?" she asked.

He watched her a moment, then nodded toward two chairs that faced the fire. She took one with a long sigh and he took the other.

"Speak," he commanded.

"Oh, I hardly know where to begin." She shook her head and felt the bone weariness she couldn't afford flood every fiber of her being. "Everyone knows the story—I have never had to tell it to anyone who didn't already have an inkling, wrong or right, about the truth."

"Just speak," he repeated, a little gentler.

"My father was a deeply flawed man."

"Are not we all?" Avondale mused softly.

"I suppose that is true. All men and women are flawed in some way. A bad habit, a strange attraction." He blinked at her and she realized she was rambling, as she was wont to do when she was nervous. She cleared her throat and tried to focus. "But my father was more flawed than most. When he died last week I found a collection of items he had stolen from others in the ranks of Society. He took things, you see. Small things, big things, things of value and not. He stole, Your Grace."

"And so you came here to continue on in his footsteps?" Avondale said with a shake of his head. "A rather dangerous calling for such a beautiful young lady."

She sucked in her breath at the way he said *beautiful*. He drew the word out and it was like he caught her with it. She stared at him in silence before she recalled the story she was telling.

In a moment, he would not see her as beautiful.

"You have it all wrong, Your Grace. I didn't come here to *take* anything," she said, reaching into her pocket, where she'd managed to stuff the brooch when he grabbed her. "I came here to return something."

She held out the item in her shaking hands. He leaned in, and when he saw what she held, he leapt from his chair and backed up three long steps. He stared at the brooch, then up to her face.

"He stole this? From me?" he whispered, his voice suddenly rougher. Filled with raw emotion.

She noted he did not try to retrieve the item. He just stared at it, his shoulders trembling. "Yes, it seems he did. I found it in his desk drawer just this afternoon when I was looking for a quill," she said.

"I do not know when he did so, I do not know how, I can only imagine why. But he took it."

"Two years ago," he murmured, at last reaching out. He still didn't take the brooch from its spot in her palm, but he brushed his fingers across it, across her hand, sending a wild jolt of awareness through her. Then he snatched his fingers away. "He took it two years ago. At least that was when I realized it was missing."

"It was…it was your sister's, wasn't it?" she pressed, even though she shouldn't.

His gaze jerked to her face and his lips thinned, turning as white as the scar that cut through them. "Yes. Did you know Anne?"

"A little," Marianne admitted. "We were of an age. I wasn't close to her, but we were friendly when we encountered each other. She was a lovely young woman. I-I'm sorry for your loss."

"Don't bother with your empty words," he snapped, stepping toward her. "Your father stole from me and now you sneak into my house, as much a liar as he was, to give it back. Why?"

She let out a long sigh at his anger. She'd known she had earned it, so it didn't surprise her. "Because when I initially uncovered what he'd done, I called the watch, hoping the things he'd taken could be returned with some discretion. Instead, this horrible inspector used my father's bad acts in order to further himself. He has spread the truth far and wide, and he has destroyed our family reputation. He is nothing less than a demon and seems to take great pleasure in hurting others. I knew if I called on him to help me return this to you, it would only add fuel to an already raging inferno. Sneaking in here with the idea of just leaving it on your desk was cowardly, I admit it. But it was an act of desperation."

"To protect yourself," he sneered.

She shook her head. "I have very little to protect. I am already considered an old maid, Your Grace. I have no illusions that my reputation will recover from this. I'm trying to protect…to protect my younger sister. She is a child, just ten. I can only pray these whispers may die down by the time she is to enter Society. I must hope for that so that she could have some chance at a future. But I must do everything in my power to make those whispers go away more quickly."

He arched a brow. "Give the girl a good dowry when she comes of age and any sins will be forgiven."

"I agree, but that is out of the question. My cousin has inherited the title from my father, as he had no sons, and the new earl is bent on removing us from sight. We have a pittance as an inheritance—it will barely be enough to keep us fed and sheltered." Tears filled her eyes as she told this stranger her plight. Hearing the full weight of it for the first time made her stomach turn. "It is an uphill battle."

He stared at her in a silence that seemed to stretch forever, then slowly shook his head. "You could have destroyed this or sold it. You didn't have to risk what you did to return it."

She shrugged. "I could not do that. It would make me no better than my father, wouldn't it? What kind of sister would I be if *that* was the example I set for Juliet?"

His expression remained cool and unreadable as he took in what she said. Then he asked, "And you think bringing this back to me makes up for what your father did?"

"It's all I can do," she said softly.

His eyes lit up briefly and he moved toward her another long step. She shifted in her seat as she watched him move. His motions were graceful but also intimidating. And yet she didn't stand or back away from him. She didn't want to.

"It's not *all* you can do," he retorted.

Now she did stand, shoving her shaking hands behind her back. "You want something from me. Something as compensation? What is it?"

He glided forward again and held out his hand. To her shock, his fingers moved across her jawline, tracing the skin there with intimate and utterly inappropriate slowness.

"What would you say if I told you I want *you*?"

CHAPTER 3

Alexander watched as understanding dawned across Marianne's face. He waited to see her disgust at the notion, for her fear because of his monstrous appearance. But there was none. Her eyes instead lit up with interest at his suggestion, coupled with confusion.

"I-I'm a lady," she stammered at last.

He nodded slowly. "Indeed, you are that. Does that mean you pretend not to understand what I desire?"

She licked her lips and his cock hardened at the swipe of her pink tongue. He wanted to feel the same across his skin. He had from the moment he first touched her and realized his intruder was a woman.

It had been a long time since he wanted something or someone so much. He found himself quite desperate for her, despite what she'd come here to do. Despite the fact that she was not the kind of woman one made this type of offer to. Despite the fact that she could talk and talk and talk, it seemed. Despite it all, he wanted her.

"You wish to…" Her cheeks flamed and her voice dropped to a whisper. "…bed me."

"Say it again," he ordered. "Louder."

She cleared her throat and glared at him before she said, "You wish to bed me."

He nodded. "For a time, yes, I want to *bed* you. But you know there will be consequences to that action. I assume you are a virgin?"

The blush of her skin grew darker. "Of course I am, Your Grace. My father was a thief—that does not make me a wanton."

"I hope you *are* a wanton once you let me touch you," he said with a rusty laugh. "That will make this so much more fun. But you *will* surrender your virginity. That will limit your future."

She pondered that a moment. "My future is already severely limited, as I've told you. My virginity isn't what will keep a man of means and standing from offering for me. Still, it will put an end to any future I might have once wished for. What will I gain in return for this?"

His eyes widened at her strength and grit. Rather than mincing or blushing or fainting, she was *negotiating* with him.

"You said you are about to be put out of your home. That your inheritance is hardly enough to keep you," he said. "How long is your cousin allowing you to have to find a new arrangement?"

"A month," she said, and her voice broke. Her fear was obvious, and for a moment he wished he could comfort her.

Of course, he did no such foolish thing. He hardened his tone and said, "I have a cottage on my estate in Avondale that used to be let but is currently empty. I would guarantee you to have it for a very reduced rent. Low enough that your purse would stretch."

She met his eyes, and he could see her interest growing. "But if anyone found out what I had traded for, it would hurt my sister even more than this mess with my father has."

He shrugged. "I have no interest in telling tales, not that I have anyone to tell them to. And if it would strengthen my offer, I would be willing to add to your sister's future dowry. I think a few thousand pounds when she turns eighteen would certainly make her a viable prospect for a man of respectability."

Her lips parted, and for a moment it seemed he had stunned her into silence. He watched as she attempted to regather herself. "A few thousand pounds," she breathed at last. "That is a great deal of money. What will you expect from me in return? What will you have me do?"

He stepped closer, drawing in a long drag of her sweet scent. Slowly, he caught her arms and pulled her tight against him. God's teeth, but she was soft and molded to him like she'd been made to do so.

"Anything I desire," he responded. "You will come with me to the estate as soon as possible. Have your servants prepare your sister for travel in a month when she will come to join you at the cottage. Until then, you'll be mine. All mine. How and when and where I desire it."

"A month," she breathed, her gaze flitting to his lips. She wanted him to kiss her, and he would. To seal the deal.

"For now you would live in my home, though you would move to the cottage once your sister arrived on the estate. We might be able to come to a discreet arrangement for more time if we were equally pleased by each other."

"And if you are not pleased with me?" she asked. "Would that mean your bargain would not stand?"

He pursed his lips. She was tenacious, he could see. That would serve him well if it were put to use as his lover. But right now she was only interested in protecting her sister.

He understood that.

"In my sister's name, I vow to you that I shall not go back on my word," he said.

What he'd said shocked him. He had never thought to invoke Anne's name in promise before.

He cleared his throat. "A month with me and that is all you will be forced to endure if you do not want more. The cottage will be yours. And the funds for your sister will go into an account that will be accessible when she is ready to come out in Society."

Marianne struggled from his embrace and backed away. Her dark green eyes speared him, holding steady, almost as if she could read him. He found himself wanting to turn away from that focused stare. To push away from it.

"This is…it is a very unexpected offer. I never would have thought such a thing would happen when I decided to come here tonight. I didn't even think you were here when I—"

"Marianne," he interrupted softly.

She blinked as if she hadn't realized she'd been speaking in a stream of consciousness. "Why would you be willing to give so much to get so little?"

"I don't know." He hesitated because he had not meant to be so… *honest* in his response. Something in this woman brought that out in him, as much as she brought out the need he had suppressed for so long.

"You don't know?" she repeated, her tone thick with incredulity. "I think you are the kind of man who always knows *exactly* what you are doing."

He frowned. Yes, he had always been precisely that. Until tonight, it seemed. He pressed his lips together. "Are you saying you don't want the bargain, my lady? It is no harm to me either way."

She blanched and said, "I-I didn't say that."

He shrugged. "All I know is that I want you. And since wanting anything is a rare enough occasion for me, I find I'm willing to pay a great deal for the pleasure of indulging myself. Will you take my offer or no?"

She licked her lips again and his cock throbbed as he waited for her to respond. Then, slowly, she nodded. "I would be a fool to refuse such a generous offer. Especially since there will be no generosity to come from any other party. Do you…will you *hurt* me?"

He stared at her, horror filling him. "No. I don't want to hurt you."

She let out her breath. "I suppose I have no other choice but to take that promise at its face. Y-Yes, Your Grace. I will do as you ask."

There was a great rush of relief that flooded his throbbing body. With a groan, he stepped forward, slid his hands across her cheeks to cup her face and dropped his lips down on hers.

By the way she stiffened and gasped, he could tell she was shocked. He waited for her to pull back, to turn her face so she could no longer feel his scarred lips on her soft and pliable ones.

But to his surprise, she didn't do that. Instead she slowly relaxed in his arms. Her hands reached up to grip his forearms, and when his tongue swept across her lips, she opened to him with a shiver of surrender and desire. He greedily took what she offered, driving his tongue against hers, memorizing the sweet flavor of her mouth that matched the scent of her skin.

Want throbbed through him, driving him to fantasies of pushing her back against the office door, lifting her skirts and taking her then and there. But he didn't. *That* wasn't the bargain. And if he was going to claim the prize of her innocence, he had to restrain himself from being the beast he was.

As difficult as that was, he forced himself to step away from her. She was trembling as she stared at him, her eyes glazed with shock and wanting, her hands shaking at her sides.

But she didn't run. She didn't turn away.

It had been a very long time since someone had stood their ground with him.

"I will fetch you tomorrow afternoon for the trip to Avondale," he said. "That should give you enough time to make your excuses and arrangements, I would think."

Her lips parted. "*Tomorrow?*"

He arched a brow. "Your month started the moment I kissed you, Lady Marianne. Are you going back on our arrangement already?"

She pressed her lips together, thinning them. "Of course not. I will do my best to make all preparations before your arrival, Your Grace."

"See that you do," he said, his tone sharp to cover up any emotions this arrangement, this exchange, had inspired in him. "You may go."

Her brow wrinkled as if she were confused, then she nodded. "Yes."

She turned and slowly approached his desk, setting his sister's brooch on the surface before she left his office. He did not follow, as much as he wanted to see if she would now leave through his front door like a guest or his window like a beautiful thief in the night.

Once she was gone, he let out the breath he'd felt like he'd been holding the entire time they were in the room together. He moved toward the desk, staring at the brooch as he neared it. The miniature along the top had been fashioned to look like Anne, something he had commissioned the year she turned sixteen.

It felt like a lifetime ago when he'd done it. When he'd still been a good brother, had the opportunity to be a good man. When Anne was still alive, when he could see her face and hear her laughter any time he desired to do so.

He touched the brooch, pain rising up in him as he did so. Anne had been the last person who loved him. The last person who thought he deserved such emotion and connection. If she were here to know the bargain he'd just made with the Earl of Martingale's daughter, she would look at him with such horror and contempt.

He shook his head and turned away from the pin. He had made his bargain. It would not last long. Once a month was over, he would likely be finished with his desire for Marianne and she would be well pleased to be rid of him. That would be the end of it. He would go back to being alone.

Just as he deserved to be.

~

Marianne had not slept a wink since her encounter with the Duke of Avondale. She felt the effects as she trudged down the stairs to the parlor, where she would break the news of her departure to Juliet. The rest of the household staff already knew. They had been ordered to make arrangements for their move to Avondale's cottage in a month's time.

She would never forget the look on her butler's face when she'd told him. He had stared at her like she had sprung a second head, and he didn't even know the worst of it.

That she was trading her body for Juliet's future. A bargain where she would surely gain more than Avondale would. Her freedom was a high cost for whatever small amount of pleasure she might bring to him.

Now, her own pleasure? *That* was another story. She had not had a moment pass since she left his home where she didn't think of that searing kiss between them. Her lips still burned with the memory and with anticipation of what else the sinfully seductive and obviously experienced duke could do to her.

She entered the parlor to find Juliet sitting with her governess. Miss Bennett had already heard the news, and Marianne had asked her to stand by to help comfort Juliet. There would be little time for Marianne to do so, herself. The Duke of Avondale had already sent word he would come for her shortly.

"You have been busy this morning," Juliet said as she crossed the room to kiss Marianne's cheek. "I didn't see you at breakfast."

Marianne smiled and shot Miss Bennett a look. The governess nodded as if understanding to be ready. "Yes, I have been busy, poppin," Marianne said. "You see, I must...I must go away for a little while."

Juliet took a step back and stared up at her in confusion. "Go—go away?" she repeated. "But...but why? Where? For how long?"

Marianne took her sister's hand and led her to the settee. "Don't be upset, darling. You know that we cannot stay in this house for long thanks to Cousin Samuel. I have found us a situation in the country where I hope we will be happy, but I must go ahead to take care of some business before you can join me."

"In the country?" Juliet repeated.

Marianne forced a smile to her face as she nodded. "Oh yes. A lovely cottage!"

She hoped that part was true. God, she hoped this entire bargain would lead to happiness and comfort for her sister.

Juliet gave a look to Miss Bennett and then worried her lip. "How long will you be away?"

"A month is all, and then you will join me," Marianne said. She reached for her sister, but Juliet stepped out of the way.

"A month is a very long time!" she gasped out. "I don't want you to go away for so long."

"I know, but—"

"I don't want you to go away at all!" Juliet said, her eyes filling with tears before she bolted from the room and up the stairway toward her chamber.

Marianne let out a sigh as she glanced at the clock on the mantel. The duke would be here at any moment. There was no time to pursue Juliet and try to make it right between them.

Miss Bennett rose and came toward her. "I will talk to her, my lady," she said kindly. "I'll help her see that you are doing what you think is best for her. That you are…*sacrificing* for her."

Marianne blinked at Miss Bennett's tone and looked at her closely. The servants would certainly have their theories and opinions about this sudden decision, especially once Avondale's carriage pulled up to collect her. Certainly, none of those could be worse than the truth of what she was doing.

"Do you think I'm doing the right thing?" she whispered.

Miss Bennett's smile softened. She was of an age to Marianne, and there was a friendliness they had always maintained. "Sometimes what is best may not be what others would consider right. I know you love your sister and you would surrender a great deal to help her."

Marianne nodded. "I would."

Of course, at present the idea of a month with Avondale didn't feel like the biggest sacrifice in the world to her. Not if his kisses were as melting as last night's had been.

"A carriage just pulled up," Miss Bennett said, making Marianne turn toward the window. It was a fine carriage, indeed, with Avondale's crest huge and blatant on the side.

"Oh God," Marianne whispered.

"I'll go up and see if I can talk to Juliet."

Marianne nodded, tears jumping to her eyes. "Take care of her. And if there is any problem, if Samuel tries to remove you before it is time to join us…please contact me immediately."

"I will," Miss Bennett said, and exited the room just as Avondale entered, Marianne's butler trailing behind with yet another judgmental expression on his face.

"The Duke of—" he began to announce.

Avondale held up a hand and his lips set into a thin line that highlighted the whiteness of the scar across them. "She knows who I am. Leave us."

Marianne was surprised when her butler did not look to her for verification of Avondale's heavy-handed order, but simply left as he'd been told. She folded her arms and stared at the man.

He was incredibly handsome in daylight. Even more handsome than she had remembered. That scar that slashed his face only made her pay closer attention to his bright eyes, his high cheekbones and his full lips. Those lips that had covered hers not long ago.

"Are you prepared?" he said, his gaze never leaving hers.

She struggled to recall how to speak and finally simply nodded.

He inclined his head slightly. "Then we should go."

"I'll call for my maid," she said, moving toward the pull by the door.

He stepped to the side, blocking her path with his big body. She had to come up short to keep from crashing right into his broad chest. She looked up, feeling her lips tremble, her entire body tremble.

"There is a carriage coming to your back door to collect your things. Your maid can ride in it," he said, his tone brooking no refusal.

She wrinkled her brow. "But…but that would mean you and I would ride alone together."

His lips tilted up further. "Oh yes, it does."

She caught her breath at the wickedness of his expression. It did something physical to her, something that made her bones liquid and heat spread through her veins. It was intoxicating and terrifying at the same time.

"But—"

He leaned in, and his warm breath slid over her lips, like a kiss though he never touched her. "Lady Marianne, it is time we begin your education. And *that* will require privacy. Make your final preparations and then we go in my carriage. Together. Alone."

CHAPTER 4

Alexander watched as Marianne shifted in her seat, turning toward the window and craning her neck as the townhouse disappeared behind them. When it was entirely out of sight, she settled back into place with a shaky sigh. There was a faint sparkle of tears in her eyes and to his surprise, his stomach clenched at the sight.

Normally he didn't allow himself such weakness, but he had a strange desire to comfort her, just as he had the night before.

He cleared his throat. "You'll see her soon."

She nodded and forced a smile to her face. "I know."

"I'm not going to hurt you," he whispered, somehow needing to remind her of that in her vulnerable state. Perhaps needing to remind himself the same thing.

Her expression softened and she reached out as if to take his hand. Her fingers stretched toward him, and he held his breath as he waited for her touch. But before she could reach him, she stopped and dropped her eyes away. A blush filled her cheeks.

"I suppose it is foolish of me, considering our bargain and why it was made. But I trust when you say you won't hurt me, Your Grace."

He pressed his lips together hard. Did she refuse to touch him out of disgust for his appearance? Or was it just her innocence?

Either way, he *would* have her. That was their bargain.

He moved to her, taking the seat next to her. Slowly he lifted his hands up to her face. Her skin was impossibly soft, her lips trembling as she lifted them toward him, her breath coming as a ragged sigh of invitation and surrender.

"Alexander," he murmured.

Her eyes widened slightly. "What?"

"I'm going to do things to you, Marianne. Things that will require that you call me Alexander."

She swallowed hard, but didn't resist as he dropped his lips to hers and kissed her. She went soft beneath him, her mouth opening to welcome him in. He smiled at the surrender. She was a quick learner and her shaky sigh told him she had enjoyed their previous encounter as much as he had.

He was going to make sure she enjoyed their next one even more. He deepened the kiss, angling his head so he could taste every inch of her sweet mouth. To his shock, she responded, darting her tongue out and brushing it across his own. His body lit on fire with that innocent passion bubbling below the surface. His cock throbbed, swelling and hardening to a painful degree.

He'd had plans for this woman. Plans that involved a bed in the inn they'd stop at along the way.

He wasn't going to make it that long.

He pushed her back, pinning her against the wall of the carriage as he groaned into her open mouth. She slipped her arms around him, her fingers pressing hard into his shoulders as she kissed him back with passion that belied her trembling innocence.

He drew back, exploring her face in the dim light in the carriage. "Turn around."

She blinked. "Your Grace?"

"Alexander," he corrected again. "Turn around."

She still looked questioning as she did so, placing her back toward him. He shivered as he lifted his hands, unfastening the buttons along her spine.

"What are you doing?" she murmured, but she didn't draw away from him. In fact, she inched back a little, a small offering she might not have even realized she made.

Which made it all the better.

"I'm undressing you," he said, pushing her gown forward. "I want to see you. Turn back around."

She was slow to do so, but at last she faced him, her cheeks flaming red, her nipples hard against the flimsy fabric of her chemise. He reached out to slide his fingers beneath the straps and drew them down to tangle with the gown, revealing her from the waist up.

Her lips were trembling, but she didn't refuse him as he stared at her body. Her beautiful body. She had full breasts, they would be heavy in his hands, and they were capped with dusty rose nipples that at present were swollen and hard with desire she likely didn't even understand.

He bent his head and traced the tip of his tongue around one nipple. She gasped at the sensation, but quickly arched against him with a low moan.

"What is this?" she murmured.

He lifted his head, watching how her face was slack with sensation even as her eyes were wide with confusion. "Pleasure," he said. "This is pleasure. And there is about to be a great deal more of it. Lift your skirts."

"Alexander," she said, her cheeks flaming.

"Do it," he ordered.

She inched them up, barely to her knees, and he almost laughed at her defiance. He rather liked her spark. He didn't want her to lose it—he just wanted her to use it on more...exciting matters.

He caught her hem and pushed the dress all the way up to her stomach. She was wearing drawers, which he reached down and caught, tearing the fabric open at the slit and baring her lower body.

"You won't wear these anymore," he said. "For the next month you will wear nothing beneath your gowns."

She swallowed but nodded slowly. She shifted in her seat, clearly uncomfortable at being so revealed. But he wasn't finished yet.

"Put one foot on the step next to the door," he said as he moved to kneel before her on the carriage floor. "And the other on the seat beside you."

"But then I'll be wide open and—"

"I want you wide open," he interrupted, his mouth watering as she stared down at him.

She bit her lip. "Are you going to claim me?"

He tilted his head at the question, spoken with such fear. Not that he blamed her. She likely knew very little about sex, as did most ladies. What she was about to give him was precious, her only bargaining chip in a world of men who would happily take advantage.

Just as he planned to take advantage, he supposed.

"I will," he said slowly. "But not here, Marianne. Not in a carriage where you wouldn't be comfortable. Tonight we will stop at an inn and rest. There will be a bed and time for me to make you ready."

"Then what are you doing now?" she whispered.

"Pleasure isn't only about putting my cock in you," he said, reaching up to take one slippered foot and resting it on the step on the door. "There are many ways to find release, for both of us."

"Release?" she asked, but she moved her other foot as she did so and opened herself to him.

He stared at the slick, sweet pussy set before him and shuddered with the power of his desire. Her constant questions should have reduced that need, but they didn't. "Release. To make you come. Have you ever touched yourself, in the dark, in your bed? Here?"

He reached out and gently swiped his thumb across the crease between her thighs. She rocked into him as he did so, her breath breaking. She turned her face and he smiled.

"You have," he said. "Have you ground against your hand, seeking pleasure?"

She swallowed hard, and then she nodded without looking at him.

"That pleasure was your release. Coming. And I can make you do that right here, right now."

She licked her lips and let her gaze return to him. "How?"

He didn't answer, but bent his head, nudging his nose along the fragrant folds of her sex. She tensed beneath that touch, lifting her hips toward him with a muffled moan. A moan that turned to a harsh cry when he darted out his tongue and traced it along the entrance to her sex.

Marianne gripped her hands against the carriage seat as sensations crashed over her. Alexander was...*licking* her. Pressing her folds open with his big hands and licking her over and over. And it was magnificent! His tongue was rough and firm, awakening nerves that she'd only just barely brought to life when she touched herself in those stolen moments he'd forced her to admit to taking in the dark of her chamber.

This was no fumbled attempt in the dark. No, this man knew exactly what he was doing.

He lifted his head from between her thighs and she shivered as she stared at him. He looked so wicked, kneeling between her spread legs, his big hands pressing her open even wider, his lips slick and his eyes dark and dangerous.

"You're thinking too much, Marianne," he whispered, his voice thick and low. "Let go."

She swallowed hard. What he was asking her to do was near-impossible. She had so much responsibility, so much she carried on her back. If she let go, even for a moment, she feared she would lose her grip and everything would come crashing down around her, around Juliet.

"Look at me," he whispered.

She forced herself to do so, locking eyes with him and losing herself in the swirling, dark depths.

"Let. Go," he repeated. An order this time, rather than a request. But also a form of permission. This man, for all intents and purposes, had purchased her surrender in exchange for her sister's future.

And she would obey him. Because she should. Because she wanted to.

She settled back against the carriage seat and closed her eyes, pushing away her worries, her fears, her nagging questions about this man and about her future. And with great difficulty, she let go.

She felt his breath against her folds a second time, and she gasped as the stroke of his tongue returned to her wet, tingling sex. She lifted into him, reveling in the sensations he woke in her. And there were so very many sensations to be explored. The stroke of his tongue, the feel of his strong fingers holding her open to him in the most wicked ways, and of course the response of her hungry, wanton body.

Her entire being seemed to hum with increasing pleasure as he licked and licked. Tingles spread from every fold and pulsed in that bundle of nerves just at the top of her sex. The one he sometimes swirled his tongue around and made her lurch and cry out with pleasure.

What he was doing, the reactions his mouth elicited, it was similar to the pleasure she brought herself with her hands, but far more intense and focused. And it built with powerful force as he focused more and more on her clitoris.

She arched into him, grinding her hips without even meaning to do so, reaching for the pleasure he promised with every stroke of his tongue. And then, suddenly, it was there, explosive as it washed over her in long, powerful waves.

Her eyes flew open and she stared at him as he continued to lick her through the crisis, holding her hips steady as he pulled more and more and more sensation free. After what seemed like an eternity, the jolts of electric pleasure subsided and he lifted his head to smile up at her.

Her heart skipped a beat. He really was uncommonly handsome. She wanted to trace both scar and jaw with her fingers, with her mouth.

He leaned up, bracing himself on the seat, and kissed her. Once again her mind emptied as she tasted the earthy flavor of her release on his tongue and melted into the driving sensation of his mouth.

"That was perfect," he murmured as he gently tugged her skirts back down over her legs. "Did you enjoy it?"

She laughed despite the intensity of this moment and the gravity of what she had just allowed this man, this veritable stranger, to do to her.

"Were my gasps and cries not proof enough of my enjoyment?" she teased.

He arched a brow and reached out to trace a circle around her nipple with the edge of his fingernail. She gasped at the sensation as desire flooded her a second time.

"Women can pretend their release, you know, far easier than a man can."

She shook her head. "There was nothing pretended about that, I assure you. It was...wonderful. Better than anything I've found on my own."

He nodded, and she thought there was a moment of relief on his face. Like he was afraid she hadn't truly wanted him or liked what they'd done. But then it was gone and he was stoic and unreadable again.

"Good," he said, his tone more formal. "Would you like me to rebutton you?"

She nodded slowly and slid her arms through her sleeves before she put her back to him a second time. He was just as swift and efficient in tidying her as he had been in making her so very undone. When she was returned to some semblance of order, he moved to his side of the carriage where he settled against the seat, watching her with those intensely bright blue eyes.

She shifted under his scrutiny. "Er, isn't there something we can do for…you?"

Those same eyes went wide. "For me?"

"Although I'm an innocent, or I was an innocent. Am I still an innocent? You've not taken my maidenhead, but—"

"Marianne," he said softly, and she shut her mouth. She was rambling. Again. But he had a tiny hint of a smile on his face, like he was not annoyed by it.

She cleared her throat and refocused herself. "I have heard told that men are very uncomfortable if they are…excited and then cannot find release."

He shifted. "Men who do not understand the value of anticipation, perhaps," he said, his voice dropping back to that low and dangerous tone. "I do. There will be hours for me to picture what it will feel like to slide home into that sweet pussy of yours, Marianne. To feel you pulse around me, tight as a glove. Hours to imagine the way you will arch beneath me as you give yourself over in every way imaginable."

Marianne's lips parted as excitement coursed through her. In truth, she had been hesitant about joining with this man. It was one thing to like his kisses, or even the wickedness of his mouth against her most private of places. But letting him mount her was quite another thing, one that was permanent. One that some of her married friends had described as less than pleasant. But when he held her stare and said those words…those wicked, heated words… she found herself wanting just what he described.

"Why don't you rest?" he said, turning his face to stare out the window. "It's a long ride and I doubt you slept much last night. You'll likely not sleep tonight either, if I do my job right. So it will be in your best interest to nap if you can."

She tilted her head, searching his face. A moment ago he had been tender and passionate with her. Now he had placed a wall between them. But what was she to do about it? Their bargain was about pleasure, but it was at his whim. She certainly had no right to press him if he no longer wanted to talk to her.

And he was, of course, right. The night before had been sleepless and she was exhausted.

"Very well," she said softly.

He reached down and opened a drawer that had been built into the bench of his seat. From it, he pulled a small pillow and a neatly folded blanket. "For your comfort," he said.

She took the offerings and carefully set up her place on the seat. She rested her head on the pillow, propping it against the wall next to her and watched him for a moment.

Finally, she took in a deep breath and said, "Alexander?"

He glanced at her. "Yes?"

"Thank you for being...kind," she said.

His mouth thinned and he shrugged. "I look out for my best interest, Marianne. Kindness has nothing to do with it."

With that, he pulled a folded paper from the gap in the seat next to him and opened it, closing off communication between them. She sighed and shut her eyes, but even as sleep overtook her, she couldn't help but think that his final words to her were not correct. And that he simply wished to hide any gentleness or softness from her.

Which made her wonder about him all the more.

CHAPTER 5

Darkness had gathered in the carriage, but the occasional reflection from the moonlight outside still allowed Alexander a good look at Marianne. She was tucked up on the seat across from him, sound asleep. Just as she had been for hours. The depth of her sleep made him wonder just how long it had been since she had really rested.

Not that it was his problem. He hadn't taken Marianne into this bargain to repair whatever damage others had done to her. He'd done it for himself. For his gratification.

She shifted a little, letting out a tiny moan in her sleep, and his body clenched. He had already gone too far with her, an innocent. A lady. Ruined her just by taking her on this trip, not to mention when he spread her wide and made her come.

And he would do more to her. So much more.

"You are a selfish bastard," he muttered out loud, flopping back on the carriage seat and looking away from Marianne. When he shut his eyes, he could still see her in his mind. Only he pictured her with a look of horror, a look of fear and heartache. He pictured her ruined, because that was the only thing he was capable of doing, ruining those around him. That had always been true and it would likely always be true. If he'd had any decency he would have sent her away the moment he caught her in his home and continued to hide away just as he had these past two years. Continued to protect the world from what he was at his heart, protect himself from what they would see when they looked at him.

Instead, he had allowed their brief encounter in London to create a scenario in which he dragged this woman into his darkness. Where he would destroy her future just to make his own a tiny fraction more bearable.

The carriage began to slow and he straightened, pulling back the curtain farther. As he had suspected, they had arrived at the inn for the night. As the carriage stopped, he watched as one of the footmen jumped down to make the arrangements. He'd already been given specific orders, and Alexander expected them to be followed.

He let out a long breath and leaned forward to extend his hand. He planned to touch Marianne's knee to gently wake her, but he found himself hesitating. It was funny, for he had touched her intimately just a few hours before. Now the idea of squeezing her leg felt too…familiar.

He didn't have to, though. Before he could muster his nerve or his heart or whatever it was that was required, she stirred on her own and her eyes opened. She looked across the carriage at him and a slow smile spread across her lovely face.

"Hello," she said, her voice still thick with sleep. Then it was as if she recognized where she was. The smile faded, and she bolted to an upright position and looked around. "Oh, we've stopped. Where are we?"

"At an inn," he explained, pulling his hand back and wondering at the odd disappointment at the act. He hadn't wanted to touch her and now he felt sorry he hadn't. Foolishness.

"Oh," she whispered, and swallowed hard. He could see her mind working, turning on what he'd told her earlier in the day: that he would take her tonight, at the inn.

He could hardly wait.

"Come," he said, tapping on the door so that the waiting servant would open it for them at last.

Alexander climbed out first and then turned back to offer his hand to Marianne. She stared at him, her green eyes boring down into him with intensity, like she could read his soul.

"Come," he repeated, more sharply this time, and she frowned as she took his assistance. Her fingers folded around his and he jolted at the touch. She did the same, those beautiful eyes widening as she darted her gaze away, as if she didn't look at him that this connection between them would fade in intensity.

It didn't, but he released her the moment she was steady on her feet and turned toward the footman who was now returning from the inn.

"You spoke to the owner?" Alexander asked sharply.

"Yes, Your Grace," the young man responded with a quick nod. "The name I gave was Smith. The room will be ready momentarily and food will be sent up, just as you requested."

Alexander nodded. "Very good. Help Rodgers with the animals. We leave tomorrow at dawn so that we may arrive home before supper."

"Yes, sir," the footman replied as Alexander motioned Marianne to join him as he walked toward the inn.

She did so silently, her eyes wide as she stared up at the building that loomed before her. Her questions were reflected on her face, her fears, but there was something else there. Something he recognized, and it hit him in the gut. He saw her desire. Her excitement. She was an innocent, that much was clear, but she was a responsive innocent. One who had been built for pleasure, it seemed.

And he could not wait to test her limits and awaken her.

～

Marianne's hands shook, but she shoved them behind her back as she and Alexander entered the inn and were greeted by a portly man in fine clothing. He had a huge mustache and a wide smile beneath it as he rushed forward to greet them.

"Mr. and Mrs. Smith!" he said, a little too loudly, but with a jolly quality that wasn't diminished even as his eyes widened when he observed Alexander's scar. "Welcome, welcome. I'm Mr. Carlisle. All the arrangements are being made."

Alexander tensed as the man looked at his face, but he began to speak and Marianne looked off away from them. Mr. and Mrs. Smith. Of course Alexander would give the man false information about their identities. About the fact that they were married. The innkeeper didn't seem the kind who would participate in the ruination of an innocent.

She frowned. Ruination. That was what she was going up into, after all. But when she thought of Alexander's mouth on her in the carriage, what they had done didn't feel ruinous. It made her feel alive. She had dreamed about it, about what was to come, in the carriage. Now he would take her upstairs and…

"My dear?"

She jumped when she realized Alexander was referring to her. "Yes?"

He smiled, but there was a tension to his mouth, one that pulled the scar across his face and brightened the white line. "Mr. Carlisle is showing us to our room."

"Of course," Marianne said with a little shake of her head and a glance for the waiting innkeeper. "I'm sorry, it was a long day of travel."

The innkeeper moved ahead of them, guiding them through a main hall and toward a set of stairs. "I can well imagine, madam. But our beds are comfortable and our food is perfection. A good night's sleep will put you to rights."

Marianne glanced at Alexander. He had already promised she

would have no sleep tonight. Right now she didn't want sleep. She wanted to…touch him. She didn't know how to do that or what would actually happen once she did, but the desire pulsed in her regardless.

Mr. Carlisle took them to the end of a long hallway and pushed open the door at the end. "Here we are. Our best rooms."

Alexander motioned Marianne in first and she gasped. It was a lovely room, big and open, with a fire burning brightly. There was a table by the window, already set for supper, though food had not yet been delivered. There was another door on the opposite side of the room, and the innkeeper bustled forward to open it. "The bedroom," he explained. "And through it to the dressing room, where the—"

"Yes," Alexander cut him off. "Thank you."

The man nodded and looked from one of them to the other. "Well, I'll leave you now. Food will be delivered into the main sitting room shortly and the other…item…will be taken care of in an hour or so?"

"Two," Alexander said, his stare focusing on Marianne. There was a smoky heat to it, one that curled her toes in her stockings and made her thighs clench against her will.

"Two," the man repeated, and then hustled for the door. "Good evening, Mr. and Mrs. Smith."

Mr. Carlisle shut the door as he exited, and Marianne started at the quiet click that indicated she was now alone with Alexander. In a chamber they would share. In a chamber where she would surrender her virginity to him.

He moved toward her, and she couldn't help but tense as he closed the distance with only three long steps. He came to a sudden stop. "I'm not going to jump on you," he said.

Her breath hitched and she stared up at him, mesmerized by the intensity of his face, the beauty and the imperfection of it. She wanted this man, propriety be damned.

His eyes narrowed. "Unless that's what you want," he whispered, moving even closer. His body heat surrounded her and she could hardly breathe at all now. He sucked up all the space and air between them with his presence. "Is that what you want?"

She swallowed, struggling to find words. It was odd, since she often babbled, especially when she was nervous. But right now she could hardly breathe. Finally, she merely bobbed her head once. His expression grew harder, more focused and purposeful, and he reached out to trace a thumb across her lips. She fought the urge to capture it with her mouth, suck it and let him drag his skin across her skin.

He caught her arm and pulled her against him, hard, tight, and then he lowered his mouth with exquisite slowness. She lifted into him, eager for his kiss, eager for him in general, and when he brushed his mouth across hers, she let out a ragged sigh of relief.

What started as gentle spiraled almost immediately into a hungry claiming of her mouth, and she lost herself in the incessant drive of his tongue and the heated grip of his hands on her arms. She recognized that he was pushing her backward, into the bedchamber, and she didn't resist. The bedchamber was exactly where she wanted to be.

He maneuvered them into the room and kicked the door shut behind them as he continued to kiss her and kiss her until her blood boiled and her vision blurred with desire and sensation. If someone had asked her a week ago if she would be here, she would have said no. She would have been aghast at the suggestion. But now that she was, there was nowhere else she'd rather be than in this room, with this man.

This man who had wrapped his arms around her and was now stripping open the buttons along the back of her dress, pulling it free like he had earlier in the carriage. She felt the fabric droop and he pulled away from the kiss to tug the entire contraption down, past her hips to pool on the floor at her feet.

"Step out," he ordered, his tone low and ragged.

She followed the order—how could she not?—and kicked the dress aside. Her chemise hit just above her knees and she blushed as he looked at her, despite what they'd done in the carriage earlier in the day. She was not accustomed to being viewed with so little on. Would she ever be?

He was still for what felt like an eternity and then reached out again, catching her hips with his big hands, drawing her forward to collide with the solid muscle of his body.

"I should not do this," he whispered, his breath catching as he stared down into her face, just inches from his own. "What little of a gentleman is left of me is telling me to stop. To let you go."

She caught her breath at the idea that he would free her from their bargain. She supposed she should thrill at that idea, but she didn't. What he suggested didn't sound like freedom to her. More like abandonment. Loss.

She pulled from his arms and lifted shaking hands to the straps of her chemise. Drawing a deep breath, she pushed the undergarment away and now stood naked, save her stockings and slippers.

"You and I have a bargain," she managed to squeak out past dry lips. "Tell me you don't plan to renege."

His eyes went wide. "No. I don't think I could even if I tried. Not anymore."

She folded her hands before her, heat flooding her from head to toe. "I-I don't know what to do."

"Take off the rest," he suggested.

She nodded, turning away slightly. She toed off her slippers and rolled her stockings down her legs, draping them over the arm of a chair closest to her. When she turned back, she found Alexander still staring at her. She stared right back, for he had removed his jacket, waistcoat and shirt while she focused on her stockings.

She'd never seen a half-naked man before. And her mouth went utterly dry at the sight of this one. He was…granite. Steel. An unmovable object. His was a body of strength, with tanned flesh overlaying what seemed like endless ripples of muscle. He had a peppering of dark hair across his chest, leading in a trail down to his trouser waist.

"Oh my God," she murmured.

"My thoughts exactly," he said, his tone thick with what she recognized was desire. Again her mind turned to the carriage. To his mouth on her, to the racking pleasure that had turned her inside out and changed her forever.

"The bed," he grunted, pointing to it. "Now, please."

She looked at the bed. When they entered the room, she had been too distracted by his touch to really take in the chamber. Now she caught her breath. It was a large bed, with crisp white linens. It faced the fire, so there was a golden glow across it, almost welcoming her to the future she had never guessed she would now be facing.

A future as this man's lover.

She climbed into the high bed and settled back on the pillows, watching as he parted the buttons on his trousers and slid them down his trim hips. She stared at what he revealed.

"Do you know what it's called?" he asked, staying right where he stood.

"That?" she whispered, pointing to the hard thrust of muscle between his legs. It had a mushroom head, a long shaft and a thatch of dark curls at its base. Where her sex was soft and wet and pliable, his looked like a weapon.

"A cock," he said. "Do you know what I'll do with it?"

"I saw…animals on my father's estate in the country," she admitted. "And once I found a very naughty book in his study. So I have some idea."

"But your mother never spoke to you of this?" he asked.

She shook her head. "I was young when my mother died, not close to marriageable age. She never talked to me about this, nor did anyone else."

He shut his eyes, and for a long moment he said nothing, nor did he move. Then he looked at her again. "It will hurt the first time. I'll do everything I can to ease the pain, but it is part of what will happen. But after, once this first time is through, there will not be pain again. Do you understand?"

"And what I've felt when I touched myself, when you…licked me?" she asked, blushing so dark that she was sure she looked like a beet. "Will that happen again?"

"I'm going to make sure of it," he whispered, and at last he moved toward her. He was like an animal, stalking its prey. Slow and steady, he never removed his gaze from her, focused and intent. She, like a rabbit facing a fox, froze, waiting for him, her breath short and her body tense with anticipation. He joined her on the bed, his big body dipping the mattress as he stalked toward her, now on all fours like the beast she could see living inside of him.

He moved over her, caging her against the pillows with his arms and staring down at her, his expression hard to read beyond intense, powerful desire. He dropped his mouth and brushed his lips back and forth against hers. She sank into the kiss once more, memorizing the feel of his mouth on hers, the sensation of the slightly raised mark of his scar rolling over her skin.

"Tell me what you're thinking," he whispered as he pulled away.

She swallowed. Despite his darkness, this man inspired honesty in her. Perhaps in part because she sensed he would settle for nothing less than that. If she lied, he would see it. And he would not allow it.

"There are so many thoughts," she began. "A thousand bouncing off each other and creating such cacophony that I can hardly discern one from the other. So where do I begin? Or do I—"

He let out his breath. "Marianne."

The interruption, her name said so softly, settled her mind a fraction.

"I'm afraid," she admitted. "Not just of what is about to happen, but of how much I want it. How much I want…you. Is that wrong? You are hardly more than a stranger and I've spent my whole life being told to guard what I am about to hand over to you."

He pushed off her, rolling to the side where he faced her, his expression pensive. "Not wrong. Ladies are taught that what they want, what they feel, is to be hidden, but it's natural to feel desire. After all, you've experienced that pleasure that comes from orgasm."

She tilted her head. "Orgasm?"

He shook his head slowly. "Release. The pleasure you felt here—" He glided just the tips of his fingers down the apex of her body, settling them gently at the soaking entrance to her sex. "—when you came. That drive to feel that release is natural, even if the arrangement we've come to is unorthodox."

He didn't move his hand when he finished speaking, but gently massaged the sensitive flesh between her legs. She shut her eyes on a ragged breath and began to lift toward him.

"This is the last chance, though, Marianne," he whispered, his breath rolling over her throat before he kissed her neck, nibbling the sensitive flesh. "Once I take you, there's no going back. So you must tell me now, is this truly what you want?"

She opened her eyes, watching as he dragged his mouth down her collarbone, over the heavy swell of her breast, and then his pink tongue stroked out over her nipple. She gasped, lifting her hips hard into his hand, feeling his fingertips breach her just a fraction as sensation rushed through her, powerful and almost overwhelming.

In that moment, the truth hit her like a slap in the face. She was doing this not to save Juliet, not out of desperation, not for any other reason but that she wanted this man. She wanted the pleasure he seemed capable of giving with just a flick of his wrist or his tongue. She wanted it for herself, with no other ulterior motive, even if she would benefit from her decision in the future.

She reached for him, tucking a finger beneath his chin and forcing him to lift his face to look at her. "Yes," she said, holding his gaze steady. "I want this. I want you. The answer is yes."

CHAPTER 6

Alexander had been with many women in his life. Before he was scarred, he'd been known as a rake, a seducer of women, and they had fallen at his feet for the opportunity for a night in his bed. Tonight should have been nothing out of the ordinary for him. Oh, it had been a while, yes. But it shouldn't have meant anything beyond slaking a desire that had risen up so powerfully in him.

But now, staring into Marianne's green eyes, seeing the innocence in her expression, but also the heat that bubbled beneath her demure surface…he felt a stirring in his heart that he didn't understand and didn't want.

He wanted it to go away.

With a growl, he rolled back over to cover her, pinning her to the bed with his superior weight. She mewled out in pleasure, arching against him with unpracticed passion that made his hard cock even harder, a divining rod that screamed at him where to go.

With difficulty, he fought the urge to simply plunge inside her tight body, and kissed her roughly. She tasted like peaches, sweet and ripe, and she relaxed beneath him with a soft sound of pleasure. When she was limp, he returned his attention to her body, dragging his mouth back to her rosy nipples, where he licked and sucked and plucked at her. He loved how her breath caught with pleasure, how her hips rolled against his, seeking what he had to offer. He loved how she shut her eyes and surrendered to sensation. Innocent or no, she was bold. She was brave.

And that spoke to him in some deep place he had thought cut off when he locked himself away from the world at large. Tonight he would allow himself this pleasure. After…well, he would decide that when he came to it.

He dragged his mouth lower, tasting the flesh of her stomach, her hip, and then parting her legs to reveal her sex just as he had in the carriage. She was already wet, and the scent of her desire drove him mad with wanting. But he wanted this to be good for her. So he pushed his own desire aside and focused on making her come, making her ready.

He spread her folds, rubbing the flat of his fingers across the entrance to her body. She gasped, turning her head on the pillows at the intimate touch. He watched her face, observing how she bit her lip, how she arched her back as he smoothed his fingers across her again, then dipped just the tip of his index finger inside.

"Alexander," she gasped, her eyes opening wide and his name a prayer as he breached her body this time.

"I want to ready you," he explained, only barely holding back a groan as her tight body pulsed around him. She was most definitely untried and he gently stretched her with his fingers. She dug her fingers into the coverlet, hissing out a sound that wasn't clearly pleasure or pain, and he stopped moving. "Does it hurt?"

"I don't know," she admitted, her breath short. "It's full."

He almost laughed at that statement, for she hadn't even begun to experience fullness yet. His cock would soon stretch her, leaving no more space between them.

And he was so ready for that moment. Judging from the slick welcome of her sex around his fingers, so was she. He bent his head, drawing his tongue against the salty and sweet essence of her body. She ground up into him just as she had done in the carriage, and within a few long strokes, her body began to shake with orgasm. He looked up at her as he continued to draw her through the pleasure, reveling in the look of pure release on her lovely face.

When the tremors had subsided, he lifted to his knees, grasped her hips and slid her lower on the bed. He pressed her thighs wider before he matched their bodies, his hardness to her softness. She looked down at the place where they would be joined, and he saw the worry on her face, but also the curiosity and lingering need.

"Ready?" he asked.

She jerked out a nod. "Yes."

He drove forward in one slick thrust and barely contained a groan of pure bliss. By God, but her tight body welcomed him, pulsing around him in the last few tremors of her prior orgasm. He looked down at her face and saw the flash of pain there, so he forced himself to hold still when all he wanted to do was pound against her hard and fast, slaking his need for her until there was nothing but blinding pleasure to wipe away everything else.

"Talk to me," he urged, hearing the strain in his voice.

She wiggled a little beneath him and her sex clenched against his cock. He dipped his head back with a harsh grunt, fighting for the control this woman didn't even fully realize she could take.

"It hurt for a moment," she whispered. "But now it's just...odd."

"And what about now?" he asked as he slowly rotated his hips.

She gasped, her eyes going even wider as she jerked her stare to his face. "Alexander?"

"And now?" he repeated, rolling his hips again.

She sucked in air through her teeth as she lifted against him instinctually. Oh, yes, she was built for this. From her beautiful head down to her curling toes. She was built for this and for him.

He moved faster now, working to balance a desire to be gentle with her with his need to come. And she met him stroke for stroke, gasping out his name as he gathered her closer and kissed her deeply.

Their hips ground together, her sex milked him, hotter and

tighter than anything he'd ever experienced before. And swiftly he approached a crisis he would not be able to avoid. Her panting breaths echoed in his ears as she neared her own release a second time and he ground hard into her to bring her there.

She let out a harsh cry, her fingernails digging into his shoulders as she nearly bucked off the bed. He drove his tongue into her mouth, catching her gasps and moans of pleasure as he drove harder and faster into her clenching body. He felt the gathering storm reaching its crescendo and with a moan, he withdrew from her body and spent between them.

His heart racing, he rolled from her, pulling her against his chest and holding her there, relieved from all the negative emotions that normally clouded his every move. At least for a few short moments.

Marianne pulled the blanket around her a little tighter and pushed her plate away. It had only been half an hour since she and Alexander had made love, but it seemed like an eternity. Certainly, she felt like she was with a different man.

In the bed, he had been gentle, careful, and he had given her more pleasure than she had ever thought possible. But here, sitting in the main room of their chamber, a table of food spread out before them, he was back to being distant, cool.

She shifted and hissed out a small sound of discomfort. Her body wasn't used to what they'd just done, and it was telling her all about it.

He frowned even more deeply than he had a moment before. "They're likely preparing a bath in the dressing room even as we speak," he said. "After I finish eating, I'll check. The warm water will help with the pain."

She wrinkled her brow as she examined him closely. He was a dichotomy, that was certain. Hard and distant, but also caring and careful. Handsome but scarred. On the outside his scars were obvious, but there was something beyond that. Deeper than that.

"You arranged for a bath?" she asked.

He arched a brow. "Contrary to my appearance, I'm not a monster, Marianne. I recognize you may be feeling some discomfort."

She swallowed hard and looked at his face closely. "You don't look like a monster, Alexander. And after today, I do not think you are one in your heart, as gruff as you may try to be."

"Don't you?" he said slowly.

She heard the dangerous warning in his tone. She ignored it, even though the man made her nervous. Even though he held her future in his hands now.

"No," she said, hating that her voice shook. "If you were a monster, you would not have been so…careful with me. You could have simply taken me and not given a thought to my pleasure. You didn't."

He was silent for what felt like an eternity, and then he leaned forward. "Wanting you to come is for my pleasure as much as yours. Don't mistake yourself, Marianne—I do what I do for my own reasons."

She frowned. He was pushing her away, that much was obvious. Although she should have allowed it, she saw something in his eyes in that moment. Pain. And it made her want to draw closer to him, despite his words.

"Losing your sister must have been very hard for you," she said slowly.

He stiffened immediately and his gaze narrowed as he pushed his plate aside and got to his feet in one smooth motion.

"I do not speak of Anne," he snapped. "Not to anyone."

He walked away from her to the fire and leaned over the flames. The dancing light caressed his bare chest and she caught her breath. Wanting him came so naturally to her. Even in this moment where he was obviously putting a wall between them.

"I understand needing to shut yourself off from it," she pressed, getting to her own feet and adjusting the blanket that covered her. "I lost my mother when I was fourteen. And then my father just weeks ago."

He faced her, his arms folded across his chest. "It seems your father did not provide much for you other than scandal. Do you not feel like it is good riddance?"

She worried her lip as sadness rose up in her. "I admit I'm angry with him. I hate that his actions created the situation Juliet and I find ourselves in. But I loved my father, flaws and all. Just as I'm certain your sister loved you."

He took a long step toward her. "I told you, I do not speak of my sister to anyone. Is that clear?"

His voice grew louder on the last few words, and she jumped at the raw pain and anger in his voice and on his face. In that moment, he looked and sounded like the monster he kept trying to convince her that he was. And yet she still didn't feel like backing away from him.

She nodded slowly. "I understand you, Your Grace."

He stood perfectly still for a moment, holding her stare, struggling, it seemed, to find a way back to the illusion of control that he showed to the world. Then he nodded once. "Very good. I shall go check on your bath."

With that, he turned on his heel and stalked away, leaving her alone. Leaving her with the realization that beneath his anger and his swagger and his coldness was something dark and deep. Something she wasn't certain she should dare to explore.

No matter how much she was tempted to do so.

CHAPTER 7

Marianne shifted in the carriage seat and let out a small sigh. "You must be uncomfortable, miss."

She jolted at her maid's words. She kept forgetting Bonnie was even in the carriage with her, her mind was so tangled. But Alexander had insisted he ride outside the vehicle on horseback when they left the inn early that morning. So Bonnie had been taken from the other carriage and placed with her to keep her company.

And Marianne had been distracted and confused ever since.

"It's just been a long few days," she admitted. "I'm fine."

That seemed to appease the maid, for she went back to her knitting and humming a popular tune. Marianne peeked out the curtains, watching Alexander ride alongside the vehicle on his horse. The man sat the animal well, his strong body hardly even bouncing he was in so much control.

Just as he always was. The night before, he had allowed her the bath, then curled against her in the bed, his big body cradling hers. In the morning, he'd woken her with soft kisses and the probing press of his cock on her backside. They'd made love slowly, passionately, and she had come three times before he found his release.

And yet, once more, the moment the passion faded, he put the wall between them. And here she was, riding inside with her maid, and him outside, like they were strangers rather than lovers.

Like she worked for him. And she supposed in a way, she did. She was his mistress, in reality, no matter how limited that arrangement was. Trading her body for what she needed, for the security of her future. That was not a place she'd ever thought to find herself in.

Nor to enjoy so much once she was in it. What a wanton she was turning out to be, thinking of this man and what his body did to hers. Even as he made it perfectly clear that he had no intention of being anything to her other than a lover, and a temporary one at that.

Outside the window, Alexander urged his horse on and suddenly the animal leapt forward and they disappeared from view. She pulled the curtain back fully, craning her neck to see where they could have gone, and that was when she saw it. A huge estate, rising up in the distance. Her mouth dropped open, for the home was five times bigger than her own father's best estate. A castle fit for a king, not just a duke.

"Great Lord." Bonnie whistled beside her as she, too, watched the giant house grow closer in the distance. "That's something. To think, you'll be duchess of all this."

Marianne jerked her face toward her maid in surprise. "Duchess? No, I'm not marrying Avondale, Bonnie."

Her maid seemed surprised for a moment, then she bent her head. "I'm sorry, Lady Marianne. I must have misunderstood."

Heat flooded Marianne's cheeks as she saw the faint look of disapproval on Bonnie's face. But why wouldn't she disapprove? Ladies were not meant to take men to their bed who they would not marry. Certainly they didn't like it as much as she had.

Perhaps she wasn't a lady at heart. Just as her father hadn't truly been a gentleman in the end.

The carriage pulled to a stop, bringing her thoughts to an end with it. Within moments, the door was opened and a footman stood there to greet her. Marianne ignored the pull of disappointment that it wasn't Alexander who helped her out. But he was already standing on a long staircase, talking to a man in impeccable livery.

As Bonnie moved off to make arrangements for her things, Marianne hesitated. Should she join the duke or the servants? Her place suddenly felt very unclear.

"Lady Marianne," Alexander called out. "Come here, please."

She climbed the steps and stood beside him as he introduced her to his butler. "Jones will take care of anything you need and ensure your maid is instructed on the workings of the household. He will also show you to your chamber. I'll see you at supper."

Marianne blinked. How efficient Alexander sounded now. How utterly disinterested in her he looked and acted as he waved her off to the butler and went inside the house.

If Jones had thoughts on her being here or her role in his master's life, he made no indication on his face. He simply led her up to a chamber and she followed, making note of the stark element that the estate had. There were few pieces of art on the wall, no portraits at all, and as she passed by, she noted half the doors to the rooms were closed up tight.

The house was half-dead.

And she was staking her life on the man who had brought her here. Not for the first time, she wondered at the bargain she had made.

Alexander sat at his desk with a pile of correspondence at his side. Every time he left the countryside for London, there were a dozen things to do when he returned. He might have shut up a great many parts of his life, but he had never shirked on his duties as duke. Too many people depended on him and his lands and holdings to let them go fallow.

Normally, he would have been neck-deep in responses and troubles, but today he sat staring at the letters, completely unable to focus on matters at hand. His mind kept taking him elsewhere. Out of this room, up the stairs, to the chamber where a very unexpected lady now stayed.

Thoughts of Marianne intruded upon him constantly, just as they had during the ride to the estate. Just as they had since the moment he had captured her in his study in London.

The woman was a menace. And he could not recall ever wanting someone more than he wanted her. Which was utterly and completely terrifying, and certainly not the bargain he had made with her just a few days before.

He wanted to separate the drives of his body from the swirling cloud of his mind and the pounding ache of his heart, but it was proving to be impossible in this case.

There was a light knock on his door, and Alexander stiffened with displeasure. His household staff knew exactly what his orders were when it came to his private rooms. He was never to be disturbed, save for if the house was burning down around him.

"Your Grace?"

He gripped his quill tighter as the light, feminine voice pierced the barrier of the door. So it was not a servant who intruded. It was Marianne, herself.

He briefly considered ignoring her, but then let out his breath in a long sigh. "Come in," he snapped, rising to greet her properly as she hesitantly entered his office.

In the hours since their arrival, she had changed her clothing and fixed her hair. Not that she needed to do either. She was lovely no matter what she wore or did. Her dark hair curled around her face, framing the perfection there and making her dark green eyes sparkle like the finest emeralds. She had a sprinkling of light freckles on her nose, as well. He had noticed them before, but now he couldn't help but stare at that tiny imperfection, which only made her more…interesting.

"What is it?" he barked out, hearing the sharpness of his tone and watching her flinch under its snap.

She swallowed hard, and for a moment he thought she might simply turn on her heel and run away. Not that he would blame her. But instead, she drew a long, deep breath and slowly closed the door behind her.

"Have I displeased you already?" she asked, lifting her chin as she shoved her shaking hands behind her back.

Alexander tilted his head, mesmerized by the strength of her character as much as the beauty of her countenance. There were few ladies of her rank who would be so bold as Marianne proved herself to be every day. Few who would stand up to him, certainly.

"Your Grace?" she whispered.

He shook off his thoughts. "You have not displeased me," he said.

She pressed her lips together, almost as if she were annoyed by his response. Slowly, she placed her hands on her hips and speared him with a withering look.

"If I have, I really must demand that you be honest with me, or this arrangement will not work. And I need it to work."

"*Demand*," he repeated, shocked that her impertinence inspired in him a desire to smile. He wasn't certain he actually knew *how* to smile anymore.

She nodded. "Yes. I am well aware of my failings, Your Grace—"

"I thought we had agreed on Alexander," he interrupted, coming around the desk and leaning on the edge.

She huffed out a breath. "Very well. I'm aware of my failings, *Alexander*. My limitations when it comes to the realm of physical pleasures. I don't have experience, as you well knew when you began this. But I liked what we shared." She turned her face and a dark blush colored her cheeks. "I liked it a great deal, actually. And I would like to learn. I want to…to *please* you."

"Have you ever seen a lion, Marianne?" he asked.

She wrinkled her brow and her attention returned to him. "A lion?"

"In a circus like Astley's or something of the like?"

She shook her head. "No. My father didn't like that sort of thing, so we never went. Why—"

"The lions are quite ferocious looking," he said, stepping toward her. "With their manes and their roar and their battle-scarred faces."

He watched her gaze flit to his own scar and then refocus on his eyes. "And?" she asked.

"But in the wild, it is the lionesses who do the hunting. They're bolder even if they do not look it." He stepped closer, his cock throbbing with every inch that vanished between them. "It turns out that you may very well be a lioness, for you are very direct, aren't you? Very brave."

She swallowed as he reached her and dragged his fingertips down her cheek. "I do not feel brave," she whispered. "I feel utterly terrified of how much I want those things we shared in the carriage and last night in the bed at the inn. I'm afraid of never getting to experience that feeling again. And I'm afraid of...of you."

He froze, leaving his hand cupping her chin gently. "Afraid of me?" he repeated. "Because of my appearance?"

"You think that scar makes you frightening?" she scoffed. "Quite the opposite. I'm not afraid of your scars, Alexander. I'm afraid of the things you wake in me. Things I've been told my whole life were wrong."

He stared down into her face, so earnest and so alive and so beautiful. Also so filled with desire, plain and pure and *his*. Suddenly he wanted to do such wicked things with her, to her. He wanted to ruin her entirely and make sure she would be branded by his touch forever.

He wanted to claim her utterly and completely and never let her go.

The last thought jolted him, and he dropped his hand from her cheek. He turned away, fighting for composure even as his heart pounded and his body thrummed with desire.

He looked at her again once he had reined in the foolish needs in his mind. "Pleasing me may shock you," he whispered. "Are you truly prepared to fully dedicate yourself to passion?"

She didn't waver or hesitate as she said, "Yes."

He flicked his head toward the door. "Lock it."

Her eyes went wide, but she did as she'd been told, tracking to the door and turning the key. Then she leaned back against the surface and stared at him. "And now?"

He lifted his hand to the fall front on his trousers and unhooked the buttons there. The flap fell forward, and he watched as she blinked at his hard cock beneath the fabric, then licked her lips swiftly. God, how he wanted her mouth on him. And he was going to have it. It would be a test of how far she'd go anyway. If she was going to resist, this would be the way to find out. It might be better for her anyway, to decide he was far too debauched for her.

"Come here," he ground out, his voice strained with the need that seemed to pulse through his every nerve ending.

She crossed the room in a few jerky steps and stopped before him. He cupped her chin, dropping his mouth to hers for a deep, probing kiss. She opened to him, lifting her hands to his forearms and mewling out pleasure as he drove his tongue into her mouth. With difficulty, he pulled away.

"On your knees, Marianne," he whispered, hoping she would obey, knowing she might not, and uncertain if he was trying to draw her closer or push her away.

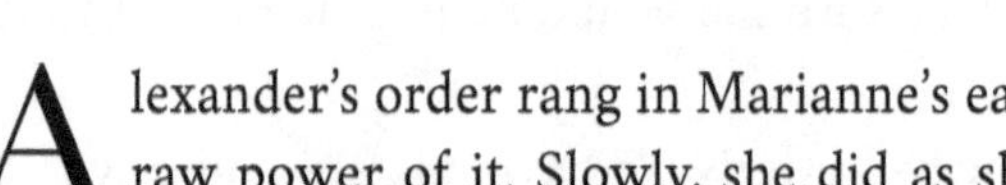

Alexander's order rang in Marianne's ears and she jolted at the raw power of it. Slowly, she did as she'd been told, settling her skirts around her as she looked up at him. His face was drawn taut with desire and his cock was right there, hard and ready. Although she should wait for his next instruction, she didn't. Instead, she reached out and caught his cock in one hand, stroking it gently.

He bucked against her with a gasp of surprise and pleasure that made tingles rush through her body. She stroked him, thinking of the pleasures they had already shared, of how he moved when he was inside of her. She mimicked his thrusts with her hands.

And when his breathing was ragged and broken, she thought of when he'd tasted her. Would he like the same? Would her mouth be pleasing to him? She wasn't certain but now, her gaze locked on his, she wanted to know more than anything. She darted out her tongue to swirl it around the head of his cock.

He made a strangled cry and pushed, driving between her lips. She took him, allowing him into her mouth inch by inch, just as she had welcomed him earlier into her sex. He held her gaze as he began to slowly thrust, and the moment where she understood his desire was very clear. He wanted to take her mouth like it was her sex. And she wanted it, too. She relaxed her mouth and reached up to grip the base of his shaft, working her hand over him as he made shallow thrusts that didn't quite reach her throat.

She rolled her tongue around him, testing his response. When he dipped his head back in pleasure, she repeated the action. To her great surprise, she wanted this. She wanted the power of it, yes, for there was a great deal of that in making this strong man moan with helpless need. But she wanted something more than that. She wanted to take away his troubles, to make him surrender to her the way she had, to make him feel as good as he had done for her.

His thrusts increased, driving a bit deeper now, and she took him as best she could, stroking his shaft as he ravished her mouth. And just as she thought he would come, he grabbed her arms and lifted her, turning her around so that she faced his desk. He flipped her skirts up, spreading her stance wide before he slid into her wet and trembling body.

He took her, hard and fast, without any of the gentleness that had been present the first two times they'd made love. And she reveled in it, pressing back to meet him, her fingers tangling between her legs to rub her clitoris. The orgasm hit her hard and she cried out as he pushed his hand against her back, flattening her against the desk's surface as he thrust again and again. At last he let out a ragged, animal moan and she felt the splash of his seed across her backside as he came.

For a while they remained like that, their panting breaths merging in the otherwise quiet room. But at last he withdrew, smoothing her skirts down over her and refastening his trouser front. She stood and faced him only to find his expression back to being unreadable despite their passionate joining.

"You see," he said. "You haven't displeased me."

She nodded. "Good."

He stepped closer and kissed her once more. Then he went back around his desk and sat down. "I have some work to do. I'll see you at supper."

She blinked at the sharp change from passionate lover to this disconnected and disinterested duke who sat before her, his attention already back on his work like she was a servant to be dismissed.

"Very well," she said, backing toward the door and letting herself out. In the hall, she looked around her, the pleasures they had just shared mingling with her anxiety about what she was expected to do and be to this man.

He was in pain. That was evident. Everything in this stark house said he had locked himself away. Everything in his expression told her that when he was forced to speak of his sister, as did his hesitance when it came to discussing his scar.

It was none of her affair, of course. She had been brought here for his pleasure. All she was giving him was the physical. But he couldn't be truly happy until he had let go of the past. And a part of her that wanted to help him do just that, the dangers of making that kind of connection with him be damned.

CHAPTER 8

When Alexander rounded the corner into his parlor a few hours later, he almost came to a complete halt. Marianne was already there. She was seated in a chair beside the fire, her legs curled up beneath her as she pored over the book in her hand. He was struck not just by how lovely she was—that was obvious. That was overpowering.

But it was how comfortable she looked that truly took him by surprise. Like she…belonged there. In his chair, in his parlor, in his house.

For a moment, that realization struck him and he wanted to… run. He wanted to turn tail and run like a coward from this slight, fascinating woman who had given him her body as trade for her safety.

"Alexander," she said, her face brightening as she stood to greet him and cut off any option he had for escape. "Good evening."

"I hope I didn't keep you waiting," he said, stepping into the room.

She shook her head. "No. I came in early to read. I didn't want to be late. I have guessed you are a man who values punctuality."

He couldn't help the smile that twitched briefly to his lips.

"Somehow I don't see you as a lady who keeps a sharp eye on the clock."

She blushed but a giggle bubbled from her lips. That sound was so light that Alexander actually stepped toward it.

"I admit, I can sometimes be forgetful when it comes to the time," she said. "I get distracted often by a book or a chat with Juliet or my father." Her smile faded. "Or I did."

His brow wrinkled at the sadness that entered her gaze. Her father had torn apart her life and yet Marianne still mourned him. Despite the fact that there was color to her gown. He tilted his head at the pretty blue that caught the firelight.

"You are not wearing black," he said.

Now the color in her cheeks darkened, but this time it looked like guilt that brought the pink there. "I...I want to," she whispered. "But my cousin only allowed me to purchase one mourning gown and I had no time to dye any other gowns. After the travel, it needed to be laundered, so I packed other items. It is not out of disrespect, I assure you."

Anger rose in Alexander's chest, washing over him in an unexpected wave. How dare her cousin create such an environment for those who were now in his care? How dare he make Marianne worry even for a moment when she was already experiencing grief and pain and humiliation?

"I will have a seamstress come," he said softly, "and a few additional gowns made for you. Once your sister arrives, I will extend the same to her."

Marianne blinked in what appeared to be disbelief. "You would—you would do that for me? For her? That is outside the bounds of our agreement."

He waved his hand to dismiss the concern. "The bounds of the agreement are what I say they are. You will have the gowns, I'll have arrangements made in the morning."

"I-I cannot repay your kindness," she whispered, and he heard the tremble in her voice. The fear and the pain there wormed its way into a heart that had been so cold for what felt like a lifetime.

He cleared his throat. "You are repaying it. Now, supper is ready. Will you join me?"

She stepped toward him and he held out his arm to her in offering. But she didn't take it. Instead, she lifted to her tiptoes and brushed her lips to his cheek. He turned to her, their eyes locking. The moment grew heavy with desire, the kind that was always between them. But there was something else there too. Something far more terrifying.

"Thank you," she whispered, her voice thick. "You do not have to be kind. I know you say that is for your own purpose, but it makes my life easier nonetheless. No one has made my life easier for a long time, so I-I appreciate it."

He didn't know how to respond to her words, nor to the warm reaction that spread through his entire body. So he merely took her arm and led her into the dining room for their supper.

Marianne couldn't stop staring at Alexander as the servants drew away the final dinner course of the night and replaced it with a raspberry tart that made her heart leap with its fruity scent.

The man was a riddle. Just like the tart, actually. Its center was bitter, but also sweet. Together, the combination was surprising and tantalizing.

Alexander was much the same. He could be so cold and dismissive, making her feel with every fiber of her being that this was a mere arrangement for him. That he gave no more care for her than he did a person he passed on the street.

And then he could be so much more. Like when he touched her, pleasured her. Or when he offered her an effortless kindness as he had in the parlor before supper.

And now he was somewhere in the middle. Quiet but not cold.

"This tart is divine," Marianne said, searching for something to fill the silence that suddenly felt uncomfortable because she had analyzed it too much. "I do love dessert."

He arched a brow. "I will pass that along to the cook. She'll stack desserts to the ceiling if she thinks it will please me."

"Ah," Marianne said with a smile. "So the servants want to please you."

He wrinkled his brow. "You sound as though that is a surprise or a discovery."

"You are so reticent to share your thoughts, Your Grace, I am forced to determine them myself. Determine anything about you, really."

He was staring at her now, his expression unreadable. Immediately she began to regret her cheeky outburst. Hadn't she been told a hundred times to not be so bold? And yet she'd done it, so it was too late to escape the consequences now.

"It's almost a game," she continued.

"A game," he repeated.

She nodded. "Yes. Certainly you are not unfamiliar with the concept. You must have played games now and then when you were a child. Though you seem the kind of man who has always been an adult."

His cheek twitched and she thought he might be trying not to smile. That buoyed her confidence and she arched a playful brow at him. He sighed. "Yes, Marianne, I know what games are."

"I love games," she admitted. "Juliet and I are always making them up. Guessing how many sweets are in a dish or how many steps it is from one side of a room to another. Anything can be a game if one tries hard enough."

She knew she was talking too much and expected Alexander to cut her off from her foolishness. But instead he leaned back in his chair and folded his arms. "Including the reading of my thoughts."

She nodded. "Certainly."

"And you're very good at games," he drawled, his voice suddenly infused with that dark sensuality that made her toes curl in her slippers.

"Er," she stammered, suddenly thrown by the glint in his eyes. She'd thought her playfulness would irritate him, but it didn't seem to have that effect at all. "I'm good enough."

"All right," he said softly. "Then tell me, Lady Marianne…how many times have I kissed you?"

Her lips parted at the very naughty twist on her concept of a game. She worried her lip slightly and bent her head as heat rushed to her cheeks. "I—"

"Come now," he said, pushing to his feet. "How is that question much different from guessing the number of steps from one side of a room to another?"

She gathered herself as best she could and cleared her throat. "It is very different, Your Grace. You see, there are many elements to a kiss. Sometimes one seems to bleed into another, so do you count those as one kiss or two or three?" Her breath came shorter as he moved in her direction slowly. "And then…and then there are the locations of the kisses. Are you asking how many times you have kissed my lips? Or does a kiss to the hand count? Or the neck? Or the…the…"

She trailed off, her words fading as he moved even closer. He felt very big now. Like he filled all the space in the room and in her mind. She struggled to continue speaking.

"And then there is the question of initiation," she continued. "You asked how many times you've kissed me. So I now have to think of any times I kissed you. Or kissed you back or—"

"Marianne," he said. That single word stopped her. She tracked his hand as he reached down to catch her arm. He brought her to her feet gently, and then she was against his broad chest, his full lips a breath from hers. "Here is an easier question. How long will it take to get to my chamber? Because I tire of this game and would like to play another."

She blinked up at him, drawn in by everything about him. Then she leaned up and brushed her lips to his. He deepened the kiss, his fingers digging into her arms as he fought, very obviously, with an animal drive to claim her without regard for where they were. She almost wished he would, at that.

"Come with me," he whispered, taking her hand and guiding her from the room.

She followed, silenced at last by the heat of his desire, by the trembling response of her own. For the moment she would set aside the confusion he created in her. For the moment all she would do was surrender.

CHAPTER 9

It had been a week since her arrival at Alexander's estate, and Marianne was no less confused by her role here than she had been the afternoon she arrived. The place was beautiful, of course, despite its stark emptiness. The gardens were perfect, the library filled with books to occupy her time, and her room was pretty and comfortable.

The servants treated her with nothing but respect, regardless of the fact that she was obviously here as a sexual plaything for their master. Even when she overheard them, when they didn't know she was there, she'd never caught a one of them say a cross word about Alexander. They were cautious around him, but it was evident he was truly liked by those who served him.

And it wasn't that Alexander didn't spend time with her. They shared meals in the evenings and then retired to his bedchamber together, where he made love to her until her body shook and she feared she could take no more pleasure. She was slowly being molded to his desires and she reveled in the awakening his touch provided.

Beyond the physical, though, she was not satisfied. Alexander could talk about literature, politics, science, and she enjoyed their discourse on those subjects. But the moment she tried to talk to him about anything personal, he withdrew. Or more accurately, he distracted her with his mouth and his hands and his cock.

Now she stood in the library, staring up at the great shelves lined with well-worn books, and she huffed out a breath. These were not the subjects she wished to explore. She wanted to know more about the man who had taken her as a lover, as a mistress. She wanted to understand why he was so afraid to get close to her. She wanted to know how he'd gotten the scars both on his face and in his heart.

Outside she heard the rustle of a maid's skirts, and she stepped out of the library and into the hall to find a young woman dusting a table.

"Excuse me?" Marianne said.

The young woman turned toward her. "Yes, my lady? Is there something you need?"

Marianne hesitated. She spent most days alone, locked away from the man who had brought her here. Today, that was not enough.

"Do you know where His Grace is this morning?" Marianne asked, trying not to frown. He had left his bed early in the day without anything but a brief kiss for her naked shoulder. Of course, that was his way.

"I believe he rode into the village," the maid said.

Marianne shifted, disappointed that there would be no opportunity for her to speak to him directly. At least not right then, when her courage was up. "Do you know when he'll return?"

"I'm sorry, my lady, I don't," the girl said, her cheeks darkening as she avoided Marianne's gaze. "He often goes to the village to meet with his tenants and do other business. That's all I know."

Marianne nodded. "Thank you, you've been a great help."

She moved past the girl, allowing her to return to her work, but as she walked, she pondered. If Alexander was gone for the day, that meant she would have a bit more freedom than when he was here in the house. And if she wanted to know more about him…well, she had a pretty good idea of where to start looking for that information.

She cast a glance over her shoulder, but the young woman in the hall had turned her back to continue her duties. Marianne sighed and walked swiftly down the hall. She stopped at the door to Alexander's study. His fortress. His cell.

She tried it and found it unlocked, so she slipped inside and shut it behind her before anyone could see her and tell her not to enter his room without him present.

As she leaned against the barrier, she shook her head. "Of course, he's not trying to lock them out. They're all too afraid to violate his orders not to come in."

She drew a long breath and looked around. She'd been in this room only once, on the day she'd arrived at the estate. She blushed as she thought of dropping to her knees and taking Alexander into her mouth for the first time. Her body hummed with the thought, as it was becoming an act she truly enjoyed and did often. Pleasuring him, making him lose control...she *liked* it.

She shook her head. She hadn't come in here to think about the physical acts she wantonly enjoyed—she was here to see if she could learn something about the man who performed them on her. And she assumed he would be back at some point, so she put her mind to the task at hand at last.

She moved toward the bookcases near the fire first. While in the library the tomes were more entertaining or educational, the books he had in here were dry. Volumes on farming, the history of the shire he lorded over, thick volumes containing maps and plans for homes and buildings. The most interesting thing about them to her was how worn each book looked, as if they were truly used by the man on a regular basis.

"He takes his work seriously," she mused as she moved away and stepped to his desk.

The leather chair behind it was well kept, and since she knew he didn't allow servants into this room, that meant he applied oil to it himself. She shivered as she let her fingertips dance over the smooth, shiny surface and then drew the chair back to sit in it.

He was bigger than she was, and the chair didn't fit her slender frame, but she scooted it closer to the desk and looked at the surface. It wasn't tidy, that was certain. Papers and letters were strewn across the top, but all of them seemed to relate to the business of Avondale, which the man lorded over. There was a ledger, open to a line of neatly written numbers and scrawled notes in the margins about debits and credits.

But nothing personal. It was as if the man had shut off all things that related to himself and now they no longer existed. But that couldn't be true. She'd seen the pain on his face when he spoke of his sister in London. And she'd felt the emotion that pulsed under the surface when they spent time together outside of his bed.

She sighed and was about to stand when she caught the glint of something metal hidden under a pile of papers. She moved them gently and caught her breath. The cameo she had returned to Alexander that had begun their wicked bargain now rested on his desk. He'd had it strung upon a gold necklace and it was now fitted in the pages of a book, almost as a page marker.

But this was no book about farming or the shire. This book looked like a worn journal. She stared at its leather cover, its yellowing pages with the cameo dangling below and her heart began to pound.

Clearly the book on this desk *was* personal. The glimpse she had wanted to get of the man who had brought her here. But to read his diary…

That was going too far, wasn't it? To do something like that would violate his privacy and that was wrong, so very wrong. But it was such a temptation, this opportunity to look into his soul and see his life through his own eyes.

Her hands shook as she slid the diary across the desk to rest in front of her. Slowly, she turned the pages open to the place he had marked with his sister's necklace. What she found was not his handwriting in the pages, but a lady's. And judging from the context, it was Anne's. This was his sister's journal, not his own. The page marked was the last one before the book went blank, signaling an end to her life.

Sudden tears flew to Marianne's eyes at the last few words written on the page.

I wish Alexander would not be so reckless with his affairs.
I wish he would come home and see me.

The page edge was worn far more than any other in the journal. And judging from its place of prominence on his desk and the marker that held its page, Marianne could only guess that this was something he looked at, read and reread over and over again. A private admonishment from someone he'd loved and lost.

A personal torture for whatever sins he believed he had committed.

Her heart ached for him, and she was about the turn the page back and see what had been written prior when the door to the study slammed. She jerked her face up to find Alexander standing there, his expression twisted with pain and anger and all the other emotions he so rarely revealed. His mouth opened and shut as she slowly stood.

He stared from her to the diary she had been reading before he said, "What are you doing?"

"Alexander—" she began.

"What the bloody hell are you doing?" he repeated, this time more loudly, his hands shaking at his sides and his voice cracking.

She moved out from behind his desk. "I-I'm sorry," she stammered. "I shouldn't have pried."

He strode toward her in three long steps and stopped just before her. He made no attempt to touch her, but stared down at her, his eyes wide and wild. "No, you shouldn't have. I have strict instructions that this room be left alone. No servant is to enter—"

"I'm not a servant, Alexander," she interrupted, placing a hand on his forearm. He jerked it away, and tears filled her eyes at the expression of pain and betrayal on his face. "I'm...I'm your lover, aren't I? Bargain or no."

"I'm paying you for your time, Marianne," he snapped, pacing away from her toward his desk, resting both hands on the top. "You are a servant."

She flinched at both his cruel words and the harsh tone with which he said them, but she recognized his reaction for what it was. This was an attempt to push her away, and a great part of her wanted to allow just that. To turn and walk away from his harshness, from his pain, because it was so big and all-encompassing. If she explored it, she knew it would bind them even more than making love to him had.

But a bigger part of her knew she *had* to stay. Over the short time they'd known each other, she had begun to...care for this man. His gentleness toward her, his quiet intelligence...they drew her in. They had made her do this foolish thing of intruding upon him.

She wouldn't walk away now.

"I would have simply asked you about your...your past, your feelings, but I knew you wouldn't tell me anything, for you never do," she explained.

He spun toward her, his eyes flashing. "So you invade my privacy and the privacy of my dead sister to get what you want?"

"It was wrong of me to do so, and I apologize. I only want to understand you," she pleaded softly. "I want to understand what kind of man is so capable of gentleness and passion, of kindness to his servants and of such a broad base of knowledge, but is the same kind who locks himself away in a castle like he is a beast who must be caged."

He shook his head. "That is the most apt description I have ever heard," he said. "And if you were wise, you would walk away now before that beast is unleashed."

She swallowed hard, his warning ringing in her ears and his anger making her hands shake. But then she straightened her shoulders, took a step toward him instead of away and said, "No."

∼

Alexander stared, his rage and pain muted momentarily by the strength Marianne presented. She stood toe to toe with him, the only indication that she was afraid was the slight tremble to her lower lip. And she shook her head slowly.

"I won't leave you, Alexander," she whispered. "You won't chase me away."

Deep inside, in a place he thought he had killed a long time ago, something in him broke. Pain spread through him, pain and heartache and desire for the connection she offered just by staying instead of running away. He had been alone for so very long and this woman…this woman made him want a different life. One he didn't deserve, hadn't earned, one he couldn't have.

Could he?

"What did you read?" he asked, his voice as ragged as his emotions.

She didn't break her stare from his as she said, "Just the last two lines your sister wrote. That she wished you would be more prudent in your affairs. That she wished you would come home and see her."

Alexander almost buckled under the weight of those two sentences. He had read his sister's diary a hundred times since her death, smiling at her girlish dreams and flowing descriptions of her life. Aching as she talked about the beginnings of an illness that would soon steal her away.

Breaking at those last two lines she'd ever written. They labeled him as exactly what he was: a monster. He'd carried that truth with him for years. It was the reason why he hid, far beyond the scar that marred him.

"You shouldn't have done it," he said, but most of the heat had gone out of his rage.

Marianne moved toward him another step, and this time when she touched him he didn't have the ability to pull away. Her fingers closed over his forearm and she touched his cheek with her other hand.

"I shouldn't have," she agreed. "But I did. And I'm not sorry that I want to understand you more. Haven't you been alone long enough?"

He flinched. "I *deserve* to be alone, Marianne. God, I never should have brought you here. Wanting you took me off guard and I should have known it would end like this. I shouldn't have allowed myself…" He swallowed hard. "…*you.*"

"Tell me what happened," she pressed, her fingers stroking along the ridge of his scar, gentle, just as she was gentle. "Please."

The pain spread, like a fist opening in his chest, and he nearly buckled from it. He'd controlled it so long that now it felt overwhelming, like waves on an ocean that could no longer be repelled by a sea wall. A hurricane that would wash away all that he was and all that he had pretended to be all these years.

"She was sick," he began, closing his eyes as tears stung there. "She was sick and I should have come home. I didn't think it was serious, though, and I…I was doing something I shouldn't have done."

She was quiet a moment, then her thumb smoothed over his lower lip. He opened his eyes and her green stare held his, soothing him like a walk in a cool wood. "What were you doing?" she asked.

He held his breath. He had never spoken of his deeds. He had never said out loud what had brought him here. And yet this woman coaxed so many emotions from him. So many things he had promised himself he would never feel again.

And he found himself saying the words.

"I was engaged in an affair with a married woman," he admitted, watching her face for a reaction of horror or anger or fear. There was none, only empathy. "Her husband found out and challenged me to a duel. I was supposed to leave for home that day, to see Anne. Instead, I faced him on the field of honor."

Her eyes went wide. "So, you—you were shot?"

He shook his head. "No, I shot him in the shoulder, disarming him. And I was so damned cocky. Such a bastard. I strode up to that man, happy to gloat over my victory. It turned out he had a knife."

She recoiled momentarily. "Oh, Alexander."

"He cut me." He turned his face so his scar faced her. "He nearly took my eye. In the end, he just managed to make me as ugly on the outside as I was inside. He was wrestled to the ground by his second and I was rushed off, bleeding and damaged. I couldn't leave London for a week as they tended the wounds. By the time I did…"

She flinched. "She was…"

He nodded. "When I arrived home, she was no longer conscious. She died in my arms without ever knowing I'd returned. Without ever speaking another word to me or hearing my voice."

He bent his head and a drop of water hit his hand. He stared at it, realizing for the first time that he was crying. He had never wept, not when Anne died. Not since. He hadn't allowed himself that luxury, and yet now the tears slid down his cheeks and burned his skin.

"Alexander," Marianne whispered as she moved to wrap her arms around him.

For a moment, he allowed that comfort, pulling his arms around her as he leaned against her, the only thing holding him up. The only person for years to crack through his mask.

"I'm so sorry," she soothed, her hands moving gently across his back. "I'm so sorry that happened to you."

He opened his eyes and swallowed back his tears. With great difficulty, he extracted himself from her embrace and stepped away.

He stared down at her, fighting to put his mask, his façade back in place.

"Nothing happened to me, Marianne," he said. "*I* created the hell I live in. I choose to stay outside of the world because I no longer merit a place in it thanks to my actions. Those actions were my fault and I *deserve* to be alone. Now I want you to go."

Her eyes went wide and her lips parted. "Alexander," she began.

He pointed at the door. "Please," he said, his tone a bit too loud. "I want you to go. Now."

He thought for a moment that she would resist. Refuse. He tensed at the idea, for if she touched him again, offered him what he didn't deserve, he knew he would take it. He'd never let it or her go.

At last, she nodded slowly. "If that is what you need, I'll go," she said softly, and moved for the door. There she paused and turned back toward him. "She wouldn't want for you to live in such pain and such loneliness. You betray her as much by the choices you make now as by what you did back then."

Those were her last words before she stepped from his study, closing him back into the room alone. Leaving her words to hang in the air and in his heart and mind, where they tortured him.

CHAPTER 10

Marianne had not seen Alexander for three days. He hadn't joined her for supper, he hadn't taken her to his bed, he hadn't even come out of his office. And she had no idea what to do. He had asked her to leave and now she wondered if he meant his home and his life, not just the room where he'd confessed so much pain to her.

Leave. That word had been ringing in her ears every moment since. Her mind was a cacophony of thoughts at all times. Where would she go? How would she survive? How would she protect her sister? But most of all, loudest amongst the fray, was how would she do without what she'd found here with Alexander? She craved being near him now, not just for the physical connection they shared, but for what he hid beneath his cold exterior.

If she was forced to walk away, she knew she would leave a piece of herself behind.

With a moan, she pushed her uneaten breakfast aside and put her head in her hands.

"Pardon me."

She lifted her face as Alexander stepped into the room. He was dressed impeccably, shaved and bathed, like their time apart had never happened. But there was something in his face, a new expression that she recognized now. Because she'd seen past the mask.

"I'll leave you alone," he began as he backed toward the hallway.

"No!" she said, leaping to her feet. "Oh, no, please don't go. I haven't seen you in so long. Won't you…won't you join me?"

He hesitated, his blue eyes flitting over her from head to toe, his longing for her clear in his expression, but tempered by a wariness that hadn't been there before.

She'd put it there by her actions, by her prying.

"In truth, I'm not hungry," he said.

She stepped forward. "Then take a walk with me," she suggested. "I've done some exploring on this beautiful property, but to have a guide who has lived here all his life would be a pleasure." He seemed to consider the suggestion a moment, and she moved even closer. "Please."

Softness entered his expression and at last he nodded. "Very well. A walk would likely do me good. I've been cooped up too long."

"Then lead the way," she said, motioning for the door. She wanted desperately to take his hand, but resisted. He was obviously struggling with what their relationship now was after their last encounter. The last thing she wanted to do was push him too hard.

She'd done that enough.

He walked out the front door and down the steps, then turned toward the long drive. She fell into step beside him, and for a while they were silent, the only sound their footfalls and the calls of birds as Marianne and Alexander moved away from the main house and down into the wooded area that surrounded it.

"Your family has held this property a long time," she said, searching for a safe topic. "And you obviously take a great deal of pride in your duties here."

He cast her a side glance. "Yes, I do. How do you know that?"

She shrugged. "I see it in the way you interact with those who serve you. And I noted that the pages of the books in your study that are about the surrounding area were well-worn from use."

His mouth tightened a bit at the reminder that she'd intruded upon his space, but he didn't draw away. Instead, he let out a long breath. "My father was a good man. Distant, but serious about his duties. I did not always follow in his footsteps, I fear. My sister encouraged me to do better, long before her death. So for the past five years, I've dedicated myself, and there have been dividends."

They crested a hill, and Marianne caught her breath. Down below was a wide, green valley with a twisting creek that fed into a calm pond.

"It's lovely," she said. "I haven't come this way before, so I've never found this."

He smiled. "Then I'm pleased to be the first to show you. This was my favorite spot as a boy. I fished here, I swam, I laid out in the sun and dreamed."

He took her hand at last as he helped her down the steep side of the hill toward the water. She clung to his fingers, feeling their warmth and strength and longing for more, even though she knew she couldn't ask for it at present.

"What did you dream about?" she asked.

He released her as they reached the bottom of the hill and his frown pulled down. She had gone too far, without even meaning to and she rushed to repair the damage.

"We all have dreams, don't we? As a girl, I had my own," she said. "Funny how they change as one grows older."

He led her to the edge of the lake, to a bench that had been placed beneath a tree there. As he motioned her to sit with him, he said, "What did you dream of as a girl?"

She hesitated. Pushing him on his past was one thing, but now that the tables had been turned, she felt anxiety rise in her chest. Still, as she looked at him, his expression taut and drawn, she knew that she owed him a glimpse of herself, as payment for the glimpse she had taken against his will a few days earlier.

Perhaps that was the only way to work out whatever was between them. With honesty. Stark honesty she had been avoiding for a very long time.

"I wanted the things all girls are trained to desire," she said, looking out over the water so she wouldn't have to see his reaction. "A marriage, a home...*children*. I never thought to dream of anything else."

"But those dreams did not come true," Alexander said. "Though I don't know why. You're beautiful and clever, gentle, and the kind of lady most men would be proud to call a wife. Why didn't you get what you desired?"

She sucked in a breath. "The world is talking about my father right now. About his stealing from his peers. They love that story, it feeds their sense of self-worth, makes them feel like they climbed over him on a ladder to the top of the *ton*." She shook her head. "But it isn't the only story."

Alexander leaned his arm on the back on the bench, his fingers gently caressing her bare neck. "What other story is there?"

She shivered with the brush of his hand and fought for focus. "My father had so many vices—the stealing is only the worst of it. He whored. He gambled too much and he was terrible at the sport. He lost far more money than he ever won. So by the time I came out I...had no dowry. Add to that the fact that I feared leaving my sister in his care and I didn't exactly encourage any man who might have had an interest."

Alexander shook his head. "You feared he would hurt your sister?"

"Not physically," she rushed to say. "He loved her, just as he loved me, in his own way. He just had no capacity to protect us. I learned that long, long ago. I didn't want Juliet to have to learn the same lesson." She bent her head. "I failed, though. She's learning it now, regardless of how hard I tried to avoid that."

Alexander leaned forward, cupping her chin and tilting her face toward his. "You are sacrificing all you are, all you wanted, for her.

One day she'll recognize that and I hope she will appreciate it." He searched her face, his expression suddenly filled with understanding. "Do you regret what you've done for her?"

Marianne swallowed hard. His expression was so intent, it pulled her in. They were one in that moment, two people joined not by sex, but by the pain they endured. They were linked by that and by the fact that they each wanted to ease the other's suffering. And by being together, somehow they did.

She shivered at that thought and all it meant. "Are you asking if I regret coming here, being with you?"

He nodded. "Yes."

She leaned up, feeling his warmth and strength surround her even before he held her in his arms. She brushed her lips against his and whispered, "No. I don't regret it. I will never regret it, Alexander, never."

He let out a long, shuddering sigh and then his mouth moved over hers. He was gentle at first, the kiss a balm on her wounds, perhaps a balm on his own. But as she slid her hands up his chest, wrapped her arms around his neck, the intensity of the kiss increased and the heat between them did the same.

He drew her over into his lap and she felt the evidence of his desire for her as his erection pressed hard into her hip. She smiled, for his need for her was exactly what she wanted. She needed him, too. She wanted to have him, right here, right now, and let his touch erase the rest of the pain she had brought to the surface when she spoke of her father.

His hands began to roam as he kissed her, brushing over her breasts, down her hips. He shifted her, and suddenly she was straddling him, her dress tangled between them and her sex pressed hard against his cock. She lifted into him, cupping his cheeks as the kiss between them deepened and began to spiral out of control.

He pushed at her dress, lifting it up, bunching it around her waist, and she responded by reaching between them to unfasten his trouser front. She pulled the fall away and broke the kiss to look down at his erection. She smiled as she stroked him once, twice, feeling him twitch in her hand, hearing him groan with pleasure.

He cupped her backside, which was now bared to the warm summer breeze, and lifted her, positioning her over his cock. They locked eyes, and she never broke the gaze as she lowered herself down onto him, filling her body with him. Feeling her heart and her soul filled by him, too.

She could have kissed him again, but she wanted to look at him. She wanted to watch his pleasure, she wanted to see him watch hers. So she began to move as he dug his hands into her hips and arched beneath her, matching her rhythm.

Pleasure came rushing forward almost immediately. Not just of her aching, twitching body, but of her entire being. In that moment, she knew this was where she belonged. This man was her home. And that realization jolted her into the most powerful orgasm she had ever experienced. It seemed to flow through her entire body, a pleasure that touched every part of her and brought tears to her eyes. She rocked into him, crying out his name as she tremored around him.

He groaned out an incoherent sound of pleasure and then pulled himself free of her, pumping against his hand as he drew her in for a long kiss.

She slipped back onto the bench next to him, tucking her feet beneath her as she rested her head on his chest. She felt the beating of his heart, strong and powerful there. The rhythm of it matched her own, and she curled her hand into a fist against it.

"I don't know why I need you so much," he whispered, his lips grazing her temple.

She looked up at him, loving every angle of his face, loving even the scar that marred the perfection there. She didn't want perfection. She wasn't perfect herself. The scar represented who this man had once been. Who he had become. And in that moment, everything in her heart became very clear.

"Alexander," she said, her heart pounding. "I-I love you."

He stiffened against her, his face going from relaxed and content to taut and unreadable. He slowly moved away from her, forcing her to sit up. Then he got to his feet and stared down at her.

"What did you say?" he asked.

She swallowed hard. "I said I love you."

He shook his head and spun away from her, pacing down to the water's edge. She let him stand there for a moment, but it quickly became clear that he had no plans to come back to her.

Her hands were shaking as she got up and followed him. "I-I'm not asking—"

"Stop." He turned on her, his eyes flashing with emotions that he couldn't hide. She could see him trying to do so, but the rawness was there, harsher and harder than it had been even when he spoke of his past.

"Alexander," she whispered.

He shook his head. "Why? Why would you say that?"

"Because it's true," she confessed, her hands shaking. "I have spent a lifetime alone, feeling lost. With you, I'm found. And I think if you look inside yourself, you feel the same way."

"I don't," he snapped, but his voice cracked. "I don't feel *anything*, Marianne, that is what you don't understand. I am not some savior you can run to, declare your love and find some ending like in a fairytale. I am a bastard, I always have been. Whatever small amount of love I had to give, it died with my sister. I will never love you back. I will never give you the life you desire. The one you deserve."

"You are punishing yourself for sins you committed years ago," she argued, unwilling to let him push her away when everything had just become so clear to her.

"No, Marianne, I'm not," he said. His voice was becoming calmer and his face harder. "I'm just fucking you. Do you understand? You are nothing more to me than a body to fuck. There is nothing else to it. Get that through your head."

She stared at him, searching for the warmth she knew he possessed. Trying to find the gentleness that lurked beneath his hard exterior. But there was none. He had crushed it, hiding it from her just as he insisted on hiding his heart.

In that moment, she realized he might *never* be capable of sharing more. That recognition tore her in two.

She nodded slowly. "I see," she whispered, praying she would not burst into tears.

He turned away from her. "I'm returning to the house. Will you go with me?"

She pursed her lips. "No. No, I'll make my own way back."

He hesitated, then set his jaw into a hard line. "As you wish, Marianne."

He turned and left her there, standing beside the water, her heart full of gifts that he was unwilling to accept. Her heart filled with an ache that he refused to acknowledge or heal because his own pain was so stark. So clear.

And she had never felt so alone in her entire life. Nor so uncertain. Laying herself on the line had not resulted in the happiness she had briefly glimpsed with this man.

And now it threatened any future she might make with her sister. Because there was no way Alexander would want her here now. His face had made that clear, as had the cruel way in which he had dismissed her.

She had no idea what to do.

Alexander burst back into the house, his chest burning with pain, with anger and with something far stronger. Something he didn't want.

Hope.

When Marianne had stood before him, so bravely making her confession of her heart, what had stirred most powerfully in him was hope.

That and fear. Gripping fear of what he could destroy if he accepted her love. He had devastated his sister. He could not bear to do the same to Marianne.

He could hardly breathe as he moved to go to his study. He needed to be alone, to think without Marianne's presence in every corner of his heart. Only even his office was not safe from her. He stared at his desk and thought of how she had intruded upon his pain there. Confronted him there. Touched him there, body and soul.

"Bollocks," he snapped out to no one in particular.

"Your Grace?"

He gripped his hands at his sides and faced the butler. "What is it, Jones?" he barked.

Jones did not respond to the harshness he was faced with, but only said, "I am sorry to bother you, sir, but you have a visitor."

Alexander fought the urge to snarl in response and tried to regain his composure. "A visitor. I am not expecting anyone. Who is it?"

"The Earl of Martingale, Your Grace."

Alexander swayed slightly. "The Earl of Martingale is dead."

"Er, the *newest* Martingale, Your Grace. He says he is Lady Marianne's cousin."

Alexander smashed his teeth together so hard that his ears rang. He stared at Jones, then let his gaze slip down the hallway. So Marianne's cousin was here. Which meant the man must have gotten wind of her scandalous arrangement with him. That he had come to save her was promising. At least she wasn't as alone in the world as she seemed to think. Perhaps this was better. Alexander could send her back with her cousin. Send her away where he couldn't hurt her and she couldn't dissolve all his walls.

He ignored the sting in his heart at that thought and nodded. "Yes, of course I'll see him." The moment he said the words, he shook his head slightly. Since he was scarred, he'd been uncomfortable meeting strangers, and yet today he was so focused on Marianne that he'd not given that a thought. Odd. "Er, where has he been put?"

"The green parlor, Your Grace."

He nodded again, his feet somehow reluctant to move even though the solution that now presented itself was exactly what needed to happen. For Marianne. For himself.

"Lady Marianne will be returning to the house shortly," he said as he forced himself to walk. "Send her to join us when she does. Until then, I would like privacy."

"Of course, sir," the butler's voice said, fading off as Alexander made his way down the long hallway to the parlor where his guest awaited. The door was shut and he drew a long breath before he opened it and joined the man who was now Earl of Martingale.

As he entered the room, the man at his fireplace turned and Alexander took the measure of him. He was older than Alexander by fifteen years. He had a round face with thinning hair and a ruddy complexion.

Of course, he felt the man take his measure, as well. There was no mistaking the stare, the curiosity as Martingale looked at his face. Slowly, Alexander closed the door behind himself before he moved forward.

"Lord Martingale," he said, extending a hand cautiously. "Good afternoon."

He expected Martingale to refuse his offer, but the man stepped forward and shook his hand firmly. "Your Grace," he said as his gaze flickered once more over Alexander's scarred face. "I realize I was not expected."

"I suppose I *should* have expected you," Alexander said with a grim frown. "Considering the circumstances."

He motioned to the chairs before the fire and the men sat down. Martingale leaned forward, draping his elbows over his knees. "The circumstances, Your Grace?"

Alexander shifted. Where was this man's righteous anger? His desperation to come to the defense and aid of his female relative? Where was his drive to save Marianne from the clutches of a man who would ruin her? *Had* ruined her. Martingale should be calling him out right now, not sitting with bored politeness in his parlor.

Yet here Martingale was able to meet Alexander's eyes easily and there seemed to be no anger in his countenance or attitude. But the only reason he would have come here was for Marianne. The two men didn't know each other otherwise.

"I assume you have come here on behalf of Marianne," Alexander said carefully.

Both Martingale's eyebrows lifted. "You think I've come to rush to the aid of my cousin? Hardly. I'm pleased to have her gone."

Alexander stared at the man in shock for a moment as he tried to process those words. "You—you cannot mean that," he said at last. "You must have guessed the nature of my arrangement with her."

Martingale smiled, but there was no warmth or generosity to it. "You've made her your mistress, yes? I can hardly blame you. My cousin is quite comely. I should have thought of that myself, honestly."

Burning anger flared in Alexander's chest and he gripped the armrests of his chair to keep from flying across the space between them. "I am surprised to hear you say that."

"She never made a good match, one that might have raised our family fortunes," Martingale said with a shrug. "She knows that she is to be on the street in short order. Making a bargain with you may be the first intelligent thing the chit has done in years."

"If you haven't come to stand up for Marianne's honor, why are you here?" Alexander asked, barely able to remain civil in the face of this man's coldness and cruelty.

Martingale leaned back in his chair, folding his fingers together with a smile. "Marianne's leaving has saddled me with another problem all together. Her sister."

Alexander straightened. "Juliet?"

Martingale nodded. "Yes. You see, Marianne has abandoned her."

Leaping to his feet, Alexander glared at the man. "That is not true and you know it. You gave Marianne a month to find a new arrangement. She has now and Juliet will join her shortly."

"Do you think anyone will believe that?" Martingale drawled, remaining in his seat despite the fact that Alexander towered over him, fists clenched at his side. "When they find out Marianne has whored herself out to a beast in the countryside, will they blame me for finding another arrangement for the child?"

Alexander felt the color drain from his cheeks. He knew Marianne loved her sister deeply. The idea that she could lose the girl would shatter her. "Another arrangement?" he repeated. "What the hell are you saying?"

"I cannot take her, Your Grace," Martingale said. "I'm not

equipped and there are no other relatives. So what will become of her, I am not certain. She might go to an orphanage, perhaps. Or a workhouse."

Alexander let out a cry of anger and grasped Martingale by his cravat. He yanked the man to his feet and twisted the fabric in his hand, effectively cutting off the air to Martingale's lungs as he shoved him back against the wall. He leaned in, enjoying how the bastard was turning purple as he clawed at Alexander's hands.

"What do you want?" he growled, and slowly relaxed his grip, letting the other man have air at last.

Martingale sucked in long breaths as his color returned to something more normal. He struggled in Alexander's grip, but couldn't escape. "I-I want money," he burst out. "You've bought one of my cousins, haven't you? And now that I see you, it's clear you care for Marianne somehow. Perhaps you would buy the other and solve both our problems."

Alexander stared at him, this bastard in a perfect outfit with his perfect hair and perfect face. He wasn't scarred like Alexander, but *he* was the monster in this room at the moment. And all Alexander wanted was to save Marianne from him. Save her from the pain of losing her sister.

Save her because he loved her.

That realization hit him in the gut and nearly buckled him. But he stayed strong because that was what she needed him to be. He slammed Martingale back against the wall once more, hard enough that the prick's head bounced against it and he let out a whining cry of pain.

"Where is she?" Alexander growled. "Where is Juliet?"

"Still at home," Martingale gasped. "She's still at home. I stopped by to see Marianne three days ago and found out where she had gone from a servant. I have not yet cast Juliet out and I don't have to. I only want some compensation for the trouble. It isn't asking much."

"Here is what you are going to do," Alexander hissed, bringing his face close to Martingale. "You are going to leave that child alone. I will come to fetch her straight away. I will come myself, and if I find that even a hair on her head has been harmed, I will cut you down in the street. In the street, sir, do you understand?"

"And what will you give me?" the little weasel asked.

Alexander was almost impressed by his singularity. Most men would have pissed themselves by now and simply be begging for their lives.

"Aside from allowing you to continue to breathe?" Alexander asked, twisting the cravat again ever so slightly. "I will pay you five thousand pounds. But for that I want more than Juliet. For that, I want your silence. You will *never* speak of Marianne's bargain with me, not to a single soul. You will *never* bother her ever again, nor make light or sport of her father's misdeeds in public or private. If you do, I will make sure you pay."

"Five thousand pounds?" the man repeated. "That hardly seems enough for—"

Alexander narrowed his eyes. "The other option is that I kill you and bury you in my garden, Lord Martingale. Do you think that I won't? You called me a beast—would you like to test that theory?"

"N-No!" Martingale burst out. Alexander released him when he tugged against his grip this time. Martingale immediately deposited himself on his ass on the parlor floor as Alexander walked away.

"Excellent. Then we've come to terms," Alexander drawled, pleased to see that Martingale's throat was red and rubbed from his cravat being tightened there. It would do the man good to see the bruised reminder of what had happened here. "Now get out."

Martingale hesitated, then nodded. "Yes. Yes, of course."

He said nothing more, but hustled from the room. Once he was gone, Alexander poured himself a drink and slugged it back, his mind twisting not on the bargain he'd just made but the realization Martingale's arrival had forced him to make.

He loved Marianne. But did that change things between them?

Did he deserve to love her after all he had done? After what he had caused in the past?

He didn't know, but he suddenly wanted to see her. He strode from the parlor and into the foyer, where Jones was watching Martingale ride down the drive like a demon army was pursuing him.

"Good, I see the trash has taken itself away," Alexander said.

"Quite, Your Grace," Jones said, his tone a little more smug than Alexander would have expected. Alexander smiled slightly at the butler.

"I was surprised that Lady Marianne did not join us. I would have thought she'd rush right in when she heard her cousin had joined us."

Jones turned toward him. "I'm sorry, Your Grace, Lady Marianne has not returned."

Alexander wrinkled his brow. It hadn't been all that long since he left Marianne by the lake, but he'd expected her to come back by now. That she hadn't…

"I need my horse," he said, trying to keep the concern from his tone and from his heart. An almost impossible task when he had a sinking feeling that Marianne's absence did not bode well. "Now."

Marianne walked along the road, but she had no idea where she was going. All she knew was that she couldn't go back to face Alexander again. Not now at least. She needed space.

She needed to figure out what to do after one confessed one's heart, only to have it soundly rebuffed.

She stopped, stepping off the path, and bent her head as tears gathered in her eyes. She balled up her fists and pressed them there, willing away the weakness of her tears. Failing miserably. She wanted to sink down into the grass by the road and just cry. Or scream.

But she couldn't. Back in London, her sister awaited. She had to figure out what to do so that Juliet would be protected.

"Oh God," Marianne whispered. "I cannot even protect myself."

There was a thunderous sound in the distance. A rider was approaching. Marianne turned to face the person and her breath hitched. Even from a distance, she recognized Alexander's frame. He was heading straight for her and he was coming fast.

She smoothed her hands over her gown and straightened her shoulders, trying to put on her bravest face as he pulled up short and swung from his horse. He tossed the reins aside and crossed the distance between them. His expression was lined with worry and anger as he caught her forearms.

"Where were you?" he asked, giving her a gentle shake before he pulled her against his chest.

She felt his heart pounding as he cradled her close, and she couldn't help it. Despite his rejection of her, she wrapped her arms around him and clung to him, breathing in his scent and his presence. Soon enough she knew she would lose both, for he couldn't want her to stay here after everything that had happened today.

She wasn't sure she could bear to stay even if he would allow it.

"Answer me," he said, stepping back. "Why didn't you come home?"

She flinched. "Home?" she repeated. "Your Grace, we both know that is not my home."

His lips pressed hard together. "You know what I mean. You said you would return after me, but I've been searching for you for almost an hour, and now I find you heading up the road that leads away from my estate? Do you know how dangerous that is?"

She folded her arms, forcing herself to take a step back from him. "I-I wasn't leaving. I don't *think* I was leaving. I just…I couldn't go back. I couldn't face you after…after…"

He bent his head. "I'm sorry, Marianne."

She caught her breath. His tone sounded so truly grieved and apologetic. But she couldn't let herself be lulled. She shook her head. "You needn't be. You could have been kinder in your rejection, of course, but you have made it clear you feel nothing for me. I just don't know if I can stay here in that cottage you have offered, after this. I would hate to cause you discomfort and I don't know if I could encounter you and—"

"Please be quiet," he interrupted.

She arched a brow. "I'm sorry?"

"You talk and talk, Marianne," he said, and he laughed. She stared, for she had never seen him smile, not in any real way, and here he was...*smiling*. And he was beautiful. So beautiful that her heart hurt to look at him.

"I—"

"Honestly," he grunted, then caught her hand, tugged her forward and kissed her.

She was so surprised by the action, she didn't fight it. She just melted against him, letting him explore her mouth right there in the middle of the road. And when she was thoroughly breathless and dizzy, he let her go.

"I shall remember that is the only way to make you stop talking. Though I must be honest that I rather love the way you chatter. Every word brings life back to my heart," he said.

She blinked at him as those words, those lovely words, pierced into her soul. But he couldn't mean them. Not after what had happened earlier. "I—"

"Please, let me tell you this," he said softly, and she closed her mouth. "Marianne, when I realized you hadn't returned, I was terrified. I have been searching for you, fearing the worst, knowing that if something happened to you, it was my fault."

She shook her head. "No. You made yourself clear from the beginning in what you wanted from me. I was a fool to allow my heart to convince me that there could be more."

"No," he said, and he reached out to take her hand. His rough palm felt like heaven in hers. "I was a fool to think that I could bring you home and not have you permeate every part of me, every part of my world. You have, Marianne. And that terrified me. It still terrifies me, truth be told. But there is one thing that frightens me more."

She stared at him. He was...softer somehow. More connected and gentle as he spoke to her.

"What is that?" she asked, her voice shaking as she tried to rein in her hopes, her dreams.

"Losing you," he said. "I don't want to lose you, Marianne. Even if I don't deserve you, I still...I still want you."

She frowned. Want. He wanted her. That was something, but could it be enough?

"I love you," he said, and his breath hitched.

"You...you love me?"

He nodded. "I do. I do love you."

Her mouth dropped open. "Please tell me you aren't playing a game with me, Alexander."

"I'm cruel, but not so cruel as that," he said, and he reached out to stroke her cheek. "I love you, Marianne. And I don't want you to run away. I want you to stay with me."

CHAPTER 12

Marianne was just staring at him, and Alexander could see the confusion and pain and fear and hope all mixed on her face. She wasn't certain of him and he couldn't blame her, for he had given her so little reason to have faith since he met her.

But *he* had faith. And he was determined to share it with her. Even if it was terrifying to him. Even if he had to overcome the voice inside of him that said to run away from this future, from this woman who was so determined to heal his heavy soul.

"There's a reason you found my sister's cameo," he said. "I believe that. I believe she led you to me. You are her final gift to me. You, a frustrating, amazing, sensual woman who can make me say and do all the things I've avoided for years. The woman who can see past my scars, and I don't mean the ones on my face."

Marianne's bottom lip quivered and her frown deepened with every word he spoke. His heart sank. Had he waited too long? Was his rejection of her earlier in the day a final moment she couldn't overcome?

"Please say something," he whispered, hoping, praying.

"You love me?" she repeated again.

He nodded. "Yes."

She was quiet for a moment, just staring at him, and then she moved forward, into his arms, her mouth lifting to his, her tears merging with his own as he kissed her deeply, passionately, and with all the love in his heart.

She drew away with a smile. "I love you."

Joy flooded him, but he couldn't surrender to it, not immediately. "There is something I must tell you."

Her brow wrinkled. "More secrets?"

He shook his head. "No. It's about Juliet." She buckled and he caught her. "It's all right, Marianne," he reassured her. Then he told her of his encounter with her cousin and the bargain he'd made.

She stared at him when he'd said it all. "I cannot believe he would do that."

"Nor could I." He nearly spat to eliminate the nasty taste her cousin left in his mouth. "But I think we should go to London, Marianne. Juliet must be fetched. I don't want to give that bastard any opportunity to renege on our bargain."

She nodded. "I agree."

"Good," he said, and motioned to his horse. "Let's go back, shall we, and I'll make the arrangements right away."

He helped her up on the animal and then swung up behind her. She settled back into his arms and he turned them back toward his home. *Their* home. His heart soared with the thought.

"At any rate," he said, nuzzling her neck gently. "You'll want her here for the wedding."

She jerked her face toward him. "Wedding?" she repeated.

He laughed. "I love you, Marianne. Don't you think there will be a wedding? As soon as possible?"

"You're asking me to marry you?" she whispered.

"If you'll have a beast like me," he said, holding his breath as he awaited her answer.

She gave it by lifting her lips to his. She gave it with the smile he felt against his mouth. She gave it as she shouted, "Yes!" to the skies.

And for the first time in years, his life had meaning again.

EPILOGUE

Six Months Later

Juliet sat by the lakeside, a fishing pole in one hand, a book in the other. As Marianne watched her from the bench at the lakeside, she laughed. "She's going to lose the fish *and* the book at this rate."

"I'll buy her another book, and I suppose I could catch her a fish," Alexander chuckled.

Marianne turned toward him, still in wonder at the fact that this man was her husband. Her love. Her life. And also in wonder at how much he'd changed since their hasty wedding just after they retrieved Juliet from London.

Oh, he was still clever and dedicated to his tenants and duties. He was still uncomfortable with the idea of a return to Society. But he was also quicker to smile, quicker to laugh. He'd taken on the role of father to her sister with kindness and patience, and Juliet adored him.

And as for his skills as a husband, he remained a passionate lover, but he was also a fine friend and partner, who looked out for her needs every day and in every way. Better still, he allowed her to do the same for him.

He caught her staring at him and reached up to touch his scar, "What? Do I have something on my face?" he teased.

She shook her head as she reached up to draw him down and kissed him gently. "I love you," she whispered.

His teasing faded and he pulled back from her lips to stare into her face. "I don't know how I earned that love, Marianne. But I cherish it. And I return it. With all my heart."

She sighed, tucking herself into the crook of his shoulder as she returned her attention to her sister. Half a year before she had been pondering the horror her life had become, fearing for the future that felt so dire.

Today she was certain of her happiness. And her love. And that was all that mattered.

LADY NO SAYS YES

THE SCANDAL SHEET BOOK 3

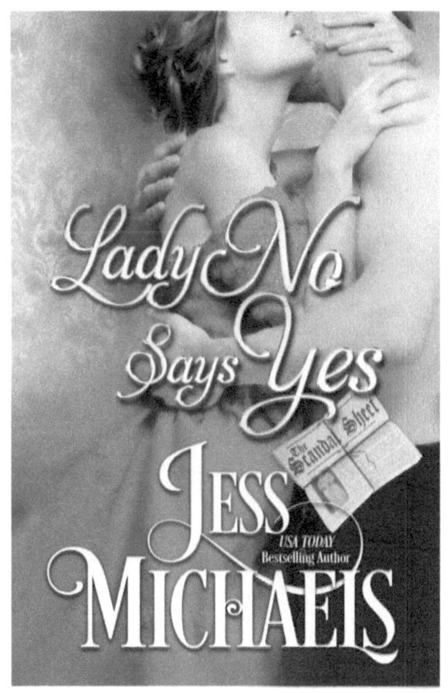

To Michael, my forever YES.

CHAPTER 1

All in Society are well-aware of the famous—or is it infamous?—Lady No. Despite her station in life, her generous dowry and the expectations of her family, the young woman refuses any man who dares cross her path. Kindly, yes, but firmly. The lady seems determined to enter into spinsterhood. Will this new Season finally be the one to see Lady No meet her match? Only time will tell. But if not, one wonders if the shine will eventually wear off her diamond, leaving her to regret the chances she did not take.

As her aunt Louisa read the latest *Scandal Sheet* out loud, Lady Sophie couldn't help but laugh. Her aunt lifted her gaze with a smirk of her own.

"Well, there you have it," Louisa said, folding the paper. "You are famous. Or infamous."

Sophie shook her head and teased, "Me? Are you saying you think Lady No is *me*?"

"Oh come, don't play coy even in jest. You know *they* call you Lady No behind your back. It could be no one else but you," Louisa said.

Sophie's laughter faded and she glanced at the folded sheet before her aunt. She could only read a few words now, but *Lady No* stood out amongst them all. It *was* her not-very-secret nickname, though she'd never felt it was said in cruelty. She was an oddity in Society, to be certain, but she was liked well enough. She had friends, and the gentlemen who she refused were, on the whole, good-natured about it. She was always kind in her set downs.

"I'm not really certain why it fascinates them so, my refusals. I simply haven't found something worth saying yes to. Shouldn't I wait to say yes until I find something worthwhile?"

Louisa had been smiling along with her, but now her face

fell a fraction. "Of course. I've been your guardian for how long now?"

"Nearly fifteen years," Sophie said softly, carefully not allowing her thoughts to turn to her long-dead parents. "And you have been the best guardian one could hope for."

Louisa smiled briefly and reached out to take Sophie's hand. "Well, I've always been proud to see that you have your own mind. And I think you are correct that you should not accept anyone into your life who doesn't appreciate that wonderful quality about you."

Sophie tilted her head. "I sense a *however* coming."

Louisa laughed. "You know me too well. *However*, I wonder at your methods, my dear. It isn't just that you have refused any marriage proposal that has come your way. You refuse everything else, too. How long has it been since you took a walk with a young man? Or danced? Or paired for a hand of cards?"

Sophie pursed her lips. She hated to admit her aunt was right, but she was. It had been many a year since she had done any of those things. Since her first season, and that was nearly four years before.

"They only want me for my money," she said. That was true.

There were other things that kept her saying no, too, but she wouldn't think about speaking them out loud. They only caused pain for both her and her aunt. Only made her think about topics best left unexplored.

Louisa shook her head. "I'm not certain you know that for a fact. You say you haven't found anything worthwhile to say yes to, but you haven't really allowed anyone to prove their worth to you, have you?"

Sophie sighed. "Perhaps," she said through clenched teeth.

Louisa laughed again, softening the suddenly serious mood between them. "You inherited your stubborn streak from me, I fear. But are you ready to accept that your actions may do exactly as this little story implies and leave you a spinster?"

Sophie pushed back from the breakfast table, smoothing her hands over the skirt of her gown as she did so. Her breath suddenly felt short and her heart was pounding. But not because she feared the ultimate end her aunt described. Certainly not.

"You know, I have never seen being a spinster as such a terrible thing," she said slowly. "After all, you never wed and you are well-loved by all who know you. Is it such a terrible end?"

To her surprise, Louisa's expression flickered briefly with a pain Sophie had never seen before. A regret very much like that which had been described in the *Scandal Sheet* paper. Sophie couldn't believe she was seeing it, for her aunt had always seemed so cheerful about her life.

Louisa pushed her plate aside and leaned an elbow on the table for a moment before she spoke. "I, like you, was afforded a great deal of freedom and independence. After seeing what your mother...*endured*, my father vowed that I would not be forced into a marriage."

Sophie winced, once again trying not to let memories of her parents flood her mind. Trying to pretend that their life together, and their death together, wasn't so strong an influence on her own decisions.

"I loved him for that," Louisa continued, tears filling her eyes. "But my choices have had consequences, alongside their advantages. I adore you, my love, and I think of you much as my own daughter, but I have never borne a child. I have never felt the warmth of a husband's touch. I am, in many ways, alone."

Sophie caught her breath. "You are speaking of the very regret the paper mentions."

Louisa nodded. "I don't express it, for what would be the point? But certainly I sometimes regret that I didn't take a different path. And I would hate to see you feel that same thing, my love. Even if it is rare and fleeting, it is painful."

With a shuddering sigh, Sophie turned and walked to the window. As she looked down onto her aunt's pretty garden below, anxiety washed over her in waves. She drew a few long breaths to quell it and then whispered, "Well, what would you have me do, Aunt Louisa?"

Her aunt held up the paper they'd been reading from together. "As this rag says, the new Season is just beginning. A fresh start. I would challenge you to say yes."

"Say yes?" Sophie repeated, pivoting on her aunt with a gasp. "What are you talking about?"

"Say yes to every opportunity put on your path," Louisa encouraged. Sophie's face must have reflected the horror those words instilled in her, for her aunt shook her head swiftly. "Within reason, of course. No one is suggesting you run off to do something wicked or that you accept any marriage proposals you are offered. I am simply talking about saying yes to those things you've avoided. Dance. Play. Walk. Go riding in the park. Not all your experiences will be filled with pleasure, I'm sure, but you may be surprised that some of them will not be as terrible as you expect."

Sophie clenched her hands in front of her. She could hardly imagine doing what her aunt had suggested. It sounded terrifying, when she was honest with herself. She would open herself up. That meant she could be hurt.

And she didn't want that.

"I don't know," she breathed.

Louisa pushed to her feet at last and moved toward her. Her warm arms came around Sophie, and she squeezed gently. "I won't force you, Sophie. I would never do that. But I'm *asking* you to do this for me. Then if you decide to take the same path I have, at least I'll be comfortable in the knowledge that you gave yourself every chance to understand what you might give up."

Sophie sighed. If Louisa saw her as a daughter, she very much loved her aunt as a mother. And Louisa so rarely asked anything of her, and had kindly accepted her quirks over the years. To refuse her seemed the height of bad behavior. Besides, it was only a Season. She would please her aunt and have some good stories to tell in the end.

She didn't have to change her mind about the ultimate path of her future, after all.

"Very well," she said with a shuddering exhalation. "I will do as you ask, Aunt Louisa. I'll say yes for a Season."

Louisa's face lit up, and it was all the reward Sophie ever could have asked for.

"Oh, Sophie, I'm so pleased!" Louisa practically danced away and she snatched up the *Scandal Sheet* from the table as she moved toward the exit.

"What are you doing with that?" Sophie said with a laugh at her aunt's giddiness, even if the cause made her nervous.

"I'm saving this," Louisa explained. "In the hopes that when the Season is over, we'll look back on this moment as a turning point in your life, my love. No matter what comes out of your agreement to say yes."

Sophie watched with a smile as she left the room, paper in hand, but the expression fell when she was alone. Her decision to say no to everything had been one she made purposefully. Giving it up was a terrifying thought. As was the idea that saying yes might change her life forever.

CHAPTER 2

The Honorable Rowan Sinclair, third son of the Earl of Terrington, was in a foul mood as he stood in the study that had, up until six months before, been his father's. Now that the official mourning period was over, his eldest brother, Alistair, had thrown himself fully into taking over. Including redecorating what had once been a warm and welcoming room and making it into a spectacle of showiness.

"You hardly wait a moment, do you?" Rowan growled, slugging back his glass of scotch in one gulp and eliciting a glare from both Alistair and their middle brother, Keaton. Alistair and Keaton had the same mother, the late earl's first wife, and looked very much alike. Rowan's mother was the second wife, the beloved wife, and he was dark where his brothers were light.

They hated him for it.

"I have no idea what you mean," Alistair sniffed as he swirled his own scotch in his tumbler.

"A ball?" Rowan sneered. "Six months to the day of Father's death?"

Keaton snorted as he paced to the window. "You are a sentimental fool, Rowan. The mourning period is over—why shouldn't

Alistair hold a ball to welcome the new Season and celebrate his ascension to the title?"

"I've waited long enough," Alistair muttered.

Rowan set his jaw. His older brothers were older than him by almost two decades, nearly into their fifties. He supposed Alistair *did* feel like he'd waited long enough for his due. But the fact that neither seemed to feel anything for the man Rowan had loved so deeply made his stomach turn. He wanted to touch the black band he still wore to honor the late earl, but resisted. It felt like showing weakness to wolves.

"As much as I know you asked me here to keep up appearances, I'm certain there is more to it than merely having me take part in your *celebrations*," Rowan said. "So what is it you want, Alistair?"

Alistair stopped swirling his drink and exchanged a look with Keaton that made Rowan's back stiffen. They seemed so very *smug*.

"I have spent the past six months going over Father's finances," Keaton said. "On behalf of our brother."

Rowan let out a snort. "Ever the bootlicker you are, Keaton."

Keaton's face darkened to a deep plum and his fists tightened at his sides. "Watch yourself, boy."

Rowan shrugged. "So you've been going over the finances. What does that have to do with me?"

Alistair arched a brow. "You think we don't know about the allowance Father gave you each month? It's how you live, isn't it?"

Now it was Rowan's turn to stiffen. His father gave him an allowance to help support his aspirations as a painter. His brothers didn't know that. No one did.

"That allowance is not something you can touch," he said. "It is a gift of inheritance by the earl. He told me many times it could not be altered."

Alistair grinned wider. "We thought so, too, for in the last years of his life Father made many changes to his documents to ensure you and your mother would be protected. But Keaton's digging uncovered a bit of wording tied to the inheritance that had not been changed, buried in a document from years ago. You see, Father originally wrote it that the allowance would be continued at the earl's pleasure. *I* am the earl now. It is at my *pleasure*, Rowan."

Rowan's stomach turned. "That isn't possible."

"But it is," Keaton said with a smirk. "Feel free to take what we've found to a solicitor. I'll provide you with a copy of the will if you'd like. It *is* written that way, Rowan."

"And my *pleasure* is to cut you off," Alistair continued, rising from his seat with a great deal of drama. "Today."

Rowan swung a little on his feet as the words sank in. Perhaps he could take this to court, but he knew his brothers. They were meticulous men and likely would not have come to this moment if they weren't entirely certain of their position. Which meant Alistair had every right to cut him off.

And destroy his world.

"How could you?" he said softly. "*Why* would you do that? It isn't as if it's some great amount."

Alistair's smug smile faltered and there was a flash of anger that replaced it. "You think you're owed something by the estate? You are not. You and your mother are interlopers who have suckled at the teat of this family for decades. I may not be able to keep her from collecting her inheritance, but by God, I will not support a man who does nothing and expects to be paid for the privilege. You may be my father's son, but I see you as little more than a by-blow, only barely made legitimate by an imprudent marriage."

Rage rose in Rowan, rage he fought desperately to tamp down. "I doubt Father would have seen it that way. He loved my mother and he loved me, and that has always rubbed under your skin. So your punishment is to ignore the earl's wishes. Good show, Alistair. You do him proud."

Keaton had the decency to flinch, but Alistair merely shrugged. "Unlike you, Rowan, I never gave a damn about Father's love or good graces. If the bastard rolls in his grave over what I've done, then that's merely a bonus."

He shook his head as he came around the large desk that had once been their father's. It was loaded with ridiculous trinkets now. A little gold statue of a ram, a ridiculously oversized mother-of-pearl tea caddy, a tortoiseshell snuffbox. Disjointed and ill-matched proof that Alistair held the power and would use it to his own ends.

Alistair sank into the leather seat and flicked his hand toward Rowan. "*You* are dismissed."

Rowan stared from one brother to the other, ignoring the pain that rose up in his chest. The hate that burned as brightly for them as theirs did for him. Slowly, he turned and walked from the room, closing the door with barely a click so they wouldn't have the satisfaction of his emotional response.

But oh, there was a response. Rowan knew what his financial situation was. Without his father's support, he had very little funds. His art had not quite taken off, though he did have a few patrons who purchased his pieces. Still, it wasn't enough to live on, especially if he were to carry on the lifestyle he had been leading. The one that led him to those patrons.

"Shit," he muttered as he strode down the hallway and out into the foyer. He had every intention of leaving, but before he could, the sound of his name came from the hallway.

"There you are, Sinclair. Christ, you were in there an age. How did it go?"

He turned, trying to keep a bright expression to his face, and smiled at his longtime friend, Percival Clement. They'd gone to school together, and Percy knew a little about his strained relationship with his brothers. That was the reason he'd asked his friend to accompany him to this ridiculous party tonight. Something he'd all but forgotten in his upset.

"It was fine," he managed through clenched teeth.

Percy's eyebrows lifted. "That bad, eh? What did old Alistair want then?"

"It's a long story," Rowan sighed. "And not one I care to discuss at the moment. Let's just go."

Percy caught his arm and all but dragged him toward the ballroom instead of the bliss of escape that Rowan desired. "Oh no we aren't. What better way to get back at those pricks than to eat their food and drink their wine and have a good time at their expense?"

Normally Percy's suggestion would have made Rowan laugh, but he had none of that left in him tonight. "I may have to pretend a good time," he said. "I'm afraid you'll have to endure my poor company."

Percy slung an arm around him as they entered the ballroom. "I always do, friend," he teased. "Now stand there looking mysterious so that the ladies all titter behind their fans, and I'll go get us drinks."

As he slipped into the crowd, Rowan backed up against the wall. Right now the last thing he wanted was to be spoken to or approached. Still, he wasn't about to just abandon his friend. Percy was trying his best to lift his spirits.

As he waited Percy's return, he scanned the room. It was a crush, of course. Alistair would have accepted nothing less. He was going to show off his new position and the money that came with it to as many people as he could. Society's favorite gentlemen and ladies milled about in the ballroom, dressed in their finery, enjoying the music. And none of them even thought of Rowan's father anymore.

He sighed as that maudlin thought entered his mind. His grief still felt so very real and alive.

"Oh, great God," Percy said as he weaved his way back through the crowd. "You look so very depressed. Come, we must find someone who is having a worse time than you are so that you might feel better by comparison."

Rowan took the drink his friend offered him with a laugh. "After tonight, I'm not certain anyone could be having a worse time than I am, Percy. This may be an impossible task you embark upon."

Percy turned on him with lit-up eyes. "A challenge! Well, you know I never turn them down. I shall find another desperate soul, let me see. Let me see…"

Percy scanned the ballroom and Rowan followed his gaze as it darted from person to person. Percy faced him at last. "What about Lady Biddenguard? She is always terribly morose."

Rowan looked at the lady in question. She held her ever-present handkerchief at her breast and sighed heavily as she looked out over the crowd. "I'm not sure. I think she rather likes being sad."

"True, she does seem to revel in it." Percy let his eyes move on. "Ah, I know, Winston Richards. His engagement to Miss Amanda Gregory just ended. You must not be as desperate as he is."

Rowan found the gentleman in the crowd. He was actually laughing at present. "Winston was tupping every whore in arm's length and he *hated* Miss Gregory. He was only marrying her to appease his father."

Percy shook his head. "You may be correct then—you are the most pathetic sack in the room."

Rowan laughed again at the teasing, but before he could reply, Percy caught his arm and shook it. "Wait, I have it. I know who is far more miserable than you are."

"Who?" Rowan said, trying to determine who had caught Percy's eye in the crowd.

"Lady No," Percy said with triumph. "Er, Lady Sophie."

"Lady Louisa's niece?" Rowan asked, though he knew full well to whom his friend referred. He was an old friend of Lady Louisa and no one could say that Sophie wasn't...fetching.

He found her in the crowd on the dancefloor. She was taking a turn with a gentleman. Her dark hair framed her slender face to perfection, bringing out the brightness of her green eyes and the fullness of her pink lips.

"She's dancing, you idiot," he said. Then his eyes went wide. "Wait,.she's dancing?"

Percy nodded and the triumph in his eyes doubled. "She is! It seems Lady No has begun to say yes! Though she appears anything but pleased about it."

Rowan stared at her again, and sure enough, Sophie looked

annoyed as the music ended and she curtseyed to her partner. She was moving off the dancefloor when another man approached her. They spoke briefly and then she was led back for yet another turn. And as she spun out of his sight, he caught the frustration and desperation in her expression.

"You know, you may be correct. Lady Sophie may indeed be the most miserable person in the room," Rowan said. "What in the world is going on? Everyone knows she doesn't dance, or engage at all with virtually any man. *Why* is she dancing?"

"You haven't heard? Well, of course you haven't, this is your first event out since…" Percy cut himself off, and suddenly he reached out to squeeze Rowan's arm in solidarity. "Well, it's your first event in a long while. At the start of the Season, she just started… accepting invitations. No one knows why, but she has a massive fortune at her disposal, so of course she hasn't had a moment's peace since she accepted her first dance a week ago."

Rowan stiffened. Her fortune. It was over fifty thousand pounds, if the rumors over the years were to be believed. He examined her more closely. She looked no more pleased to be taking a turn with her current partner than she had with her last.

Which meant she was accepting these requests from gentlemen for some other reason than her own desire to find a mate.

Rowan had not considered marriage. It wasn't that he was opposed to the institution, but it wasn't on the top of his mind. He'd never focused much on one lady over another. He took lovers, he enjoyed sex immensely. But he wasn't ready to settle down.

Only now that prospect seemed like one that could solve a great many problems. If he found a lady with money, rather like the one dancing past him right now with a scowl on her face, his brothers and their schemes would matter not.

Perhaps whatever was driving Sophie could make a match between them something mutually beneficial. She was certainly comely. He'd always been attracted to her, despite the fact that she avoided him as strenuously as she avoided any other man.

"You are worlds away," Percy said. "Tell me you aren't pondering the charms of Lady Sophie now that she has become Lady Yes."

Rowan pursed his lips at the question and the tone with which it was said. In truth, he'd always respected Sophie's independent spirit. Why should she say yes to some fool just to do what Society expected?

"No, just curious as to why the sudden change," he said. "Perhaps I'll call on her aunt and see if I can wheedle the truth out of her. We've always been friendly."

Percy's brows lifted. "If you could solve the mystery, you'd be the hero of the Season, I'm sure."

Rowan shrugged. "I'm not much interested in the title. And to be honest, I am not interested in staying tonight either. I'm going to go."

Percy looked ready to make an argument against the departure, but then he sighed. "Very well. I can see that you are truly troubled by whatever went on between you and your brothers. I hope you'll consider talking to me about it."

Rowan nodded. "I will. Later."

Percy said his goodbyes and Rowan made his way through the crowd to the foyer where he asked for his horse to be brought around. But as he waited, he found himself thinking not of Alistair and Keaton and their dastardly ways, but of Sophie and the mystery of why Lady No had become Lady Yes.

And if he just might be able to use that change to his own advantage.

<h1 style="text-align:center">CHAPTER 3</h1>

Sophie limped into the parlor and flopped herself into a chair across from her aunt. Louisa lifted her brows as she handed over a cup a tea. "Something troubling you?"

Sophie nearly snorted at the dry delivery of her aunt's question. "I think I made a very bad bargain with you," she said.

Louisa smiled into her cup as she took a slow sip. When she'd swallowed, she said, "It's only been ten days. Are you reneging already?"

"It may have only been ten days, but it feels like a lifetime," Sophie said, setting her teacup aside and rising to her feet to pace to the window. "I have danced with buffoons, walked in gardens with utter idiots and had everything under the sun explained to me as if I were a fool who could barely feed myself. It is exhausting!" She pointed to her slippers. "Also, I'd like to point out that I can hardly feel my toes today thanks to them being trod upon by that horrible Duke of Landonburg at last night's soiree."

"That horrible Duke of Landonburg is the most sought after bachelor in Society," Louisa said gently.

Sophie huffed out a breath. "If he didn't have gads of money, he wouldn't be, I assure you. He is dull as dry toast, Aunt Louisa! I thought I might die of boredom right there on the dancefloor."

"Well, that is a bit dramatic, isn't it, my love?"

Sophie sighed heavily and retook her seat. "Perhaps a little, I admit. But I do not need his funds, so it is so frustrating to have to feign interest when he went on about the benefits of crop rotation for the entire duration of our dance."

"I suppose one could argue it is positive that the man is interested in his country duties, for they impact a good many people," Aunt Louisa offered weakly.

Sophie narrowed her gaze. "Are you trying to marry me off to the Duke of Landonburg?"

"No!" her aunt replied with a laugh. "Of course not. I only don't want to see you give up. Your sudden acquiescence to dance and interact with gentlemen has stirred a great deal of interest, my dear. You are not seeing the best quality of men yet, that is all."

Sophie pursed her lips. She would not say it to her aunt, but she was disappointed as much as frustrated by just that fact. Somewhere in her heart she'd dreamed of being surrounded by eligible, interesting men who might set her heart to beating faster.

"You look sad, dearest," Aunt Louisa said softly.

Sophie shrugged. "It is only that it seems like those who have approached me are only interested in my money. Or think I should be willing to settle for theirs. I suppose I thought there might be more...*spark* in this endeavor."

"I know it's difficult, but please keep trying," Louisa encouraged as she reached out to take Sophie's hand.

Sophie nodded. "I will continue the bargain, aunt, but only because I adore you. I hope I won't disappoint you, though, when I say that I cannot imagine any man striking my interest this Season."

"You could never disappoint me, dearest. Now, I am about to have a guest for tea. Would you like to join us?"

Sophie shook off her problems. "Who is joining you?"

"Rowan Sinclair."

Her aunt continued speaking, but Sophie didn't hear anything more. Once Sinclair's name was spoken, it was as if the air was drawn out of the room. She sat calmly, but inside she was clawing for breath, for purchase.

The dashing third son of the Earl of Terrington had always been a friend to Louisa. She appreciated his independent streak and his somewhat inappropriate humor. But in Sophie, he inspired quite a different reaction.

He terrified her.

He was too handsome, too certain of himself, too…just *too*. She didn't like that when he was near her, she wanted to just look at him, with his dark hair and bright blue eyes and dimples that only brought attention to his full lips. She didn't want to notice his broad shoulders and his fine physique and the way he moved with such certainty and grace.

Men like Sinclair were not safe. They swept a woman up. They made a woman's heart beat faster, like she'd claimed to want if only in her own mind. But it was an out-of-control quickness. One that meant she was surrendering reason.

And Sophie wanted no part of that kind of madness.

"I have a bit of a headache, actually," she said, rising in the middle of whatever her aunt was saying. "Too much bad wine and dance partners, I suppose. I think I will not join you and Mr. Sinclair."

Her aunt kept her gaze on her for a beat too long, then she stood, as well. "Certainly, my dear, I will make your excuses. Go up and rest yourself. I'll come check on you after he's gone."

Sophie forced a smile and leaned in to buss her cheek

. "You are too good to me, Aunt Louisa. I hope I'm not too much of a trial for you."

Louisa touched her face gently. "Never, love. Now run along."

Sophie followed the instruction and turned from the room. But as she headed up the stairs toward her comfortable bed and away from the threat of the storm that was Rowan Sinclair, she couldn't help a sense of unease. About the bargain she had made with her aunt. About the man who would now enter her parlor and intrude upon the sanctum she found such peace in.

Rowan stood in Lady Louisa's parlor, waiting for his hostess to join him as he stared up at a portrait that hung on the parlor wall. It was of Louisa and her niece, seated close together, their hands intertwined. They shared the same green eyes, though Louisa's hair was a fading blonde. And the older woman was, of course, more lined with age, though she remained quite handsome.

They were as close as mother and daughter, though he supposed they would be. Everyone knew that Sophie had lost her parents when she was very young and Louisa had raised her for most of her life.

Which meant he would have to be very careful with how he proceeded with Lady Louisa. Friendship or not, he doubted she would be happy if she thought he was sniffing around her niece for Sophie's fortune.

In truth, he wasn't very pleased with that idea, himself. But the twenty-four hours since the ball had been rather awful. He'd received his copy of his father's will, and Percy had helped him obtain a solicitor that very morning. The man had only to read over the document once to say that Alistair was within his rights to remove Rowan's funds. That fighting for otherwise in court would likely result in nothing but a lot of lost money that Rowan now didn't have.

Which meant he was back to the options he'd been tossing and turning over all night. He was bad at investment, never had the head for it. He didn't want to fall on the kindness of friends. His art didn't yet make enough to support him.

But plenty of men married for the dowry of their intended. It was mercenary, but expected. And at least Sophie was attractive.

Very attractive, really. He'd always found her in the crowd. Always appreciated the way she moved.

"Rowan Sinclair!"

He turned from the portrait as Lady Louisa entered the room, both hands outstretched. Her smile was wide and welcoming, and he returned a grin of his own as he moved toward her and allowed her to kiss each cheek as a welcome. He had always genuinely liked Lady Louisa. Five years before he'd been seated next to her at a dinner party and they'd been friends ever since. She was intelligent and amusing, kind and eccentric.

"My lady, you are a vision as always," he said as he waited for her to sit and did the same.

She slapped his forearm good-naturedly. "You are a flatterer and a flirt, sir," she teased.

He leaned in. "Always, Lady Louisa."

"It's been an age since I last saw you," she said, leaning forward to prepare his tea.

"Too long," he agreed, and meant every word. "I think we last shared tea…six months ago?"

"Just after your father's death," Louisa agreed, and her tone became more somber. "How are you holding up?"

Rowan stiffened. "As well as can be expected," he admitted softly.

"And are those wretched brothers of yours giving you too much trouble?" she pressed.

He darted his gaze to her. There was something in her tone that made him wonder if she knew his dire circumstances. But that was not possible. He'd only discovered them himself just last night.

"They are pleasant, as always," he said, keeping his tone dry and neutral.

She nodded. "Well, they may mellow now that Alistair has the power he's always wanted."

Rowan shook his head. "He does revel in the power," he muttered, his mind going to his brother's smug expression.

Louisa sighed. "You cannot wish to discuss this topic."

He laughed despite himself. "No, I do not."

She tilted her head and looked at him more closely. "What brings you by, Rowan? I was surprised to receive your request to call."

"Can a man simply wish to see an old friend from time to time?"

She sipped her tea before she answered. "Perhaps you come here to inquire after Sophie."

His eyes went wide and he stared at her. God but the woman was a hawk—she didn't miss a thing. And she was entirely unreadable in this moment, he couldn't tell her reaction even a fraction. He would have to tread carefully.

"And why would you say that?"

She folded her hands into her lap without breaking eye contact with him. "We have already established that half a year has passed since our last tea together. I cannot help but think the timing of this new call isn't a coincidence. After all, her change in demeanor is on the wind, isn't it?"

He hesitated and then nodded. "It's the talk of the town, of course. After all, how often does a woman go from refusing even the casual interest of gentlemen to dancing with any one of them who asks? Who *wouldn't* talk?"

"I admit that there is reason for the general interest," Louisa said. "But I'm more curious about your interest specifically, Rowan. You and Sophie have bumped into each other over the years in Society and through our friendship, but I've never sensed a deeper connection. So I wonder why you come all the way here to inquire. Is it more than wanting to be the center of knowledge?"

He swallowed. "Lady Sophie and I are of an age," he said, choosing every word carefully. "No one could say she isn't beautiful. And I know she is also intelligent."

"Not every man appreciates such a thing in a lady," Louisa said softly, almost wistfully.

Rowan wrinkled his brow. "I would not be interested in a stupid wife."

Louisa's eyes went wide. "Are you considering taking Sophie to *wife?"*

Rowan swallowed. He hadn't really said that thought aloud yet, though he'd obviously been considering it thanks to his financial situation. Now that the words were on the wind they felt like a collar pulled too tight around his neck.

"Your pale face tells me volumes," Louisa said when he was silent for too long. "You know I've always liked you, young man. I will not lie and say that I haven't thought you would make my Sophie a good match."

Rowan blinked. Here he'd thought he was stepping into almost enemy territory. "I-I am shocked," he admitted. "*Your* Sophie has never seemed interested in me."

Louisa shrugged. "She is...*fearful* of what she thinks love is. But her lack of interest could change, I think. With the right man."

"By the way you are looking at me, it seems you think I might be that man."

Louisa inclined her head slightly. "Perhaps. I hope so, I admit, for both your sakes. Are you interested?"

He nodded slowly. "I...am."

"Good!" Louisa's face lit up. "Then I am going to give you some information that will put you ahead of the pack of mercenaries who are currently trodding all over my niece's feet and trying to convince her to overlook their lesser qualities."

"Information?" Rowan repeated, completely astonished by this turn of events. "Please, I am fascinated."

Louisa looked over her shoulder, as if she were checking for spies, then whispered, "The reason Sophie is saying yes to every fool who approaches her is because of me."

Rowan wrinkled his brow as Louisa then explained a shocking challenge laid out to her niece. When she leaned back in her chair, he stared at her in utter shock and disbelief.

"So she *must* say yes to any offer that comes her way," he repeated, trying not to let his mind wander to the wicked things *that* would allow.

Louisa twisted her mouth. "Within reason. She doesn't have to accept any marriage proposal she doesn't truly desire. And of course she wouldn't do anything…untoward."

Rowan clenched his fists at his sides. It was hard not to picture the lovely Sophie doing quite a few untoward things in that moment. "Why tell me this?"

"Because if you know, you may take advantage of the situation," Louisa said. "Use it to get past Sophie's walls, to get to know her. To allow *her* to know you. After that, it would be up to you two to see where it went."

Rowan considered the facts. Louisa had no idea of his financial motive when it came to Sophie. A deception that didn't feel very good when she was looking at him with such hopefulness in her stare.

But Sophie could solve his problems. And they *could* be a good match.

Louisa had certainly opened a door with this secret.

"Does she know you're telling me this?" he asked.

Louisa burst out laughing. "Gracious, no! And I expect you will not tell her, nor anyone else, about this. But will you use what you know?"

He thought again of his mercenary needs and sighed. "I wouldn't be opposed."

Louisa clapped her hands together. "Most excellent! Then I would suggest you find yourself an invitation to the Applegate ball tomorrow. Sophie will be there."

"You don't think I should press my suit today?" he asked.

"She needs a day off from gentlemen," Louisa explained. "And *you* need time to plan your attack."

Rowan shook his head. "You sound as though I'm about to enter into a war with her."

Louisa arched a brow. "Darling, don't you know? Love is a war. But I've given you all the tools you need to win. I just hope you'll utilize them well."

CHAPTER 4

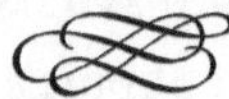

Sophie stood off to the side at the Applegate ball, wishing the floor would open up and devour her whole. She had never minded a ball before. She liked catching up with friends and listening to the music and admiring the dresses worn by others in attendance.

But now that she had to say yes to any man who asked her a boon, she felt tight, anxious. Like she was waiting for some horrible thing to drop out of the sky and crush her. Already tonight she had danced four times, and each partner was more stifling than the last.

She sighed as one of her dearest friends, Hannah Blankenship, approached. Hannah threaded a hand through her arm and looked out over the crowd with her. "It's a sorry lot, isn't it?"

Sophie smiled at the question. Hannah was the toast of Society at present. She was so lovely that every man wanted her. So Sophie knew she understood the quandary she faced.

"I wish I could say there were good prospects here, but I have not enjoyed my dances thus far."

Hannah shook her head. "I still don't know why you are partaking in dances. If I didn't have to, I certainly wouldn't."

Sophie hadn't told Hannah or any of her other friends the truth about why she was suddenly saying yes. On some level, she feared their reaction since all of them admired her so much for her ability to retain her independence.

"Oh no, it's Lord Witherspoon," Hannah whispered, elbowing Sophie.

Sophie flinched, not from the gentle thud of Hannah's elbow against her ribs but because Viscount Witherspoon was thirty years older than her and he burped whenever he spoke. Not to mention he was coming right for them.

"Our best chance is to split up," Sophie hissed. "Good luck!"

Hannah scurried to the punch bowl and Sophie took off through the crowd, toward the entrance to the ball. She intended to go to the ladies retiring room, but as she exited the ballroom and turned toward the side parlor, she saw yet another group of men standing about, clearly waiting for the ladies to exit. None of them were gentlemen she wished to spend time with, so she veered away, up the opposite side of the hall and to an open door at the far end.

She moved inside and closed it behind herself, leaning back as she caught her breath. The fire had burned down low and the room was dim, not meant to be intruded upon by guests. Which made it the perfect escape from prying eyes and seeking men.

"Wretched, wretched things," she murmured aloud.

And just as she did so, a person sat up from a reclining position on the settee that faced the fire. He turned toward her, and she caught her breath in surprise.

"Good evening, Sophie," Rowan Sinclair drawled, leaning his arm across the back of the settee in a casual manner.

"Rowan!" she burst out, too shocked to refer to him more properly. "Blast it all, you scared the dickens out of me."

He chuckled, a rich sound that filled the room and settled in her blood. It also made those deep dimples pop up in the hollows of his smooth cheeks. The appearance made her stomach do funny things. Things she didn't like. Things that were the very reason she avoided this man whenever possible.

She folded her arms. "It *isn't* funny. I didn't realize you were here, I'll leave you to your…well, whatever you were doing."

She pivoted to escape him when he said, "Won't you stay?"

She froze. He was asking her a question. One she *could* say yes to. One that according to her bargain with her aunt, she *must* say yes to.

Damn and blast it all.

She gritted her teeth and fisted her hands at her sides, keeping her gaze firmly on the door as she ground out, "Yes."

She turned and found he had pushed to his feet and was now leaning over the fire, stoking the flame so they were no longer in half-darkness together. Not that being alone with the door shut was proper at all, but at least with light it felt less…scandalous.

"May I get you a drink?" he asked, motioning to the sideboard and its bottles arranged in a line.

This time Sophie didn't have to be tricked into nodding her head and responding, "Yes, please."

He smiled as he moved to pour them each a sherry. His back was to her as he said, "I can only hope this will be a vast improvement from the watered down wine inside that insufferable party."

She couldn't help a half-smirk at his comment. "It's more water than wine, that is for certain. Honestly, I think it might just be cordial. There is no sting to it."

He faced her, holding out the glass for her. "I like a bit of sting. It makes life more interesting."

"Some would disagree," she said with a shrug. "Some *like* a watered down existence."

"Not you?" he pressed, motioning to the settee.

She hesitated before she took a place there and watched him take his own. Not too close to her. Not quite far enough.

"It seems we have few enough years on this earth not to experience as much as we can," she replied with a shrug.

She waited for his expression of shock, for an admonishment. After all, most men didn't approve of her desire to truly live. Ladies were not supposed to crave adventure or excitement or…*anything*.

But he didn't scold or sniff. If anything, his smile grew wider. "Then you and I are of a mind," he said. "I feel the same way."

"Yes, but *you* are allowed to pursue life's pleasures," she said with a sigh that wracked her from head to toe. "As a woman, I'm not. My options are far more limited."

He seemed to ponder the words for a moment. "I suppose I haven't thought of it in those terms."

She glared at him. "Of course you haven't."

"You know me so well, do you?" he asked.

She turned her gaze away. "I know your type," she said. "Rakes with no troubles who do as they like and never have to deal with the consequences."

He leaned back. "Did I harm you in some way that I am not aware of? I do not think I deserve such censure."

She jerked back toward him. She had said too much, let her rumbling feelings overflow in the presence of someone she didn't exactly trust. And now he stared at her like she had grown a second head or begun speaking in tongues.

He also had a look of...hurt. Like she'd actually said something that pricked him.

She sighed. "I'm...I'm sorry, Mr. Sinclair. I've been out of sorts tonight and I shouldn't have spoken to you in such a fashion. You've always been a friend to my aunt. And I certainly don't know you well enough to accuse you of anything, do I?"

"Why don't you know me well enough?" he pressed, scooting just a touch closer.

She blinked in confusion, both caused by his question and his proximity. Something about him set her on her head. "I beg your pardon?"

He leaned in a bit closer, his masculine scent winding its way into her nostrils. Pine, leather, warm skin. "Why don't you know me, Sophie? As you say, I've been a friend to your aunt for many years. And yet you avoid me."

"You are forward, sir."

"I'm honest. And I'm asking you to be. Do you not like me?"

She bit her lip. "Yes. No."

He laughed gently. "Which is it?"

"I don't *dislike* you," she conceded. "I like that you are kind to my aunt. But I don't know you. I...I avoid knowing you because you make me...make me..."

"Yes?"

"Nervous," she squeaked out at last, turning her face as heat flamed in her cheeks.

He didn't say anything for what felt like an eternity. She felt his stare on her even though she didn't dare look at him. Not when she'd said something so...true.

"I see," he said softly. He reached out and his fingertips brushed her chin, tilting her face back until she was forced to look at him.

He felt so much closer now. So much bigger in the small room on the small settee. And she swayed toward him ever so slightly.

"You don't have to be nervous," he said, his deep voice low and hypnotic in the otherwise silent room. "You can trust me."

She shook her head. "No, I think that is not true."

His lips twitched in another hint of a smile. "My reputation precedes me. Perhaps trust is too strong a word. But you needn't fear me, Sophie. You never need fear me."

They sat like that, too close together, for what felt like an eternity. And Sophie realized, in that moment, that she wanted this man to kiss her. To touch her. She found her eyelids dipping closed and her lips tingling as she tilted her face up ever so slightly.

But instead of brushing his mouth to hers, Rowan cleared his throat and stood up. She stared at him as he turned his back to her. "We'll be missed if we don't return to the ballroom soon."

She shook her head. Oh yes, the ballroom. She'd all but forgotten that they were in someone else's home, at someone else's ball. Slowly, she stood, her knees trembling enough that she reached back to steady herself on the settee arm. "You are correct, of course."

He turned toward her again. "Perhaps you'd do me the honor of dancing with me, Lady Sophie."

She jerked out a nod. "Y-yes," she whispered.

He smiled again and offered her his arm. But as she took it, she realized she hadn't said yes to him because of the agreement she'd made with her aunt. She'd said yes because she wanted to dance with this man.

And that was both shocking and utterly terrifying.

Rowan was keenly aware of every one of his fingers as they curled around Sophie's hip while the two of them turned about the dancefloor together. He had approached her with mercenary thoughts in his head, but now that they were together, he was truly enjoying the moment.

Sophie was unlike any woman he'd ever known. Her independence afforded her the option to say what she truly thought, and he found her honesty refreshing. That she wanted adventure and excitement and a future that wasn't bland and regular was even more attractive to him.

But what he thought of more than anything, as he guided her around the floor, was the look on her face when she'd been sitting with him in the parlor. He was no monk. He knew desire and pleasure. And Sophie had wanted him to kiss her.

More to the point, he'd very much wanted to kiss her. More than kiss her, truth be told. But since that hadn't been his intention in that moment, he'd been taken aback by the powerful desire and had turned away from it.

Now he was regretting that action. Or inaction.

"Why did you become friends with my aunt?"

He shook off his thoughts and looked down at her. She had a contemplative look on her face. Like she was trying to figure him out. "*Why?*"

She nodded. "Don't mistake me, my aunt is wonderful. I don't doubt that anyone who meets her is bound to adore her. But you are not of an age with her. It's a strange friendship."

"Perhaps it seems so," he conceded softly, and he found Lady Louisa in the crowd. "Your aunt and my mother are friends, of course, so as a young man I knew a bit about her. But I was seated next to her at a supper party at a very…difficult time in my life."

"How so?" she pressed.

He shifted, for he never spoke of his troubles, or very rarely so. But Sophie was soft and quiet and not demanding. Not digging. At least not for any cruel purpose. He found himself wanting to tell her.

"My father died six months ago, but he had been sick off and on for a very long time," he said past the sudden lump in his throat. "He first fell ill around the time I was seated beside your aunt. And she… she was very kind to me. Not the false kindness that is often shown by those in the *ton*, but something very real."

Sophie seemed to ponder that a moment as they spun in time to the music. "I am sorry about your father," she said.

"Thank you. I know you've experienced the same kind of loss," he said.

Her mouth turned down. "Only you loved your father," she murmured.

His eyes went wide. "I'm sorry, I had no idea that your relationship with yours was strained."

"That is one way to put it," she said, stiffening in his arms. "That he was an untrustworthy bastard who was cruel to my mother until the day he killed her in the accident that took them both is another."

Rowan caught his breath. Everyone knew of the story of Sophie's parents. They'd been riding in a phaeton together in the park fifteen years earlier, too recklessly, it turned out. The vehicle had crashed, killing them both instantly and orphaning the young woman in his arms. A tragedy that was whispered about, clucked about, from time to time. He had never really considered what she thought of it. What she felt about it.

Certainly he'd never imagined it was *anger* that burned in her when the memory struck.

Sophie shook her head and muttered, "I should not have said such a thing. I do not speak of it—I have no idea why I was suddenly inspired to do so."

"I'm not sorry," he said softly, and found it was true. "I would like to be friends with you, Sophie."

"Why?" she asked, her attention returning to his face.

He cleared his throat. "Because you make me nervous, too. Which means *you* are an adventure waiting to happen." He leaned a touch closer as the strains of the music ended. "Would you be friends with me?"

He saw the struggle across her expression. The fleeting moment where she seemed to want to run. The fight to find an answer. Then she nodded. "Y-yes."

He smiled, though there was something unsatisfying about her single-word answer. Was she saying yes merely because her aunt had forced her into a bargain, or did she truly want to be a friend to him? To get to know him?

It was a jumbled situation, that was certain.

She pulled her hand from his, her cheeks suddenly flushed with color. "I-I should go."

She didn't wait for him to respond, but rushed from his side. He watched her career through the crowd, past her aunt and her friends and all the mercenary gentlemen who were waiting to press their suit. She passed it all and exited directly onto the terrace.

He didn't recall making the decision, but he found himself striding after her. He pushed through the terrace doors and found her standing at the stone wall, staring up at the moon above. He caught his breath at how lovely she was in the moonlight, and there was nothing in the world that could have stopped him in that moment.

She gasped as she turned toward him, watched him approach her wordlessly. She gasped again when he put his arms around her, bent his head and brushed his lips to hers. She was supple against him, molded to his chest as her trembling hands lifted to grip the lapels of his tailored jacket.

Her lips were impossibly soft, and he tilted his head for better access as he lightly traced the bee-stung swell of them. She caught a breath and he delved deeper, tasting the hollows of her mouth as she made a low moan in the back of her throat that hardened his cock and boiled his blood in his veins.

Reluctantly, he drew back, steadying her gently before he stepped away. They stood panting, staring at each other, for what felt like an eternity before he said, "*That* is what I should have done in the parlor, Sophie."

Her lips parted in what appeared to be shock, and he could see her mind racing again, just as it had in the ballroom. He didn't wait for her reaction, for her arguments, for her decisions about what she should or shouldn't do. He merely smiled at her. "Until we meet again, my lady."

Then he turned on his heel and left the terrace, left the ball, left her standing there to ponder what had just happened between them. And knew that he would do exactly the same thing.

CHAPTER 5

"What do you think of Rowan Sinclair?" Sophie asked, hearing the tremble in her voice even as she continued stitching on her needlepoint.

Without looking up, Sophie was well aware of Hannah's gaze. There was a beat of silence, then another, and heat flooded her cheeks, much as it had on the terrace after he kissed her so shockingly and thoroughly.

"Rowan Sinclair," Hannah repeated, her tone carefully neutral. "I think he's very handsome. I think that you danced with him at the Applegate ball three nights ago and insisted that it meant nothing to you. Were you not completely honest about that fact?"

Sophie shifted in her place. Normally she spoke of her concerns to her aunt, but Louisa was not likely to approve of her sharing a scandalous kiss on a terrace, agreement between them or not. Even if she were, Rowan was a friend to Louisa. Sophie couldn't imagine baring her soul about the man to her.

"I don't know," she admitted through clenched teeth.

Hannah tossed her needlepoint on the settee next to her and leaned forward with a grin. "*That* sounds promising. Do tell all, for I know you've always liked him!"

"I have not!" Sophie argued. "I think nothing of the man."

"Posh!" Hannah said on a laugh. "You are constantly watching him from the corner of your eye and making little comments about his attire or his comportment."

"Gossip means nothing," she argued.

Hannah arched a brow. "It wouldn't mean anything if you ever gossiped about *any* other man in our acquaintance. But he's the only one. And why wouldn't you be interested? He *is* handsome and dashing and has a bit of a dangerous air about him."

Sophie couldn't argue that fact. Rowan had felt dangerous on the terrace a few nights before. Her thoughts and dreams of him since had been equally so.

"What happened?" Hannah pressed.

Sophie sighed. "Fine, since you are insistent. We bumped into each other in the parlor. We had a very...odd conversation there."

"About what?" Hannah asked.

Sophie shrugged. "I don't know. Adventure. The expectations of men versus women."

Hannah's brow wrinkled. "Heavy topics for a passing conversation."

"It didn't feel heavy. It just felt...normal." Sophie said with a frown. "Then we danced. But afterward he followed me out onto the terrace and he...kissed me."

She said the last two words as one quick, smashed-together sound, but there was no hiding it from Hannah. She gasped, clapping a hand over her mouth as her eyes went wide. "He *kissed* you!" she squealed.

Sophie flinched and looked over her shoulder. "Gracious, tell the whole house, will you?"

Hannah shook her head. "I'm sorry, I'm sorry, but that is *shocking* news. I couldn't help but react. Heavens, Sophie! He kissed you?"

Sophie felt the heat in her cheeks, brought about by both the revelation of her secret and her memories of that moment. Of Rowan's mouth on hers, hot and hard and insistent. Of his taste, mint and sherry and something that was potently male. Of the feel of his strong arms around her. Of her body's shameful reaction to all those things and more.

"Yes," she whispered.

"What was it like?"

She shifted in her seat. "It was…I don't know how to describe it."

"Well, try, won't you? I'm fairly certain my father is about to barter me off to some dreadful man. I want to know what kissing is like before I have to share my first with someone…horrible."

Sophie stared. "Hannah, you cannot be serious. Would he do that?"

Hannah bent her head. "I don't know."

"Oh, Hannah!"

"I-I can't talk about it, it's too terrifying. Please, just give me your news. It is happy, at least, and it takes my mind off of whatever terrifying paths it wishes to take."

Sophie frowned. Here she had been swirling around and around in her head about what had happened with Rowan. Something so silly when compared to what Hannah had just described. After all, agreement or not, Sophie still had control over her own future. Her aunt would never force her or barter her away.

"I *wanted* to kiss him," she admitted to both her friend and, for the first time out loud, to herself. "In the parlor I wanted to, but he pulled away and I felt a little foolish. So when he came across the terrace and caught me in his arms, it was like a dream. A—a fantasy."

Hannah smiled. "And what was it like?"

"Sweet," Sophie said, and turned her face with a blush. "Hard and passionate. Unexpected. Rather like the man who bestowed the kiss upon me."

"So what will you do?" Hannah asked. "Does this mean you are courting?"

Sophie burst out laughing. "Oh, I think not. A kiss might mean something to me, but could it to a person like Rowan Sinclair? He's known as a rake. A rogue. I'm sure it wasn't something he put much thought into. A fleeting desire. He likely hasn't thought of it since."

Hannah's mouth quirked and there was no mistaking the disappointment in her stare. "And here I thought I'd witness a true love story. They're all the rage, you know."

Sophie flinched ever so slightly. "Everyone always appears to be in love at the beginning, Hannah. It doesn't mean that sentiment will last. Yes, there are a great many supposed love matches in the swirl of Society lately, but if there is one thing I know, it is that looks can be deceiving."

Hannah frowned, concern on her face, and Sophie tensed. She didn't want to discuss this any further. So she forced a falsely bright smile on her face. "Are you coming to the Waterfield ball tonight?"

Hannah shrugged. "I'm brought to every ball, aren't I? My father insists. So yes, I'll be there."

"Good," Sophie said. "It will be nice to have a friend in the crowd."

"And if Mr. Rowan Sinclair joins the party?" Hannah teased.

"Then I suppose he will likely ignore me," Sophie whispered. "And that will prove my point that whatever was between us was meaningless."

But as she said the words, they stung her more deeply than she knew they should.

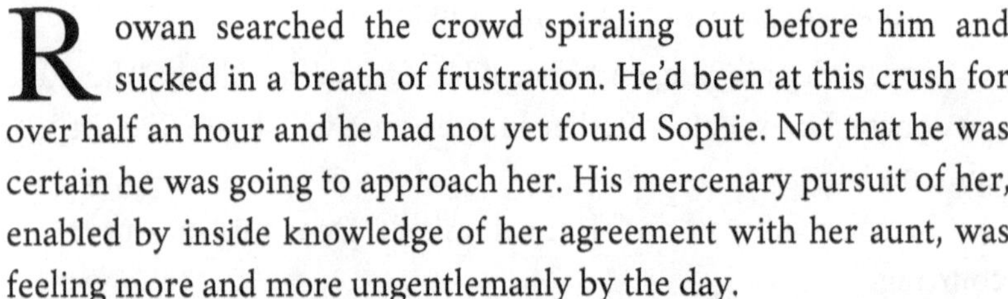

Rowan searched the crowd spiraling out before him and sucked in a breath of frustration. He'd been at this crush for over half an hour and he had not yet found Sophie. Not that he was certain he was going to approach her. His mercenary pursuit of her, enabled by inside knowledge of her agreement with her aunt, was feeling more and more ungentlemanly by the day.

Of course, he hadn't been thinking of any of that when he kissed her three nights before. No, that had been about pleasure and desire, not a need for anything but to know her taste. And that taste, that feel of her in his arms, was all he'd thought about since.

Madness, considering he'd known the woman for years and not been driven by such a drumbeat of need.

"Rowan!"

He turned to find Lady Louisa coming to his side. His heart leapt, both because he had no idea if his friend knew what he'd been doing with her charge, and also because her presence made it clear that Sophie was indeed in attendance.

"Lady Louisa," he said with a smile that suddenly felt too wide. "What a pleasure."

"It is," she agreed. "You look handsome, as always."

He laughed at her compliment. "That red suits you well, my lady."

She glanced down at her gown. "Thank you. I hesitated in the fabric, for red is awfully bold for a woman of my advanced age, but Sophie insisted. She says life is too short not to wear red."

He nodded. "Your niece is wiser than her years would imply. Is she...is she in attendance tonight?"

He had hoped his question would seem nonchalant, but from the way Louisa jerked her gaze to his face, it would seem it was not.

Her lips twitched. "She is," she said slowly. "I believe she just finished dancing with Lord Smithly and has decided to have a breath of fresh air on the terrace. If one wished to find her, that would be a good place to look."

Rowan tensed. The terrace. Not the same one where he'd kissed her, of course, but still...

"Perhaps she would not like to be disturbed," he suggested.

She arched a brow. "I'm sure she wouldn't. But that doesn't mean company isn't what she *needs*, does it?"

"I wouldn't know about that," Rowan said, though his errant mind took him back to the soft sound of pleasure Sophie had made when he touched her. Need was something he could read quite well in that circumstance.

Which was, in truth, slightly terrifying.

"It is up to you, of course," Louisa said with a slight incline of her head. "Now I see a friend waving—I must go. Lovely to see you as always, Rowan."

She slipped off into the crowd, leaving Rowan to his own thoughts. And to stare off across the room toward the terrace doors that would lead him to Sophie.

Now he knew where she was. And he just had to decide what to do about it.

~

Sophie crept down the winding path through the garden, darting her eyes around for other guests. The night was warm and the path lit by lanterns, so she didn't doubt others might be around. She didn't want to *see* others.

Saying yes was exhausting. She didn't like any of the men who pursued her. At first it had been the quality of her partners that troubled her, but now more appealing men were circling her. Lord Smithly, the last man she'd danced with, was actually very charming and even handsome.

The problem was that she compared him to...to...

"Sophie?"

She froze on the path at the sound of the warm, deep voice of the very man she now compared all others to: Rowan. She didn't have to look to know it was him. She didn't have to see his face. She knew his voice. Worse, she knew the feel of him, the presence of him.

She didn't want that. She didn't want him. She didn't want to *want*. And yet he kept popping up, suddenly and unexpectedly, and she couldn't say no. That had nothing to do with her aunt's suggestion of a Season of Yes.

"Sophie?" he repeated, now with more concern to his voice.

More question. She couldn't stand with her trembling back to him all night, much as she'd like to do so.

At last she slowly turned and looked at him. He was bathed in moonlight—it danced off his dark hair and his lean face, it brightened his eyes. It made him glow like some unattainable treasure in a silly children's story.

"Rowan...Mr. Sinclair," she squeaked out. "I didn't see you earlier."

"Nor I you," he said, moving closer, almost with caution. Like he was afraid she'd run like a spooked rabbit in the woods. It didn't seem like the worst response. He was certainly a wolf in this scenario.

"You were looking for me?" she asked, hearing the tremble in her voice. Hating that it was in her hands and her knees, too, especially when he took yet another step closer.

He nodded. "I was. All through the crowd and finding myself very disappointed when I didn't see you amongst the revelers."

"I was there," she said, turning away slightly, for she feared he could read her face. Read her desire for another kiss. Read how afraid she was of him and everything this attraction to him represented. "Dancing, even."

"So your aunt said," he drawled. "Lord Smithly, eh?"

She darted her gaze toward him. His tone was light, but his mouth was drawn down in a frustrated expression. "Yes," she admitted. "He is a fine enough man, I suppose."

"He is that," Rowan said, and moved even closer. "Fine enough."

She swallowed hard, for he was edging into her space now. Just as he had when he kissed her all those nights ago. She found herself staring up at his lips, picturing them sliding over hers again until she could no longer bear her own weight from the pleasure of it.

His hand reached out and he cupped her cheek gently. She shivered out a breath she hadn't even realized she'd been holding.

"Why are you running?" he asked, his voice so low now. Rough.

She shifted which made his fingers slide across her skin, sending waves of sensation through her entire body. "I-I'm not running."

"Oh, yes you are," he corrected. "I know the look of it. Why, Sophie?"

"Because he wasn't…they aren't…he wasn't…" she stammered, finding herself unable to complete any of those sentences. Finding they all ended with one word: *you*. She ran because none of those men was Rowan.

And he seemed to understand that, read it in her expression or her mind. His eyes went wider, his fingers bunched against her cheek, and then he wrapped an arm around her waist. He tugged and she fell against him, lifted her hand to his chest to support herself as she looked up into his eyes.

He held her there for just a moment and then he bent his head, closer and closer, until his lips brushed hers. Unlike the first time he kissed her, when there was something vivid and wild and out of control in the act, this time he was gentle. Almost too gentle. He was teasing, and frustration grew in her at the knowledge. She wanted more. She wanted that animal desire that had coursed between them the last time.

She wanted to feel again, but she was so inexperienced that she had no idea how to manage the kiss in that direction. But she thought of that night when he'd first kissed her. He had put his tongue inside her mouth and it had felt so good.

So she slowly parted her lips and then traced the crease of his mouth with her tongue. He jolted in surprise, but his mouth came open and she took the opportunity. Once again he tasted of mint and sherry, of desire and danger, and she tilted her head to get more of it. More of him.

He made a low, animal sound in his throat and then he gathered her closer before he drove his tongue against hers, the wolf reawakened by her boldness. She lifted into him, going on instinct, going on pleasure, and felt one of his hands trail down her side, across her hip, and then he shockingly grabbed her bottom and ground her against him.

Sensation exploded through her and she let out a cry against his mouth. And in that moment there was another sound in the air. Voices.

He pulled away, all but shoving her behind his back to offer her protection with his body as they both stared in the direction of the sound. People were coming down the walkway toward them. Far enough away that they very likely hadn't seen the shocking things they'd been doing. Close enough that an interception was only moments away.

Sophie stared up at him, at his jaw clenched tight and his eyes focused on those who would intrude upon their moment. He looked dangerous. He looked perfect.

"Please, I can't...I can't..." she whispered.

His focus jerked back to her. He held her stare for what felt like an eternity, then nodded, caught her hand and drew her away from the path. She followed wordlessly, trusting him to take her someplace safe. Someplace quiet. Someplace where she could regather herself before she was forced to return to being Lady Yes.

They twisted and turned, and at last he came to a stop in front of the hothouse situated in the back corner of the estate grounds. He glanced toward her, uncertain, it seemed, in this moment.

"Is this...all right?" he asked.

She nodded. "I only need to regather myself."

He said nothing more, but pushed the door open and motioned her inside. The evening air had been cool and dry, and she gasped at the muggy heat inside the glass building. All around them were flowers, tended by Lady Waterfield, herself, if gossip was to be believed. Sophie sucked in a deep breath of fragrant air before she heard the door behind her shut softly.

And now they were alone.

She turned toward him. He was standing five feet away, just at the door, and all he was doing was watching her. Careful, cautious… but also heated.

Inescapable.

"Perhaps this was a mistake," she said, more to herself than to him.

He arched a brow. "You didn't want to be in the garden, did you? Nor return to the party? Why question yourself now?"

She clenched her teeth. "Because I'm expected to be there."

He shrugged. "Expectation is overrated."

She narrowed her gaze at him. "Says the man who lives up to his own reputation of perfection."

"My reputation?" he repeated, amusement in his tone.

"Yes," she said. "You are the bored, lay-about third son of an earl, aren't you? Off seducing women in gardens?"

Now his lips pursed. "I don't recall *seducing* you, my dear. Yes, I kissed you, but you haven't exactly pushed me away, have you?"

She shifted and turned her back on him. Looking at him was so dangerous. He drew her in when she did. He made her…want.

"I-I should have. Pushed you away, I mean."

"Why are you so afraid of what is between us?" he asked softly. "It goes beyond the normal simpering that young ladies are taught when it comes to what men desire."

She worried her lip, still not looking at him. "I-I'm not afraid," she said. Lied. She lied.

"Your voice trembles," he said. He was moving on her, but she was still too nervous to look at him. "And it belies any denial you make. You're afraid."

She turned and found him right behind her, so close that she nearly careened into his broad chest. She lost her breath as she looked up at him, lost any ability to argue.

"But you also like it when I kiss you," he continued, his voice hypnotic. He was reaching for her again, smoothing a hand across her cheek, down to cup her neck. "You want to deny it, but you can't. Can you?"

She struggled, trying to find the denial but unable to. Because he was right. Finally she sighed. "I can't."

He leaned in and kissed her once again. Immediately she lifted into him, her arms coming around his neck, his hands pulling her tighter, closer. Their mouths crashed together in reckless, abandoned desire, and her body began to pulse with feeling she'd never felt, sensations that were both fascinating and terrifying.

She broke the kiss with a harsh cry, but couldn't bring herself to leave his arms. She stared up into his face, so close, so handsome, so focused on her.

"I-I don't know what this is," she gasped out. "I don't know what to do, Rowan."

He tilted his head, his expression gentling. "It's desire, Sophie. Need. Pleasure. Those things aren't wrong, no matter what someone has told you in the past."

"It feels…*dizzy.*"

For a moment, he seemed to be pondering what to do next. Then his face grew even more wolfish. "Does it tingle? Here?" He brushed his hand gently across her breasts, jolting her with the intimacy of his touch. Her nipples sang when he stroked across them in such a shocking way.

"Yes," she gasped, both a prayer and an answer to his question.

"And between your legs?" he pressed, though he didn't move to touch her there, but just continued to brush his fingers across her nipple slowly, gently.

She blushed but couldn't deny him. "Y-yes," she admitted. "It feels hot there. Tingly. W-wet."

He muttered something, a curse perhaps, and then he slowly began to back her up through the greenhouse. Farther and farther into the dark, away from the door.

"I can help," he whispered as he eased her back onto a bench that was hidden in the corner of the room. "I can make all that pressure ease."

"You would ruin me," she gasped, though in this moment she

didn't think that sounded like the worst thing in the world. She had married friends who actually seemed to like what their husbands did in the dark of their bedrooms.

He shook his head. "There are ways to give you ease without ruining you."

She pursed her lips. She hadn't heard of that before. Of course, she hadn't exactly asked questions. Desire was so frightening to her. Still was, in truth, as she sat with this man standing above her, offering her…

Well, offering her something.

"I don't know," she whispered.

He slowly dropped to his knees, and they were face to face again. "I want to make you come, Sophie."

"Come?"

"It will be so pleasurable," he promised. "Please, will you let me?"

She swallowed. He was asking her a question. One she could say yes to. And though her aunt had likely never thought of this situation when she made her bargain with Sophie weeks ago, now she had to decide. Did she say yes? Or did she say no?

"Yes," she whispered, almost without realizing it.

CHAPTER 6

Rowan could hardly believe that Sophie had just agreed to let him touch her, pleasure her. This had not been his plan when he approached her in the garden, but here they were, alone in the steamy darkness, her body trembling as he leaned up on his knees and claimed her mouth once again.

He'd always liked kissing. He was a proficient at it, if his lovers were telling the truth. He could do it for hours, truth be told, allowing desire to build in a slow, powerful burn until there was nothing left but throbbing need.

Sophie took him to that place in moments. His cock was like stone, rubbing uncomfortably against his trouser front, his body whispering all the things he wanted to do to the lady who was moaning against his lips, her trembling hands smoothing gently across his chest. He couldn't do, wouldn't do, any of those things his body desired, of course. He might be on a path that he didn't like, but there was still a gentleman in him. He wouldn't force her hand by claiming her.

But he was certainly not above seducing her to push her toward his plans. Not when the thought of it was so damned pleasurable.

He dragged her to the edge of the bench, forcing her legs to part to give him a place. She shivered, her tongue driving into his mouth with an increased abandon that set him on fire. He'd never thought she was passionate. Her reputation of always saying no had led people to say she was cold.

She was not. Her fingers glided into his hair, her heart pounded hard enough that he could feel it—her body was like an inferno. She gasped when he slid his hand down her side, curling it around to cup her breast for a second time. Just as it had been the first time he touched her so intimately, her nipple was a hard outline beneath her thin gown. He stroked his thumb over it, measuring her every reaction, from the catch of her breath to the arch of her back to the way she trembled.

He wanted more. As much as she could give. He wanted it now.

He gripped a handful of silken skirt in his fist, tugging it up over her calves, her knees. She gasped a second time and jerked her head back to look at him in the dim light. Her eyes were wide, uncertain but also filled with undeniable need. He held that stare, unwavering as he glided the skirt higher, over her thighs. Only then did he look down at what had been revealed.

She had lovely legs, and they were clad in a finely stitched, almost sheer stocking that was silky to the touch when he let his hand settle on her knee.

She jolted. "Rowan!" she gasped, a question and a plea.

He leaned in and brushed his lips against hers until she relaxed slightly. "I'm not going to ruin you," he promised a second time.

He didn't wait for her response but began to nibble his way along her neck, down to the slope of her gown. He dragged his mouth over her breast, wishing he had time to strip her naked, to worship her as she deserved to be worshipped.

She made a strangled cry as he placed a hand on each thigh and gently pushed, giving himself more space and revealing her in the moonlight that filtered into the hothouse. Her drawers were easily parted, and he stopped breathing as he looked at the slick, fragrant flower of her sex, there for him to pluck so easily.

She turned her head. "You shouldn't. *I* shouldn't."

He glanced up. Her hands were gripped against the edge of the bench, her breath was short, she worried her lip.

"You're right," he whispered. "But I'm still going to do it. You still want me to."

She nodded, and the wordless consent was all he needed. He leaned in, brushing his fingertips against her first. She jolted at the first contact, her hips lifting slightly toward him in a natural yearning for the pleasure he would give. Some part of her understood that, even though she'd never experienced it. Even if it frightened her because she'd spent her whole life being told that what he wanted to do was wicked. Wrong. A cause for ruination and despair.

He wanted to replace all those fears with powerful memories. To wake that passion he could see inside of her. To make her crave what he could give rather than fearfully brace herself.

He stroked her again, parting her outer folds with his thumbs. She was slick already, aroused by his kisses, by the way he'd touched her so far. Her responsiveness only drove him with more fevered purpose. He drew a long whiff of her sweetness and then ducked his head to stroke his tongue across her at last.

The riot of feelings that cascaded over Sophie as Rowan touched her in this utterly sinful, completely inappropriate, fantastically wonderful way was almost indescribable.

She was shocked, of course. His mouth was on her. His *mouth*. And he was kissing her with abandon in her most personal and private of places.

But her reaction, both body and soul, was not what she knew it should be. She should be outraged and horrified, should push him away and tell her aunt.

Instead, her body flared with heat and pleasure unlike anything she'd ever experienced. She dipped her head back, holding tighter and tighter to the bench's edge as he stroked his tongue across the entire entrance of her trembling sex. Electric pleasure sizzled through her, and she let out a tiny cry she could not have kept inside for all the riches in the world. That sound only seemed to drive Rowan, for he held her more firmly in place with his big hands on her thighs and darted his tongue across her with purpose.

She lifted against him on instinct, her breath vanishing with the pleasure that grinding on his tongue created. This was...*magical.* This was spectacular. This was everything, and she surrendered to it and to him.

He must have felt that shift, that softening of her guard, for he increased his strokes, focusing his tongue on the hidden bundle of nerves she occasionally brushed in her bath or her bed. The pleasure she felt from that innocent touch was magnified by his wicked mouth. It built, driving her toward a cliff that she couldn't see and didn't fully understand. She just knew that what she felt was building, rushing out of control.

He sucked at her, and suddenly all the sensation reached its natural crescendo. She bucked against him helplessly, letting out keening cry after keening cry as pleasure unlike anything she'd ever experienced rushed over her. There was no stopping it, no fighting it, no changing it. It just was, and she had to ride it to its end as he continued to pleasure her through it all. Until she was weak with it and sagged against the bench, her breath short and her body flushed in the aftermath.

Only then did he lift his head from between her thighs. He looked up at her, searching her face, seeing her in a way that made her even more uncomfortable and exposed than the wicked things he'd just done. She turned her face, shoving at her skirts as he shifted to take a place beside her on the bench.

"*That* is pleasure, Sophie. And it's only the beginning," he whispered, his voice rough and low and sensual. She was shocked that her body responded to the sound, still aching for more of what she'd just experienced.

She stood, pacing away from him, her hands shaking, her knees unsteady. He watched her, silent for a long moment, and then he said, "Sophie."

It was just her name, but his voice saying it forced her to turn toward him. Made her want to fall into his arms. Her blood went cold at that realization as she stared at him. He was utterly calm, completely in control. The only outward sign of what they'd done was his mussed hair, where her fingers had threaded. A few sweeps and he would be perfect again, untouched and unchanged by what they'd done.

Meanwhile, she would never be the same.

"We—we should not have done that," she whispered.

He arched a brow. "You regret it?"

She caught her breath. Regret it? She *should* regret it. She should be horrified by what she'd done, not want to repeat it. Not want to do even more. That was part of the problem. Her reaction was wrong and terrible.

"I-I don't—"

"You didn't do anything wrong," he said softly. "No matter what your friends or the stuffy women of the *ton* might tell you. Pleasure is natural, something to be celebrated and sought, not shunned."

She folded her arms. "So say you, a man. Someone who can take his pleasure without consequence. Meanwhile, I must now live with what I did. What I allowed you to do. If anyone found out, I would be labeled a wanton. My future prospects could be damaged."

"What happened to living a life of adventure, without fear?" he asked as he pushed to his feet. When he moved toward her, she forgot all her clever answers and solid reasons for pulling away from him.

She forgot everything but that moment when his mouth had

drawn intense pleasure from her. A sensation she hadn't even known could exist.

She blinked, trying desperately to bring herself back to the present. To recall why what he suggested was unsafe and unsavory, despite the pleasurable results of it. And that was the danger of his actions, of her reaction. A few stolen moments and all her reason was gone. She was ready to throw everything to the wind for him.

She'd seen the results of such a loss of control before. Up close. Personal. The consequences of her mother's obsession with her father had led to her going driving with him even when he'd been drinking. Had led to the accident that had torn them both away. They'd led to Sophie's world being destroyed.

And here she was, standing at the edge of the very same cliff with Rowan Sinclair.

Rowan Sinclair, a confirmed rake. Rowan Sinclair, a seducer of women. Rowan Sinclair, who was looking at her like he knew he could draw her in at any time, suck her life away, make her follow him to the ends of the earth with just a crook of his talented fingers.

"There are some actions that go far beyond adventure. Into foolishness. Into places where I never should have gone." She pushed past him, toward the door. The hothouse was suddenly too close, too dark, too intimate. She needed to flee.

But he didn't let her. He caught her arm and tugged her back against his chest, forced to look up into his impossibly blue eyes. Eyes she could lose herself in. A man she could lose herself in.

"I don't want to lose myself," she said, not meaning to voice it out loud, but there it was. "This was a mistake, Rowan, no matter how pleasurable it was. And I can't repeat it. I'm sorry, good—good night."

She tugged her arm from his grip and he let her go. He had no response, but simply watched her as she walked away. It was funny that his silent regard was harder to escape from than any sweetly whispered words. Somehow, though, she managed it, and stepped from the steamy greenhouse and back into the world. Reality.

Which suddenly seemed far less sparkling than it had before.

~

Rowan lifted to the balls of his feet and scanned the ballroom a third time. Still, he found no trace of Sophie. Just as he hadn't when he looked for her in the garden. Just as he hadn't when he sought her out in the numerous parlors. She had disappeared.

And all he could think about was her crumpled expression when she whispered that she didn't want to lose herself. He'd always seen her as so strong. So independent of spirit and mind. From the outside she looked untouchable, unbreakable, but now he'd seen a glimpse into the truth of her.

She was afraid. Afraid of the passion he'd awakened in her. Afraid of the idea of giving herself over to the care of another person, even for a moment. *That* was why she said no. *No* was a cloak she wore, a shield she carried. Beneath was the soft and vulnerable heart of a woman.

And he was a bastard for having ulterior motives when it came to her.

"You look sour."

He turned to find Percy coming toward him, a drink held out in offering. He took it but didn't partake. "Do I?" he mused softly.

"I assume your desperate search to determine what has driven Lady No to become Lady Yes has come up short, despite your best efforts?" Percy teased.

Rowan turned his face. "Her reasons are her own," he said softly. "It's wrong to pry."

Percy leaned back, eyebrows lifting. "When just a short time ago you were determined to be the hero of the Season?"

"I was not," Rowan said, frustration rising in his chest. "I was curious, as I'm sure many are. The feeling has passed."

"But you have been dancing with the lady. Spending time with her. You haven't turned that to your advantage?"

Rowan flinched. Turned it to his advantage? That was exactly what he'd been trying to do from the moment he discovered Sophie's secret. Turn it to his advantage.

"Unless your motive for spending time with the young woman are something less probative," Percy continued. "Her purse is—"

"Stop," Rowan said through clenched teeth.

Percy's brow furrowed. "What? I'm just—"

Rowan caught his lapels and shook him. "Stop. Now."

Percy backed away, his eyes wide as he pulled from Rowan's grip. "There now, Sinclair, there's no need for that. Jesus."

Rowan stared at his friend. A man he knew to be good and decent and filled with nothing but good humor. Yet a few ill-placed words and Rowan had been willing to come to blows with him.

Over Lady Sophie.

"I'm—I'm sorry," he muttered.

Percy held his gaze for a beat, then motioned toward the door. "Come. We need a far stronger drink than the weak swill this lot calls sherry."

Rowan nodded silently, and followed his friend from the room and down the hallway to an open parlor. They entered, and Rowan sat as Percy poured them each a glass of scotch. Rowan downed his in one swig before Percy could even take his seat.

"What's wrong?"

"They cut me off," he admitted.

Percy's eyebrows lifted. "Your brothers?"

"Completely. I depend on the allowance, I've never done much to save it. It's…"

"It's complicated," Percy said. "Because of your art."

Rowan bent his head. Only a handful of people knew of his passion. "Yes. I have never made what I do public. I have tried to build myself as an artist on my own merit, rather than on the curiosity of those who might buy a piece. I have kept it quiet to protect my family name. And now I have nothing. So I admit that when I started to pursue Sophie, her purse did have something to do with that. What kind of a man does that make me, Percy? What kind of a bastard does it make me?"

"The same as a dozens of other bastards in our acquaintance," Percy said with a shake of his head. "Money and power make most marriages in the Upper Ten Thousand go 'round. But I know you, my old friend. This self-abusing thing you are doing has nothing to do with what you don't feel. It seems to me that you are torturing yourself with what you do."

Rowan pushed to his feet. Percy was treading dangerously close to ground he didn't want to walk. Didn't want to look at.

"Do you care for this girl?"

There was the question in a nutshell. The one he'd never fully expected to ask himself or have asked to him. "I have…no answer to that."

Percy seemed to ponder that for a moment. "I see. You've circled her a long time. Far longer than just the last week or so."

"I suppose I have, considering my long friendship with her aunt," he conceded.

"Is that why you formed the friendship?"

Rowan blinked. "That's ludicrous."

"Is it? Because I watched you watch Sophie for at least a year before you became her guardian's friend. I don't doubt you and Lady Louisa do connect, but was that your true motivation?"

"I would have spoken to Sophie long before if I had feelings for her," Rowan said, folding his arms and glaring at his friend.

"Would you have? You, who have never been said no to in your life? Would you have truly risked Lady No's cut direct?"

"What are you saying?"

"That perhaps the money and this sudden drive in her to say yes are just catalysts for you to pursue what you've always secretly wanted. And now that you feel closer to it, you're afraid."

"Afraid of what?"

Percy hesitated, and then he said, "Actually losing something you care about. Like you did your father."

Rowan walked away. Percy's words cut so close to the bone. Far closer than he'd ever thought they could. Probably because there was truth to them.

Yes, he'd watched Sophie over the years. He'd admired her spirit and her wit far more than her beauty and her dowry. But he'd never come too close. Neither had she.

And now he knew what it was like to lose something he'd had and loved more than anything. His father had been Rowan's lifeline, his calm ear and advice, his sharp conscience when he needed that. Losing him had been devastating. It still was. Perhaps it always would be.

And perhaps there was some truth to the idea that it made him reach for Sophie. So that he wouldn't lose her without even trying for more.

So where did that leave him?

"She's afraid of something deeper," he admitted softly.

"So are you." Percy folded his arms, daring Rowan to deny it.

"Perhaps I am at that." Rowan let out a long sigh. "Perhaps that's why it will never work."

Percy cocked his head. "I hate to hear that," he said softly. "That you would walk away from something because it felt too…real. That sounds like a deathbed regret I wouldn't wish on my worst enemy."

Rowan shrugged. "It's something to think about," he conceded slowly.

"Indeed. And I assume you are now going to excuse yourself to consider it at length."

"You know me too well," Rowan said, squeezing his friend's arm. "Thank you."

"You're welcome," Percy called after him as he exited the parlor. "Call on me if you want to drink some of your troubles away during the thinking part."

Rowan laughed as he left his friend behind, but there was nothing joyful in his heart. It was now a jumble that he had to sort out or else risk hurting everyone involved in the situation. Something he very much didn't want to do. For himself. For her.

CHAPTER 7

"I'm worried about you, dearest."

Sophie looked up from her book and smiled as Louisa entered the parlor. "Oh, you needn't."

Her aunt arched a brow. "You have been sick enough to avoid all Society functions for a *week*, Sophie. Don't tell me I needn't worry."

Sophie pursed her lips. She felt guilty for her subterfuge in telling Louisa she didn't feel well. It had been true when she'd convinced Louisa to leave the ball a week before. After her encounter with Rowan she'd truly been out of sorts, body and mind.

Now her continued "headache" was a ploy. One she could clearly not continue if she didn't want her aunt calling on doctors to bleed her.

"Do you feel *any* better today?" Louisa said, taking the seat beside her and pressing the back of her hand to Sophie's forehead.

"I am, Aunt Louisa. My head is certainly clearer."

Of course, that was a lie. A week away from Society had given Sophie room to breathe and to think, but the results had been less than perfect. She couldn't stop thinking about Rowan. About what they'd done and how it made her feel. Nothing could clear those thoughts from her mind, not even when she shamefully touched herself at night, bringing a shadow of the pleasure he had drawn from her.

It only made it worse.

"Do you think you might be up for an event tomorrow?"

Sophie sighed. She couldn't hide forever. And she knew that Louisa truly enjoyed Society. When Sophie stayed home, her aunt often did as well, so she was selfishly denying her guardian that simple pleasure.

"Of course," she said with a forced smile. "What are the invitations?"

"Lady Terrington is having a garden party tomorrow afternoon at two at Mr. Sinclair's residence."

Sophie nodded agreeably, but her mind emptied of everything but one man as her aunt spoke. Lady Terrington was Rowan's mother.

"And since it is their first hosted event since the death of the earl, I feel I must go to support my friends," Louisa was finishing.

Sophie was brought back to the present with those words. Rowan had not spoken to her about the loss of his father six months before, but she knew that he mourned Lord Terrington deeply. It was common knowledge how close the earl had been to his second wife and third son.

"Of course," she said, pushing her feelings aside for the sake of her aunt, but also for Rowan and his mother. "I'm sure they would very much appreciate the faces of...of friends in the crowd."

Louisa beamed. "I knew you would understand. I will send our acceptance immediately. And I think you should wear that new green gown, darling. It is stunning and makes your eyes so bright."

Sophie swallowed hard and nodded. The green gown had a rather daring neckline. It might very well give easy access if a man wanted.

She pushed to her feet and paced away from her aunt and from her own troubling thoughts. She had to control herself, damn it. And this was the perfect place to practice that control. After all, she couldn't avoid Rowan forever. Even after this Season of Yes was over, she would encounter him. She had to practice her ability to be unmoved. To forget what they'd shared.

And tomorrow she would put that ability to the test.

Rowan wiped his brushes clean and stepped back from his work. He stared at the image he had created in the past week when he'd been trying to figure out his tangled emotions. What he'd painted spoke more volumes than he could have done in a month of deep conversation.

He sighed and slung a cover over the piece as his mother entered his studio. He smiled at her when their eyes met. Deep within them he saw her grief, lingering since the death of her beloved husband.

"You don't need to have this party," he said as he moved toward her and kissed her cheek.

She laughed softly and wiped a smudge of paint from his face. "Your older brothers are swirling about town, creating their own narrative about your father. I feel I must react so that everyone sees the love that is still felt for him."

Rowan pursed his lips. His older brothers *had* been talking about their father. Cruel little backhanded jabs meant to make the earl seem less decent than he had truly been. Nasty comments about Rowan's parentage or legitimacy.

God, how Rowan hated them for it. Not for himself, but for the woman before him. The mother who loved him and adored the man she lost. *She* didn't deserve this extra pain.

"Perhaps I'm being unfair to you, though," she said. "Having this event here rather than at my little home. You've been avoiding Society for the past week, I know. I recognize you may not wish to play host now."

"You know I'm happy to do whatever you desire," he assured her.

She reached up to touch his cheek, and through the sadness she still carried on her shoulders, he saw all her warmth and love. All her support. He had not told her about his brothers' removing his settlement. She would try to share her own, and she barely had enough as it was.

And he somehow doubted she would approve of his pursuit of Sophie. At least not the ulterior motive of her fortune. His mother had never been that kind of woman, no matter what his brothers said to the contrary.

"I've had several more acceptances for tomorrow's event," she said, stepping into the room to look at his paintings. They were propped against walls and balanced on easels in a haphazard way. She smiled at the landscapes that represented the flowing hills around their old country home.

The one he doubted the new earl would ever let them visit again.

"Who has accepted?" he asked, not truly interested but filled with a desire to support her.

"Lady Wintergreen, Mrs. Swarthart, and Lady Louisa and Lady Sophie."

He froze and lifted his gaze to his mother's face. She reflected no ulterior motive of her own as she glanced at him.

"I didn't realize you had invited Lady Louisa and Sophie," he said, hoping he sounded nonchalant. Fearing he did not.

She smiled. "We are both a friend to Lady Louisa, and I've heard you and Sophie have been becoming friends of a sort yourselves as of late. Are you not pleased?"

He bit his tongue. Oh, he was so very pleased at the idea of seeing Sophie. Too pleased. He wanted to touch her, to kiss her, to hold her. It was all he'd thought about in the past week.

"I know it will be a very happy party, Mama. And I'm always glad to see my friends."

She didn't answer, for she had moved across the room to stare at a portrait he'd finished about ten days before. She had not visited his studio since, and now he saw how much the picture moved her.

"Your father's painting," she whispered, her hand fluttering out as if she could touch the canvas and feel her late husband's cheek beneath her palm.

He moved to stand beside her and wrapped an arm around her. They stared together at the portrait of the man himself. Rowan had painted him as seated, his arm slung back over the chair, looking toward what, he wasn't certain. It was a casual pose, one that reflected the hint of a smile.

In what he had painted, Rowan saw his own eyes, his own jaw. He saw everything his father had been, heard the voice he loved so dearly echo in his ears. Still there, but perhaps not remembered as perfectly as it once had been.

"It's for you if you'd like it," he said softly. "If it does not hurt you too much to see it."

She pivoted toward him, her eyes bright with tears and her face lit with a smile. "I love it as I loved him. Of course I would want to have it. It is a treasure."

She leaned up to kiss his cheek and then wiped her eyes as she moved away from the picture. "And what is your latest project?" she asked, moving to pull the tarp from the painting he'd been working on when she entered.

"No!" he cried, stepped forward to stay her hand gently. "I-I am not ready for that one to be seen."

She faced him with a look of concern, and then she nodded. "Very well, love. Now come, I have a few details I'd like to discuss about tomorrow with your butler, and I feel more comfortable if you are there to approve or disapprove my arrangements."

He followed her from the room, but couldn't help his backward glance at the painting he had not revealed to her. Not yet. Not to anyone.

Because showing what he had created on canvas would reveal what he'd written on his own heart. And he wasn't ready for that.

❧

Sophie smoothed her skirt after she stepped from her aunt's carriage onto the circular drive at Rowan's estate. She looked up at the home with interest. She had never been here before. Truth be told, she wasn't certain she wanted to be here now. In his home? That felt like enemy territory.

Which was ridiculous. This was a test, that was all. One she just simply had to pass. There was nothing else to it.

Louisa smiled as she stepped down beside her, and the two women linked arms as they came up the steps to be greeted by Rowan's butler. The man led them inside and took their wraps and hats and gloves, then guided them through twisting halls.

Sophie drank in the surroundings as they walked. It was not a large home, but it was beautifully appointed. She was especially impressed by the large number of paintings that adorned the walls. Landscapes and portraits, as well as scenes. She didn't recognize the artist, but she longed to stop and look at the details.

Those thoughts fled her mind when the butler took them through a parlor and an open set of French doors that led to Rowan's garden.

"Lady Louisa and Lady Sophie," he announced. Everyone turned, and Sophie's gaze swept over them. She knew all in attendance, of course. Lords and ladies she had interacted with almost all her life. Some she'd count as friends, but in this moment she saw none of them. Not really. They were all blank faces until her eyes found Rowan.

He stood near the terrace wall, dressed impeccably, looking as beautiful as he ever had. And he was staring straight at her, his hand gripped in a fist at his side, his expression impossible to read.

Her heart dropped into her stomach, her toes curled in her slippers, and suddenly her mouth felt dry as a desert.

"Louisa!" Sophie jolted as Rowan's mother, the Countess of Terrington, appeared from what felt like nowhere and embraced her aunt briefly.

"Darling, you are beautiful," Louisa said, reaching up to touch the black fabric of the countess's mourning gown. "How are you holding up?"

Lady Terrington smiled, and Sophie saw the sadness in the expression. "As best I can. It helps to have friends near. Sophie, you are lovely as always."

Sophie reached out to squeeze the other lady's hand. She knew Lady Terrington only peripherally, as a friend of Louisa's, but she'd always liked the countess.

Of course, now she found herself wondering if the lady would be so kind and welcoming if she knew the wanton surrender Sophie had given into in the greenhouse with Rowan.

"Come say hello, dearest," Lady Terrington said, motioning past Sophie's shoulder.

Sophie stiffened, not ready to turn around. Rowan was there, she could feel him even if she didn't see him. She was keyed in now to his presence, the weight of him when he was near. The smell on the air, the way her body reacted. Damn him.

"Ladies," Rowan's deep voice said as he stepped up to his mother and forced himself into Sophie's line of sight. "Welcome. So nice to see you both."

Louisa moved forward first, taking Rowan's hands as she said something to him. Sophie had no idea what it was, for she was too lost in that moment in Rowan's bright eyes. They held hers even as he talked to Louisa. Sophie stared at how his mouth moved. That wicked mouth that could do such wicked things.

"Sophie?"

She blinked as she realized Louisa was speaking to her. "I-I'm sorry. I was woolgathering," she stammered as heat flooded her cheeks.

"Rowan was just asking if you would like a drink," Lady Terrington said with a gracious smile. "Our cook has created a marvelous punch for this warm day."

"Certainly," Sophie said with a quick glance at Rowan.

He bowed solicitously and then moved into the crowd to find their refreshment. Louisa and Lady Terrington began to talk again, and Sophie drew her first full breath as she took a step away to gather her composure.

She needed to stop this. Being around Rowan could not make her a ninny. What had happened between them was a mistake, but she could rectify it. There was no need to allow herself to be forever changed.

She *wouldn't* allow that.

As she made that vow to herself, she watched as Lord Benton walked toward her through the crowd. He was a young man, not unhandsome, with an earldom to come to him when his father passed. She'd never thought much of the man, in truth, but now she forced a smile as he joined her and thankfully truncated her spiraling thoughts of Rowan.

"Good afternoon, my lady," he said.

"Good afternoon," she returned. "And what a lovely afternoon it is."

He nodded. "I agree. It is why I came to ask you if you might walk with me in the gardens below."

Sophie stiffened. Her duty was to say yes to this man even though she had no desire to do so. She was exhausted after all her sleepless nights and troubling thoughts during the past few days.

But as she pondered that, she caught a glimpse of Rowan coming back through the crowd, drinks in hand. His smoldering gaze fell on her, and there her body reacted again. Out of control, thrilling and so inappropriate.

She caught her breath. "Yes," she burst out, the loudness of her tone making both her and her companion jump a little. "Yes, I'd like that."

The viscount smiled and offered her an arm. As she took it, she watched Rowan's expression shift a bit. His smile fell, replaced by a scowl, and his expression pinned her. Now not seductive, but accusatory.

She ignored it and pivoted, all but dragging Lord Benton from the terrace and down the stairs toward the gardens. She refused to look over her shoulder to see what Rowan was doing. She didn't care. She shouldn't care. She was not going to care.

If it took a hundred viscounts to make that clear to herself, then she would walk with a hundred viscounts.

And *none* of them would move her as much as Rowan Sinclair did.

CHAPTER 8

Rowan couldn't help but narrow his gaze as he watched damned Lord Henry Benton reach out to pluck what looked to be a petal from Sophie's hair. And she smiled. She *smiled* at him. Henry Milquetoast Fucking Benton, who had never said anything interesting to anyone in his entire damnable existence.

The jealousy that burned in Rowan's chest was hard enough to handle. He wasn't used to such a strong, angry, twisting emotion. But it was that he didn't deserve the jealousy that cut him all the deeper. Aside from stolen ecstasies in the hothouse, he had no claim on Sophie. He'd made none yet. She was making it very clear she didn't want those advances.

Except that every once in a while she glanced up toward the terrace, toward him, and he saw the flicker across her face. The reflection of his own desire, the conflict that matched the one in his throbbing heart.

At last, the pair turned toward the stairs and ascended back to join the rest of the party. Benton leaned over her hand and kissed it before he stepped away. Rowan had never wanted to punch a man more.

The moment Benton stepped aside, Rowan moved. He didn't

plan to move, it just happened as he strode across the distance between him and Sophie. She stiffened, folding her arms and straightening as he reached her.

"Come with me," he ground out through clenched teeth as he clasped her arm in his hand and drew her across the terrace. He felt the curious eyes on them as he took her through the doors, through the parlor, into another where no one could see or hear them.

She wrenched away from him and watched as he inappropriately shut the door behind him. He leaned against it, trying to regain a bit of control and composure before he spoke.

"What the hell do you think you're doing?" she snapped.

He blinked. In truth, he had no answer for that very valid question. He'd dragged her from a party in a most public way over jealousy he had no right to.

Except he felt it, just as he felt the connection that was so powerful between them.

"Benton?" he snapped out.

The color left her cheeks and she spun away from him. "What about him?"

"You would walk with him, Sophie?" he asked.

Her shoulders lifted, tension filling her every fiber. She didn't look at him. He wanted her to look at him.

"What I do is none of your affair," she said softly.

He moved on her then, without meaning to, just as had happened on the terrace. It was like he couldn't stop himself. She stole his control.

"Isn't it?" he growled as he stepped in front of her, forcing her to glare up at him. "I think I could make a good argument that I have every right, considering."

Her lips parted. "Considering what?" He arched a brow and she gasped. "How *dare* you! You would throw up what happened between us in my face?"

When she said the words, shame filled him. She was right.

"I-I'm sorry," he stammered. "That was incredibly ungentlemanly. Worse, it was unkind. You don't deserve that."

Her expression softened. "I didn't expect your apology."

He shrugged. "You should. I can admit when I'm wrong."

"Then why say what you did in the first place, if you knew it was wrong?" she whispered.

He took a small step toward her, closing almost all of what distance remained between them. Her breath hitched and that tiny sound hit him in the groin. His cock began to throb, harden, making his lust very known.

"Because the last time I saw you, you were shuddering beneath my tongue. And the first thing you did today was walk away from me. And I hate that. I shouldn't care, Sophie, but I do care very much what you do. And with whom."

"Rowan," she whispered.

He smiled. She had said his name so many ways in the past few weeks. He loved each one. Just as he loved…

He loved her.

He drew back a fraction as that realization hit him. He *loved* her. That was why she was all he could think about, that was why he needed to be near her at all times, that was why he was so uncomfortable with the idea of using her or the knowledge he had about the bargain she'd made with her aunt.

He loved her, and it had nothing to do with what he might gain from a union with her. All he wanted from that union was the right to call her his. To share his life with her.

All of his life. Now he just had to convince her to open up and see the same future that flashed so beautifully before his eyes.

"Will you come with me?" he asked softly.

She tilted her head. "Now?"

He nodded and extended his hand to her. "Please."

She hesitated, but only for a beat of time. Then she took the hand he offered and followed him.

~

Sophie didn't truly understand what was happening, but she could feel that something had changed. Rowan had been angry, and then his stare had shifted and it was like the weight of all her problems had been pulled away. There was only him.

He squeezed her hand gently as he took her to a closed door far from the parlors and the party. "I have no right to ask you to share any part of yourself until you see *me*," he said.

She shook her head. "What do you mean?"

He didn't answer, but simply turned and opened the door. He motioned for her to enter, so she released his hand and did so. She caught her breath. This room had very likely once been a parlor, but it had been transformed. There was a little furniture within and an easel in the middle with a canvas covered in cloth. Other paintings leaned against the walls.

Every one was more beautiful than the next.

She turned toward him as he entered the room and watched her. "What is this, Rowan?"

"My—my studio," he said, and color filled his cheeks as his gaze darted away.

She took a sharp breath and looked again at the art, thinking of the other paintings she'd seen on the walls about the estate.

"*Yours?*" she whispered. "Are you saying that you painted these?"

He nodded slowly. "I did."

She couldn't help it—she staggered forward and bent to examine the pieces more closely. "Rowan," she breathed as she took in the expert brushstrokes, the fine composition and color choices and the emotion that brightened each scene. "My God, they are *wonderful*."

"Thank you," he said softly.

"But how—what—?"

He smiled. "I know you have many questions. Women in Society are meant to be accomplished, but the men are not given such leeway."

She pondered that. It was an opinion she'd never considered. "I suppose you are right. I've never known a man who painted, especially one who did so this proficiently."

Rowan moved forward, his gaze sliding over the works as he murmured, "I showed a talent with paint at a young age," he explained. "My father and mother both encouraged me in the work and even brought in masters to teach me. Of course, it is complicated. My father's name could be sullied by such a thing. And I didn't want to trade on it at any rate. About five years ago, I began to try to sell my wares, under another name."

He motioned to the signature, and she leaned in to look closer. "W.R.?" she asked.

"William Reynolds," he explained. "My *nom de plume* of sorts."

"I like Rowan Sinclair better," she said, daring to hold his glance.

His pupils dilated slightly, his lids lowering. It was a possessive look, and her stomach clenched with desires she was beginning to accept were undeniable.

"Would you like to see my latest piece?" he asked as he pointed to the easel in the center of the room. "Not another soul has looked at it but me."

She blinked. "You would give me such an honor?"

He didn't respond with words, but by taking her hand and drawing her close. He pressed a gentle kiss to her lips and then moved her to the piece. He took a deep breath, and she saw his uncertainty in that moment. This man who was always so sure and centered and all too arrogantly perfect was now *nervous*. About her. A role reversal if there had ever been one.

With another little sigh, he pulled back the cloth. Sophie stared at the picture, her hand coming up to her mouth in shock. The painting was of her.

She was seated on a bench in a garden, her body half-turned, as if she'd had her name called by the painter. Her hair was loose, framing her face, and her gown was beautiful, the same color as her eyes. The portrait version of herself had a wide smile and bright and expressive eyes.

"Rowan," she murmured. "I don't know what to say!"

He pursed his lips. "Is that good or bad?"

"It's wonderful," she whispered. "I've had portraits commissioned by my aunt over the years, but never one so special and wonderful as this. You make me look far more beautiful than I am."

His brow knitted as he looked from the picture to her and back again. "No," he said. "*You* are far more beautiful than I could ever capture, even if I painted you a dozen times. A hundred." He moved toward her, his fingers threading through hers slowly. "And I would very much like to paint you a dozen times. A hundred. A thousand."

She blinked. "I don't—I don't understand."

He drew another deep breath, his face still taut with uncertainty. "I know."

Then his mouth was moving to cover hers and she lifted into him, opening when she knew she shouldn't, sighing with relief and pleasure when his tongue breached her lips.

He pulled away, stroking his fingers over her cheek lightly. "I know you don't want passion—"

She jolted. "No, it isn't that I don't want it. I want you, Rowan, I do."

"Then what?" he asked, so gentle. As if she could let her walls come down at long last and he would be there. That she could surrender all her nos and at long last say yes and know she would be protected. He touched her cheek again. "Tell me."

She drew a shuddering breath. He'd been so honest, so open to show her this glimpse into his life. His art. If she wanted him to understand, the time had come for her return that honesty. "I suppose it's because of why I became Lady No," she said, her voice shaking. "I've always said it was because I did not want to play with fortune hunters, and I suppose that is partly true. But the real reason I've hesitated is because of my—my father."

He wrinkled his brow. "You've mentioned him before. The strain of your relationship, even though you were very young when he and your mother died."

She nodded. "Yes, I was a child, but I wasn't a fool. My mother adored him, but he was a liar and a philanderer. He dangled love just out of her reach, giving her just enough that she felt she could catch it. Snatching it away the moment it was in her fingers. I saw what that did to her. How it broke her. She was willing to do anything to keep him, to capture him. She would say yes to anything he asked. Even go riding in the park when he was blind drunk after a night of carousing." She dipped her head as she recalled watching the two of them stagger into her father's fancy phaeton that fateful morning.

"She said yes to anything. And so you decided to say no to everything," he whispered.

She nodded, the pain of those words like a stab to the heart. "Yes. Until…until you."

He moved closer. "But you and I are not your parents."

"I don't know if that is true." Her voice broke, tears gathering in her eyes. "When you touch me, I lose all control. Do you see how abjectly terrifying that is to me?"

He tilted his head. "I hadn't thought of that. How much your past would make you fear this. Me. Us."

She nodded. "Perhaps I cannot overcome that fear. Not even with you."

He drew her against his chest for a moment, his arms closing around her. She rested her cheek to his chest and heard the steady thud of his heart against her ear, felt the way his breath rose and fell. Slowly, she allowed her breath to match his. And somehow, some way, the peace she wanted came to her. She drew away, looking up at him in wonder.

He was smiling back. Gentle and loving. Giving and caring. "Sophie, I'm not your father. I'm *not*. I know I've always appeared idle and feckless like he was. Bored and looking for something to occupy his time, for good or for bad. But it isn't true."

She knew that. Of course she did, on some level. "Why do you do it then?"

He motioned around them. At the artwork, including the portrait of her. "Because of this. My behavior is an act, a way to obtain *entre* into the places where I might sell my work. The truth of me is far more than that."

She stared at him, seeing him in a new light now that his creativity surrounded her. "And what are you?"

"Passionate. About my painting, about my life, about *you*. I want to touch you so very much. I want to show you how good passion can be. How it can ground you, not just sweep you away. And that when it does sweep you away, it will always bring you home again. To me."

Tears stung her eyes at those beautiful words, more seductive than even his touch. "They'll be waiting," she said, glancing over her shoulder at the closed door. "There will be a scandal if we're gone too long."

He was silent for a beat, and then he said, "Perhaps. But what will the scandal matter if we wed?"

She staggered back, breaking from his arms with a gasp of shock. "Marry? You wish to marry me?"

"I do," he said without hesitation. "I wish to marry you, Sophie. If you will have a man like me."

Sophie lifted her cold hands to her suddenly hot cheeks. This was not at all what she had intended for this day. She'd planned to come here as a test of her willpower, to avoid Rowan to show herself that she could. But not only was she standing in the middle of his studio, surrounded by the art that felt so intimate, pondering surrendering her body to him...but he was asking her to be his bride.

And even though she'd spent years as Lady No, what she wanted to say, to scream, to cry to the rooftops and beyond...was *yes*. Yes to the thrill this man put to her belly. Yes to the passion that made her body tingle. Yes to the life filled with art and adventure and laughter and everything good and interesting.

Yes to being his bride.

None of it had anything to do with her promises to her aunt to become Lady Yes. All of it had to do with Rowan Sinclair and his impossibly blue eyes and his incredibly deep spirit.

"It's soon," she squeaked instead.

He laughed. "Is it? I've been told I've always been interested in you."

She couldn't help her smile. "Have you? For I've been told the very same thing. Is that possible?"

"That I've always watched you and tracked you and secretly wondered what it would be like to touch your cheek or hold your hand or call you my Sophie?" His gaze softened. "I'm starting to believe that is possible."

"Would you…control me?" she asked.

His eyes went wide and a bit feral. "Control you? Would you like that?"

She blinked. "To be controlled? I—no. Wait, what does that mean that makes you look like you want to ravish me?"

"Ravishing you does sound delightful," he laughed. "There are some ladies…and gentlemen, truth be told…who like to be controlled in the bedroom. Bound and ordered about. I assume that isn't what you mean?"

She shivered, for bound and ordered about by Rowan didn't actually sound so very bad. "No," she said slowly. "What I meant was if I were to marry you, would you…*control* me. Give me no say in our life, give me no financial future aside from your own, keep me under lock and key unless you wished me at your side."

His expression softened. "Is *that* what your father did to your mother?"

She nodded swiftly, even as heat filled her cheeks. "Yes."

"Let me make this clear, Sophie. If we were to wed, we would be equal partners. Our lives would be led together, but I would have no quarrel with your having your own ways and friendships and interests. I have no need to be your keeper. Your lover and your friend? Oh yes, I would want to be those."

She squeezed her eyes shut. What he was offering was so... right. Oh, there was a tiny voice of doubt that still lingered at the back of her throat, in the corner of her mind, but she pushed it away.

"I will marry you, Rowan," she said, opening her eyes to look at him evenly as she said the words. "I will marry you."

He grinned, and the look made him so handsome that she could not resist anymore. She closed the distance between them in a few steps and wrapped her arms around him. She lifted to him as he lowered to her, and their mouths crashed together in a passionate kiss unlike any they'd ever shared.

Yes, in this kiss there was the desire that had pulsed between them from the first night she'd encountered him lounging in the parlor, but there was also something more. She felt a connection when their mouths met, when their tongues tangled. A promise that made her feel complete where she'd never known she wasn't whole. A sense of belonging that warmed her from head to toe.

She parted from him just enough to whisper, "Will you... touch me?"

His eyes went wide. "You don't care about the scandal?"

She shook her head. "Let it come."

His mouth found hers again, and he backed her away from his work, to a darker corner of the room, where a settee was hidden beneath a tarp. He broke from her just long enough to pull the cover aside and then he lowered her onto the cushions. She settled back, watching him, her body already twitching with the pleasure she knew he could give her. Now it was going to be so complete. So real. So perfect.

"I want to do this slowly," he said with a frown as he began to hitch up her skirt. "And with far fewer clothes, but just like last time, that is not possible."

She blushed as her skirt came up over her knees and his hands brushed her thighs. "Can you…can you not have me this way?"

He swallowed hard. "Have you?" he repeated, his voice cracking. She nodded. "Please?"

He leaned down, his weight covering her, and he kissed her. She lifted into him and felt the full length of him against her, including the hard thrust of him pressing to her stomach. She knew a little about what happened next, and that steely length both frightened and intrigued her.

"If you want this, I suppose it can't hurt. You've agreed to be my wife," he murmured, she thought more to himself than to her. "And God, but it's too much temptation to deny." He touched her face gently, tracing the line of her cheek. "Let me ready you."

"How?" she whispered.

He smiled, and it was wolfish. "Like before."

She gasped as his mouth moved to her throat, to the scooped neckline of her gown, down lower to press kisses over her stomach, her hip, and finally he dropped to his knees and positioned himself just as he'd been a week before: worshipping between her thighs. Her body quaked with the memory. With the reality as he spread her sex open and began to lick her.

She lifted against him. She knew what to expect this time, and she wanted it. Needed it. Needed that slick and heated and powerful release that would make her world a starburst of pleasure.

He eased her toward it, stroking her full length, teasing her clitoris, making her body tremble with need. But instead of letting her find release, as he had last time, when she was on the edge, ready to explode, he pulled away. She whimpered as he stood, but the whimper turned to a gasp as he unfastened the placard on his trouser front and let it drop.

She sat up slightly to stare. This was what the fuss was about. This thick, hard mass of erect flesh that now moved at her like a divining rod to water. She reached out, fascinated at how very different their bodies were, and stroked her finger across his length.

He sucked in a breath, and she jerked her hand away. "I'm sorry."

"Don't be sorry," he choked out. "Just keep touching me."

She lifted her gaze, saw the tension coiled in every muscle of his body. She'd created that. She had power, just as he did.

And in that moment, she wanted to use her power. She caught him in her hand, reveling in the soft and hard dichotomy of this thing. That some used for wrong, but that could also make her feel so very right.

She stroked him with her palm and he gripped his fists at his sides, his neck straining.

"You'll put it in me," she said softly.

"Yes." His tone was strangled.

"Will it hurt?"

He nodded slowly. "Yes, at first. If I've done my job right, then not too much."

"Will you do it now?" she asked, rubbing her thumb across the swollen head, wondering at the drop of liquid that escaped the tip.

"Jesus, but you test a man," he murmured, and he moved back over her, his mouth hungry against hers. She sank into him, her arms around his neck, smelling his skin and his hair and his body that she wanted so very desperately.

He wedged himself between her legs, his narrow hips forcing her wider so that her sex opened. Heat filled her cheeks, but she didn't pull away. What he was doing felt too damned good to ever stop it.

He reached between them, his fingers finding the slick heat of her, stroking her gently, parting her folds, teasing her until her body hummed with anticipation.

"God, I want you, Sophie," he growled against her ear as his tongue traced the shell there. "Now. To make you mine."

She nodded as she buried her face into his shoulder. Her heart was throbbing with want and fear and surrender all at once. He rubbed the head of his member against her, and she jolted at the thickness of him against what felt like an impossibly small entrance.

"Relax," he whispered, his deep tone hypnotic, gentle. She found herself following that order even as he continued to stroke her. Stroke her. Then he pushed forward and her body somehow let him in.

There was pain. It was not something she could deny. A burning sensation of flesh that should not be stretched. His mouth found hers again and he kissed her deeply, sweetly. With every inch he took, his mouth distracted her, and suddenly he was fully seated and the pain was gone, replaced by a wonderful fullness and completion. She wiggled beneath him, flexing her internal muscles around his girth.

He moaned her name and then moved his hips, withdrawing and pushing forward once more. The pleasure she felt from his mouth rushed back, different this time. More intense. More wonderful. More united because he was inside of her and they were one body with two throbbing hearts.

He met her stare with the next thrust, rotating his hips to grind against her. A flare of powerful pleasure was the result, and she dug her nails into his still-clothed shoulders as her eyes went wide.

"Rowan," she whispered.

"Let it come," he said, his gaze still holding hers with focused intensity. "It's yours."

He stroked into her again and again, and she was lost in it, this magic that she'd never known existed all around her. This thing that was so right and so foreign and yet so much like coming home.

The pleasure hit her then, with wild beating wings that tore her from the earth as she writhed and cried out beneath his still-thrusting body. She watched his face, which was now tense as he focused on her spiraling pleasure. Then his eyes fluttered shut and he made a deep, guttural grunt before she felt the heat of his seed flood and fill her.

He collapsed over her, panting as he kissed her temples, her neck, her shoulders. She smoothed her hands over his broad back, whispering meaningless endearments that fell from her mouth like water.

"You are magnificent," he said, tucking a hair behind her ear when both of them could speak coherently again.

She smiled. "I've never thought...I never knew. Will it always be like that?"

He nodded slowly. "It will. In fact, it will be better, for we won't be rushed. And I'll learn your body, as you'll learn mine. What you want and like will become second nature to me."

She leaned up and brushed her lips over his. "It seems it already is."

He grinned and then pushed off of her, parting their bodies as they each groaned in disappointment. "We should go back. Face the scandal."

The word *scandal* should have made her breath catch and her heart throb, but instead Sophie found herself laughing as she got up and fixed herself as best she could. "The best unions start with a scandal, so I've heard."

He touched her cheek with the back of his hand and smiled softly. "I hope that is very true. Now come."

She took his arm and let him lead her from the studio, back to the terrace where everyone else was still gathered. And in her heart, she felt something she'd never understood before. A hope that she'd always feared to name. Never thought she had.

But here it was, in the form of a man she had always avoided, somewhat feared...and now was going to be hers for the rest of her life.

CHAPTER 9

The scandal did come. Both of them had known that it would, but to Sophie's surprise, it had not been in any way damaging. The week since her engagement had been filled not with censure, but with knowing glances and playful jabs about the lengths one went to in order to land a rake. No one seemed very surprised at the match, and Society at large seemed to celebrate the end of Lady No and the beginning of Mrs. Sinclair.

"You look happy," Louisa said as she took her place next to Sophie and touched her hand.

Sophie shot her a playful look. "You may gloat if you'd like, you know."

Louisa had the kindness to at least look shocked at the suggestion. "Me? Gloat? Why?"

"Oh, don't be coy now!" Sophie laughed. "You came to me weeks ago with this bit about living a life of regret and letting in the possibility of more. I did so, against my will, and here I am, engaged and, as you say, happy. You must have a *tiny* desire to gloat at that."

Louisa leaned back in her chair, and her smug smile said it all. "I'm pleased to hear you say that I am always right," she said.

Sophie's lips parted. "I said no such thing!" she teased. "But…I suppose you are."

"I knew Rowan would be the right match for you, too," her aunt said with another of those smug grins. "And that if I could have him use our bargain—"

Sophie's smile fell and she stared at her in confusion. "Wait… Rowan knew of our bargain?"

Louisa clapped a hand over her mouth. "Damn," she said through her fingers. "I should not have said that."

Sophie sat still, shock flooding her. Her hands shook, her blood pounded in her veins, her head spun and hummed.

"You look as though you'll faint," Louisa said, concern heavy in her tone as she caught Sophie's hands and squeezed. "Rest back, darling, breathe."

Sophie tried, but breath felt impossible. "When?"

Louisa shifted. "When what?"

Spearing Louisa with a fierce look, Sophie snapped, "When did you tell him about our agreement?"

"The day after his brother's ball." Her aunt frowned. "You are angry with me."

"Yes!" Sophie burst out, shaking her hands away and standing to pace the room. "How could you? Our agreement was between you and me—how could you bring someone else into it? Especially someone like Rowan Sinclair?"

"Your fiancé," Louisa reminded her gently. "Sophie, come now. My subterfuge worked out, did it not? You love him, don't you?"

Sophie swallowed. Love him. She had been avoiding thinking about that since his proposal. He hadn't said that word, though his sweetness had touched her heart so very deeply.

"I—"

"Look into your heart," her aunt whispered. "Where you are so afraid to go after what happened between your mother and father. Do you *love* him?"

Sophie squeezed her eyes shut, but tears still swelled and slid down her cheek. "Yes," she admitted, and then gasped in a breath. "Yes, I love him."

She heard Louisa rise, heard her come across the room. She didn't open her eyes until Louisa wiped a tear from her cheek. "I told Rowan and I will tell you: love is a war. I only equipped him with certain advantages. What happened after that is—"

"Real?" Sophie whispered. "I want it to be, but what if he used what you told him against me? What if it is all a manipulation for his own means?"

"And what would those be?" Louisa asked, wrinkling her brow.

Sophie shrugged. "I don't know. I don't."

"You may be angry with me, but please don't let this give you an excuse to distance yourself from him," Louisa said with a smile. "Go talk to him. Tell him what I told you. Allow him at least the opportunity to explain himself. Doesn't he deserve that? Don't *you*?"

S ophie shivered. "I've closed myself off for so long. Now I've opened myself to a man who...to be honest, he terrifies me, Aunt Louisa. In the best ways, but terrified still. He can see me, and he shares things with me. He makes me want things that I always saw as dangerous and he makes me promises that I so want him to keep."

"Then give him the chance," her aunt said. "Go to him."

Sophie gasped in the breath that she'd been unable to find earlier and managed a weak smile for Louisa. "Unchaperoned?"

Louisa's arched brow was her response. "Your scandal is already afire, my dear. And since you will marry, I see no reason not to look the other way."

"Very well. I will go." She got up. "There is no time like the present, I suppose. I'll march over there and confront him and... and..."

"And see what he says," her aunt finished gently. "Once you have, come home and I will apologize again for my interference."

Sophie kissed her cheek. "I hope I will need no apologies, and will come home happier than ever."

But as she left the room to make her arrangements, Sophie couldn't help the leaden feeling deep in her stomach. The fear that when she confronted Rowan, his answers wouldn't be satisfactory and her illusions of love would fade away like music on the wind.

~

Sophie smiled at Rowan's butler as she stepped into his foyer just an hour later. She liked her future husband's servants and she wanted them to feel the same way about her. "Good afternoon, is Mr. Sinclair in residence at present?"

The man's face fell and he glanced over his shoulder as if he were concerned. "He is not, my lady, I am sorry."

She tilted her head. "It's Barton, isn't it?" He nodded, and she continued, "You seem troubled, Barton. Is there something I can do?"

"It is only that Mr. Sinclair stepped out on business for an hour and his…his…"

Before he could finish, the door to a parlor at the end of the hall opened and a round, angry-looking man appeared. Sophie took a step back in surprise. It was Rowan's eldest brother, the Earl of Terrington, who stepped into view.

"Damn you, Barton, where is the bloody tea?" He moved a few steps down the hall and suddenly stopped when his beady eyes found Sophie standing with the servant. "Well, well…if it isn't little brother's lady love."

She pushed her shoulders back and took a step up the hall. "Lady Sophie," she said, holding out her hand even though she didn't want this odious man who had only brought Rowan pain to touch her. "I understand you are waiting for Rowan's return."

His face pinched. "We are, my dear. Barton, bring the damned tea. Lady Sophie, why don't you join me? I'm sure my brother Keaton and I would love to get to know you better."

Sophie glanced at Barton. He did not look pleased. Slowly, she nodded. "Very well. I would like to wait for Rowan regardless, and I suppose since we will be family soon, it would be very pleasant to get to know you."

He offered an arm, which she pretended not to see as they walked up the hall together and back into the parlor where the earl had come from. She entered cautiously and looked around. Another man, slightly less portly than his elder brother, stood at the fireplace, staring up at the portrait of Rowan, his mother, and his father. There was a forlorn look to the other man. Almost pained.

"Look what I found, Keaton," Terrington drawled as he stepped toward his middle brother. "Rowan's new fiancé, Lady Sophie."

Keaton jolted and turned to her with a scowl. "Sinclair," he barked out with a slight lift of his hand for a greeting.

Sophie pressed her lips together. So much for the warm family welcome. These men were as dreadful as she'd always heard told.

"I am happy to find you here," she lied. "After all, we will soon be…family."

Terrington snorted. "Such as it is."

She ignored the barb as a maid appeared in the doorway with a service. She set it on the sideboard, and Sophie smiled as she said, "I'll pour. Don't trouble yourself."

The girl bobbed out a curtsey and left the room with a concerned glance at the two men. Sophie drew a long breath and began to pour the tea.

"How do you like it?" she asked the earl first.

He glared at her. "Sweet. Three sugars. No milk."

She did the preparation and turned over his cup before she put her attention on Mr. Sinclair. "And for you?"

"With a splash of whiskey," he muttered. "But just milk will do."

She frowned as she prepared his cup, then did the same for

herself. When she had taken a seat, the two men did the same facing her from the settee in what could only be called an icy silence.

She shifted with discomfort, trying desperately to find a topic that would be appropriate. "I am sorry about the death of your father," she said.

The men exchanged a look, and Terrington barked out a laugh. "I'm certain you are."

She drew back. He was being purposefully rude, and a great part of her wanted to give him the same in return. If anyone had ever deserved a set down...but she thought of Rowan and bit her tongue.

"It's been a fine Season," she tried instead. "Have you been to any interesting balls or parties?"

"None," Keaton Sinclair growled as he took a sip of tea.

She sighed. "I am trying to be polite. Is there any topic of conversation that would tempt you to do the same while we wait for Rowan's return?"

Terrington tilted his head as he set his teacup aside. She shifted beneath the weight of that stare. It was focused and hard and had a cruel bent to it. She didn't like it. She wanted to be free of it. And she pitied Rowan for having to endure it all these years. Their contempt for the man she loved was palpable.

"I have a topic I would very much like to broach, actually, since you are here and we are being forced to wait."

She swallowed but lifted her chin to face his nastiness with all the calm and collected sophistication she had been taught by her aunt. "And what is that, my lord?"

"Are you aware you are being married for your money, or are you too stupid to see that my brother is using you?"

CHAPTER 10

Rowan stepped into his foyer and smiled at Benton as he approached. A smile that fell when he saw his butler's pinched, unhappy expression.

"What is it?" he asked, his stomach clenching. He knew that face. There was generally only one cause for it.

"*They* are here, sir."

There was no need for any other explanation. Rowan knew who *they* were.

"Wonderful," he grumbled, his good humor fading. "How long?"

"Three quarters of an hour, sir. But they...they are not alone. You had another caller and she was swept away by them."

"Christ, did they get hold of my mother?" Rowan asked, running a hand through his hair. The countess could hold her own, but he hated to think of those jackals surrounding her.

"No, Mr. Sinclair. It's...it's Lady Sophie."

Rowan staggered, feeling all the blood drain from his face, rush to his racing heart. He shook out his tingling fingers and said, "Where?"

"The Blue Parlor, sir," Benton said, motioning up the hall.

Rowan raced forward, rushing to the room, fearing...he wasn't even sure what he feared. But he knew his brothers, he knew their hatred for him and their drive to destroy anything he loved or that mattered to him.

And the only thing that truly mattered to him was her.

The door to the parlor was partially open, and he shoved through it and skidded to a stop as he looked around him in fear and torment. Sophie stood at the window, and as she turned his heart stuttered. Her cheeks were streaked with tears, her hands trembled. When she saw him, her expression hardened and she lifted her chin and stared at him like he was...

The enemy.

His shifted his gaze to Keaton and Alistair. Both of them had risen from the settee upon his entrance. And they both looked smug as they smiled over at him.

He had no idea what they'd said to her. Or perhaps he did.

"Sophie, are you well?" he asked, moving toward her in three long steps.

She backed away, raising her hands to ward him off. "Don't," she hissed.

He spun on his brothers. "What did you say? What did you do?"

"Merely told her the truth, Rowan," Keaton chuckled.

Alistair shrugged. "Funny how you've spent your miserable life pretending to be so good, so much better, and yet you would lie to this charming creature."

Sophie swallowed and her soft, wavering voice drew his attention. "Is it true, Rowan? Is it true that you are destitute?"

"Sophie," he began, holding up a hand as he moved more cautiously toward her this time. He needed to touch her. He needed to make her see that he wasn't the bastard he'd been described as by these two circling vultures.

"Tell me the truth," she hissed, wiping at fresh tears that sparkled on her cheeks, accusing him as much as her words. Her pain was palpable and it cut him to his very core. "Is that the real reason you pursued me?"

"Please," he whispered, and she flinched.

"Is *that* why you created a situation where we would be forced to wed?"

He stared at her for a beat. Two. The time stretched out forever, and finally he bent his head. She deserved the truth. If he had any chance of surviving this, he needed to give that to her.

Even though he knew full well that the truth would not set him free. It would destroy him.

"Yes," he whispered, lifting his gaze to her and holding it steady. "When I began, I was thinking of your inheritance."

She made a sound in her throat that was unlike anything he'd ever heard. A sound of torment and heartbreak. It pierced the room like the cry of a wounded animal, and it took everything not to drop to his knees as she spun away, her shoulders shaking with the force of his betrayal.

He spun toward his brothers and found them staring, grinning, eating this up. "Why?" he gasped out, hardly able to find breath. "Sophie and I are nothing to you. You'd already won your victory when you stripped me of my allowance. Why interfere in this?"

"Because you deserve nothing good in your life, Rowan. You took our father, you took a portion that you never deserved," Alistair said, his nostrils flaring and his cheeks flaming. "You took his love. And now I've returned the favor."

Rowan stared, taken aback by the raw emotion in his eldest brother's voice and on his middle brother's face. He'd known they hated him for years. Today it was clearer than ever.

"You get out!"

He jumped as Sophie strode across the room, her eyes snapping rage. This time it was not directed at him, though, but at his brothers. And it was bright and glorious and strong and powerful enough that Keaton actually flinched.

"You two have done what you came for," she said, running right up into Alistair's face. "You are cold, heartless snakes and you should be ashamed of all you are and all you have been. You are not fit to shine his boots."

Alistair glared down at her. "Even now you defend him?"

She narrowed her gaze. "I will not ask again. Get out."

His brothers exchanged a look and then pivoted together. They pushed past Rowan and out the door without another word. Not that it mattered. As Sophie said, they had done what they came to do.

They had destroyed his world. Or at least helped him destroy his own. Either way, it was done now.

Rowan paced back to the door and softly shut it, granting them privacy. As he turned back, he said, "Thank you for that, Sophie. I did not deserve it."

She lifted her gaze, and it was so fucking empty and pained. "No," she murmured. "You did not. And now I'm going home."

She moved to walk past him, to walk out of his life forever. Panic lifted in him, something so sharp and harsh that it nearly set him on the ground. He lunged forward and caught her arms, holding her steady. She thrashed for a moment.

"Please, please!" he cried. "Please let me explain."

She pushed from his arms and backed up, her breath short as she stared at him. "And just how do you intend to do that, Mr. Sinclair?"

He flinched at her use of his formal address. And at the coldness in her tone and stare that accompanied it. He sucked in a breath and said, "By telling you the truth. All of it. From the very beginning. Please. Please, let me, and then I swear I'll let you go even if it kills me to do so."

Sophie stared at Rowan with a cacophony of emotion rioting within her. Topmost was the betrayal. His brothers had told her such horrid things, laughing as they did so, giving evidence for what Rowan had done. And then he'd admitted it.

But something else rose through all that heartbreak and pain. She was shocked at how desperate Rowan seemed. How emotional. He was panicked. He'd always been so strong, so unbothered, so in control, that seeing him now like this, she couldn't help but be moved.

Of course, she knew that his terror might have to do with losing her purse rather than her heart.

But there was only one way to find out.

She folded her arms, wishing she could put on armor in this moment when she felt so hurt and so vulnerable. "Fine," she said through clenched teeth. "Give me your explanations, Rowan. Tell me what exactly you did and how you think pursuing me for my money should make me feel."

Relief washed over his features and he motioned her to the settee. She glared at him but slowly made her way there. She sat on the far side, her legs turned outward to put space between them. He sighed and took a place on the other side of the settee, not pushing in, not crowding her physically even though she could see he wanted to.

"Thank you," he whispered. "May I get you anything?"

"Just talk," she said, turning her face slightly.

He swallowed. "You have seen my art."

She stiffened as she thought of that beautiful portrait he had done of her came to mind. It had meant so much to her, for he had clearly put so much of his heart into it. Would it be spoiled too when this was done?

"What about it?" she asked, trying to keep her tone cool.

"I told you that my father and mother supported me in my pursuits," he said. "But I had to paint under another name, so as not to associate such a thing with my father's title. The scandal if it came out would have been terrible. Men of my station don't make art. That's what those of Society would say. So I kept it private, and lived on the allowance given to me by my father."

"But your brothers cut you off," she said, flinching as she recalled their pleasure when they told her so.

"Yes," he said. "The night of Alistair's first ball as earl, he called me to his study and he and Keaton crowed that my allowance had been given as a boon at the earl's pleasure. Unlike my mother's inheritance, which they could not touch, mine could be taken away by whoever held the title. They stripped me of everything."

"And lo and behold, the next day my aunt told you that this Season I had agreed to say yes to anything I was asked."

His mouth dropped open. "Yes. Did you know all along?"

She shook her head. "No. My aunt let that fact slip earlier today. I was upset and worried you might have an ulterior motive in your use of that information. I came here so you could tell me that you didn't. Instead, I found so much worse."

He leaned in closer, and she shivered as his body heat swirled around her. She did not want to want him. And yet she still did, because he was Rowan and she loved him. Foolishly, perhaps.

But she still did. Being near him made this so much harder.

"I'm so sorry, Sophie," he whispered, his voice rough and raw with emotion that she wished was real. "If I had known you were coming, I would not have gone out. I would have met with you and, I hope, assuaged your fears."

"But would you have told me you pursued me for money?" she snapped, glaring at him.

He shut his eyes. "I don't know. Yes, your aunt told me about your agreement. That the reason you were suddenly involving yourself in Society after so many years of saying no to everything and everyone was that you had promised her this Season of Yes. I was reeling from being cut off and entirely uncertain. I admit that… that in the beginning, your purse was as attractive to me as you were. That I thought perhaps I could benefit from what I knew."

She bent her head and released her breath on a sob she wished she could hold back. She didn't want to show him her pain or her weakness. But she couldn't hold it in.

She refused to look at him as she lifted a fist to her lips and tried to control her tears. "You were just like the others. The others who didn't want me for who I was. Men like my father who would marry for their own gain and never give a damn about their wife."

He flinched at the comparison. "I'm sorry."

"Sorry, but you intended to be just like him. Cruelly and purposefully."

She moved to rise, but he caught her hand and held her in place. "No!" he cried, his frustration clear. "That is not what I did. I started out with the idea that I could solve my financial problems through you. Yes, I did, I admit it, and I hate myself for it. But Sophie, that is not how it ended."

She tugged on her hand, but he did not let her go. In fact, he pulled her closer so she stumbled into his lap. His arms came around her, drawing her to his chest, and she felt his heart throbbing.

"I fell in love with you," he said, tilting her head gently so she was forced to look into his eyes as he said those words. "Do you understand? I love you, Sophie. For you. For everything you are and everything you make me want to be. I love you for your beauty and your wit. For your charm and your humor. For the way you look at me and see me and accept me for who I am. For the way you defend me, as you did today when my brothers attacked, even though I know you hate me right now. I love you for so many more things, but none of them is your inheritance."

She squeezed her eyes shut, those beautiful words piercing the wall she was trying so desperately to erect. But he said what she'd wanted to hear since they made love.

He said it, and God forgive her, she wanted to believe him. And yet...

"Anyone who was desperate to keep what I could provide would say the same," she said, pushing from his lap and pacing away from the touch that confused everything.

He stared up at her, his expression helpless and pained. And then it changed. And he nodded. "Very well, you want proof. I will provide a way to show you I'm true. Don't give me the money."

She blinked. "What?"

"Your inheritance is run by your aunt, yes? She may choose to take it if she wished."

"I…suppose," Sophie said cautiously. "She would never deny me, though."

"She wouldn't. She would change the terms of the dowry. The money would go to you. In your name alone, with specific instructions that I could not touch it. You would control it and I will ask for nothing."

She shook her head. "So you would expect me to provide for our roof and everything else. I might control it, but you would benefit."

"No," he said, rising. "I would be your husband. My duty is to provide. And I would. I will sell my art, under my real name, my brothers be damned. If it is not enough to give you a life, a future, I'll…I suppose I would find a way to do so. I have friends who are in industry. I could be a man of affairs or assist. Hell, I would work the docks if it meant I came home to you. If I could clear your mind of all your fears that I'm not true."

She stared at him, shocked by the ease with which he turned away her fortune. For a man such as him, a man who had been raised in privilege, the idea of pursuing a vocation was an anathema. There would be some in his circles who would cut him off if he did so. The same if he revealed his talent in art. Men of his ilk were meant to be idle.

But he was saying that for her, he would not be.

"You would truly do this," she whispered.

He nodded immediately. "I told you, Sophie. I love you. I *love* you. I would do anything in this world not to lose you."

Tears stung her eyes once more, but this time they were tears of pleasure. She saw the man she loved looking back at her. She saw his honesty.

"When I thought you had used me," she said on a gasp, "it cut me to shreds."

"I'm sorry," he said, easing closer. "I could call those two out at dawn for being so purposefully cruel."

"I'm sorry you had to endure them all these years," she whispered. "But the wonderful thing is that you never will again."

He stared at her. "No?"

She shook her head slowly. "No. Because the fortune you are so willing to let go of to keep me is vast. But it is *ours*. I want it to finance the life we both deserve. I want it to support your wonderful talent. I want it to grow our family and our future. Because…I love you, Rowan."

He staggered back a step, almost as if he didn't dare believe what she was saying. "You do?"

She nodded. "I do, with all my heart. And it terrifies me to feel it. But it also thrills me, because when I look at you, I see my future. The good and the bad, the wondrous and the tragic, but shared together. One heart facing it all."

Now he moved again, and this time she didn't step away. He caught her in his embrace and dropped his mouth to hers, devouring her lips as he trembled with the force of his emotion.

"I thought I'd lose you," he murmured between passionate kisses that melted her knees. "And I realized that it would kill me to live without you."

She drew back, lifting her hands to cup his cheeks gently. "Now you'll never have to," she said. "Because I am yours in spirit, in soul and…" She reached between them, gliding her hands down between their bodies until she found the front fold of his trousers. Immediately he began to harden as she stroked him. "And body."

His mouth found hers again, and he backed her to the settee. He laid her across it, his hands going into her hair, his body grinding against hers with promise. She lifted into him in return, aching for the moment when they would truly be one again. She needed that now, needed to feel his love and his passion for her. She needed to reconnect.

His mouth grew gentler on hers as his hands slid down her body. He cupped one breast, squeezing, rubbing a thumb over her hard nipple beneath her silky gown. She caught her breath at the sensations that echoed through her body at that touch. She throbbed all over, but especially between her legs.

His hand slid lower, and he caught her skirt, tugging it up, bunching it between them. He pulled away as he parted the slit in her drawers and dragged a finger across her wetness.

"Someday, I will take hours to do this," he promised. "I will learn every inch of you. But for now, I just want you to have pleasure."

She nodded, pressing her lips to his jaw, the part of his neck that peeked out above his cravat. He was unbuttoning the fall front of his trousers and his hardness pressed between them, hot and hard and ready. She was ready, too.

He wedged himself between her legs on the narrow settee and leaned forward. There was no pain this time. Just pleasure as he stretched her open for him. She groaned and lifted, taking him the rest of the way.

He stared down at her, eyes wide and filled with emotion and wonder. She reached up to cup the back of his neck and drew him down, kissing him as he began to move. He ground slow circles into her, drawing her inch by inch to the edge of madness and release.

"I love you," he whispered. "I love you, Sophie. I love you."

She clung to him as the pleasure crested, rocking her body with wave after wave of sensation. He continued to move within her, his eyes squeezing shut, his neck straining, and then he let out a groan of her name and she felt him pump into her before he collapsed against her body, smoothing her hair as he whispered soft words of love against her ear.

They lay like that for a while. She was in such a dream state that she couldn't have said how long. Finally, he pressed another kiss to her lips, then sat up, drawing her with him as their bodies separated.

He smiled as he stood, tucking himself back into place. She did the same, though she knew there would be no way to entirely return to the state she'd been in when she arrived. Not in body, nor soul. This man loved her.

And she loved him.

She caught his hand. "You gave me a plan, Rowan, a way to prove to me that you are not interested in my purse."

He nodded slowly. "And I meant it."

"I will not allow you to give up your dreams. What is mine will be yours, my love. And with it, I know we'll build something even bigger and better."

He shook his head. "Sophie, I didn't tell you I loved you or make love to you to convince—"

She lifted her fingers to his lips gently. "I know. I was hurt by what I perceived to be true. But I know you, Rowan. I know your heart. And I believe you. But there is only one thing I wish to retain from your original declaration."

He stared at her for a moment. "You are too good, my love. But name what you'd keep and I'll do it gladly."

"I do want you to paint under your real identity."

He blinked at her, the blood draining from his cheeks. "You realize we may face censure for such a thing. We *will* face it."

"Anyone who would censure us would not be worthy of us," she said. "Do not forget, I am Lady No. I am accustomed to looking fools in the face and thwarting them."

He tilted his head back and laughed. "Lady No. I think it time to retire her, don't you? In trade for Lady Loved. Lady Adored. Lady Mine."

"And with you, Lady Yes," she added as she wrapped her arms around him and kissed him one more. "For the rest of my life, yes, yes, yes."

ALSO BY JESS MICHAELS

Theirs

Their Marchioness

Their Duchess

Their Countess

Their Bride

The Kent's Row Duchesses

No Dukes Allowed

Not Another Duke

Not the Duke You Marry

Regency Royals

To Protect a Princess

Earl's Choice

Princes are Wild

To Kiss a King

The Queen's Man

The Three Mrs

The Unexpected Wife

The Defiant Wife

The Duke's Wife

The Duke's By-Blows

The Love of a Libertine

The Heart of a Hellion

Forbidden

Deceived

Tempted

Ruined

Seduced

Fascinated

To see a complete listing of Jess Michaels' titles, please visit:

http://www.authorjessmichaels.com/books

ABOUT THE AUTHOR

USA Today Bestselling author Jess Michaels likes geeky stuff, Cherry Vanilla Coke Zero, anything coconut, cheese and her dog, Elton. She is lucky enough to be married to her favorite person in the world and lives in Oregon settled between the ocean and the mountains.

When she's not trying out new flavors of Greek yogurt or rewatching Bob's Burgers over and over and over (she's a Tina), she writes historical romances with smoking hot characters and emotional stories. She has written for numerous publishers and is now fully indie and loving every moment of it (well, almost every moment).

Jess loves to hear from fans! So please feel free to contact her at Jess@AuthorJessMichaels.com.

Jess Michaels offers a free book to members of her newsletter, so sign up on her website:
http://www.AuthorJessMichaels.com/

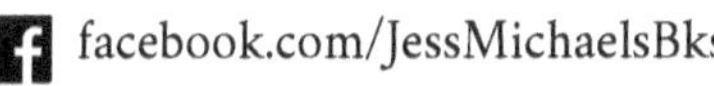

facebook.com/JessMichaelsBks

instagram.com/JessMichaelsBks

bookbub.com/authors/jess-michaels